Stories of
Life in Old Hawai'i

Stories of
Life in Old Hawai‘i

Caroline Curtis

illustrated by
Oliver C. Kinney

Kamehameha Schools Press
Honolulu
1998

Kamehameha Schools Bernice Pauahi Bishop Estate

Board of Trustees
Richard S.H. Wong, Chairman
Oswald K. Stender, 1st Vice Chair
Lokelani Lindsey, 2nd Vice Chair
Gerard A. Jervis, Secretary
Henry H. Peters, Treasurer

Education Group
Michael J. Chun, Ph.D., President
Rockne Freitas, Ed.D., Vice President/Director of Operations

Principal Executives
Nathan T.K. Aipa, Legal
Rodney Park, Administration
Yukio Takemoto, Budget & Review

Previously published as *Life in Old Hawaii,* copyright © 1970
This edition copyright © 1998 by
Kamehameha Schools Bernice Pauahi Bishop Estate

All rights reserved. No part of this book may be reproduced
in any form or by any electronic or mechanical means,
including information storage and retrieval systems,
without permission in writing from the publisher,
except by a reviewer who may quote brief passages in a review.

Inquiries should be addressed to:
Kamehameha Schools Press
1887 Makuakāne Street
Honolulu, Hawai'i 96817

The paper used in this publication meets the minimum requirements of
American National Standard for Information Sciences—
Permanence of Paper for Printed Library Materials,
ANSI/NISO Z39.48-1992.

Printed in the United States of America

ISBN 0-87336-046-X

Contents

Preface vii
    Acknowledgments viii
House Building 3
    The Site 3
    Framing the House 6
    Thatching 9
    Gifts 13
    The Dedication 14
    Legend of the First Pearl-Shell Fishhook 18
Kapa-Making 25
    In the Upland 25
    Wauke Bark 29
    Dyeing and Printing 32
A Morning on the Reef 39
A Morning on the Deep Blue Sea 43
Upland Gardens 49
    A Visit of the Overseer 49
    The *'Uala* Field 51
    The *Kalo* Patch 55
    Kalo Slips 58
    Rain 63
    After the Rain 70
    Planting 81

Matmaking	85
Capturing a Tiger Shark	93
Lūʻau and Salt	97
Lūʻau	97
Salt	99
The *Hula* School	103
Laka, Goddess of the *Hula*	103
Chosen	106
In the *Hālau*	110
Graduation	113
Kahana and His Master	119
Woodcarving	119
Tattooing	122
With the Birdcatchers	127
The Baby is Named	127
The Consecration	129
On the Way	131
Life in the Forest	137
Birdcatching in Other Districts	138
The Great Surprise	140
Canoemaking	143
Palani Fishing	143
Hauling	146
The *Moʻo* of Nuʻuanu	148

Pupils of Linohau	151
In the Upland	154
By the Sea	158
The Consecration	160
An Expert	161

Makahiki 167
    Purification 167
    The Coming of Lono 168
    Games 172
    'Ulu Maika 175
    Evening Games 178
    Hula 182
    Pahe'e and *Hōlua* 186
    The Return of Lono 188
    Prayers for the Year to Come 193

The Training of a *Kilo* 201

Aku Fishing 205

Nāwai the Netmaker 217

On Land and Sea 225
    Signs 225
    Stilts and Flying Fish 227

The Stonecutters 231
    In the Master's Yard 231
    The Journey 234

    The Workshop of the Adzes 238
    The Load of Adzes 241
    Lost 246
    The Island 249
Hiwa 255
    Kalo Wehiwa 255
    Prayers for the Precious One 257
A *Kahuna* of Healing 261
    "Funny Child" 261
    A Pupil 263
    Maile Becomes a *Kahuna* 268
Fishponds and Torches 273
Year's End 277
    Hukilau 277
    Surfing 279
    Other Pastimes 282
Glossary of Hawaiian Names and Words 287

Preface

Writing in the nineteenth century, Hawaiian historian Kepelino said, "However diligently the foreigner seeks, he cannot find all. He gets a fragment here and there and goes home." That is very true. I have read what is available, but changes came so rapidly after 1778 that much of the information about the life and customs of long-ago Hawai'i is lost.

My greatest help has come from Mary Kawena Pūku'i. As a little girl in Ka'ū, on the island of Hawai'i, she lived with a wise grandmother who told her much about the old ways and beliefs. Young as she was, she listened with deep interest and felt herself a part of the life of the early days. Later, as a translator for Bernice Pauahi Bishop Museum, she enlarged her knowledge. I hope this book will kindle in boys and girls, and in interested adults, the feeling which Mrs. Pūku'i has passed on to me about life in old Hawai'i and will increase their respect for the wisdom and skill of the Hawaiian people.

Like other peoples living close to the earth, the early Hawaiians were constantly aware of the creative forces underlying and permeating their daily lives. To the gods who emerged from this awareness they turned to ask for help and blessing for their undertakings and to give thanks for success and for all the good things of life.

Acknowledgments

My sincere thanks to Mrs. Mary Kawena Pūkuʻi for the information that made possible the writing of this book. Also thanks to Adria Croft, Donald D. Kilolani Mitchell and Winifred M. Mitchell for help in preparing the manuscript. Publication [of the original edition] was accomplished through the efforts of Louisa Palmer, [previously] long-time principal of Hanahauʻoli School, and Jack Darvill and Cecil Keesling [both also previously] of The Kamehameha Schools.

C.C.

Stories of
Life in Old Hawai'i

Editor's Note

Hawaiian words used in the text, other than proper names, are identified through the use of italic type. These words are usually defined in the sentence in which they are first used or in the Glossary at the back of the book or both.

Most Hawaiian words, like most words in English and other languages, can have more than one meaning depending on how and where they are used.

Many Hawaiian words form plurals through the use of preceding articles or by changes in the diacritics (accent markings) within the words. For example, *kahuna* is a singular form and *kāhuna* is a plural form. So sometimes it appears one way and sometimes another.

House Building

The Site

"Here is wood for a new house,
Wood for a sleeping house.
The gods of the forest
Have given wood,
'Ēā."

Down the forest trail came a long line of men, chanting as they walked. Each man carried a backload of wood, small *kauila* trunks and branches, bound with rope, then tied to back and shoulders.

The men slipped in mud. One tripped over a root and almost fell. "*E*, Malu," he called, "it is time to stop for another rest. This *kauila* wood is heavy."

Malu was at the very end of the line. "We shall stop soon," he answered. "One more turn and we shall be out of the forest."

"Good!" called another man. "Then we can feel the wind!"

"And we can see!" yet another added.

When the men reached the forest edge they untied each other's loads. Most of them lay in the shade to rest tired backs and legs. A few sat looking down the mountain toward the ocean.

"I like to look down at our homes," one said. "The people look so tiny."

"That is so!" laughed Pūpū. "See those boys climbing for a bunch of *niu*. How small they seem! And there is a girl getting water from the stream. It may be my daughter. I cannot tell."

"Look, Pūpū! I believe that is your wife. But what is she carrying? She has a bundle as big as herself."

"It is my wife," Pūpū answered after a long look. "I know! She is going from her matmaking cave. She has finished the mat she was making for Keao." Pūpū looked at Malu with a smile, for Keao was the girl whom Malu would soon marry.

"Our *kauila* wood is for a sleeping house for Keao," old Lako said. "Where is it to stand, Malu? I hope a wise *kahuna* has chosen the spot."

Puakō spoke quickly. "You are right, Lako. The *kahuna* has chosen a spot where nothing will keep blessings from the door."

"And where our sleeping house will not harm your house, O Puakō," Malu added. He gave a friendly look to the older man who was Keao's father.

"I see the houses of Puakō—the men's eating house and the one for sleeping," said Pūpū. "Just beyond that is a large house shining in the sun. That house I do not remember."

Malu laughed. "That isn't a house—yet," he answered. "It is just a pile of *pili* grass ready for the thatch. So many have helped to gather grass that the pile is very big. Perhaps we have too much."

"Much grass is needed to cover sides and roof," said Lako. "You are lucky to have your own sleeping house. When I married Ana we shared a crowded house with her many sisters and their families. Later Keao and Malu will have more houses of their own. All will be near ours. This way we can care for little ones when they come."

"The sun goes toward his resting place," said Malu. "Let us be on our way." Backloads were tied on once more. Chanting, the men moved toward their homes beside the ocean.

Framing the House

Early next morning men and boys gathered near the big pile of *pili* grass. "Lako will tell us what to do," said Malu. "I have never built a house and Lako has built many."

At once Lako set everyone to work. "The platform is well laid," he said, "big stones below and small above. Malu will not have to sleep in a mud puddle! Now little, smooth stones must be spread on top to make a smooth floor. That is work for you two."

The boys chosen hurried to the beach.

"Shall we leave the bark on the *kauila* logs, Malu?" Lako asked.

"I like smooth wood in a house frame," the young man answered. "When bark is left on I always think, 'This is the house of a lazy man!'"

"You are right," laughed Lako and set boys to peeling bark from the logs brought down the day before.

Men had the job of digging post holes. Rain had fallen in the night. At first the ground was soft and digging with the *'ō'ō* went fast. Then dry, hard earth was reached and work was slow.

While others were busy with these jobs Lako and Malu were looking over the *kauila* logs. "See this crooked one!" Lako exclaimed. "The man who carried this from the forest wasted strength. If we should use it in the house frame it would bring bad luck. All must be straight, strong and smooth."

"Here is a rotten place," said Malu.

Lako examined the log. "The one who cut that log and carried it down is still a child," he said.

Most of the logs were good. Lako and Malu examined each and sorted them into different piles. "These are the posts," said Lako. "Cut them all the same length, Malu.

Except these," he added. "These two must be left taller to be the end posts which will hold the ridgepole. These others must also stand at the ends of the house. You must cut the upper ends of every post into a point."

Sudden shouts were heard.

"O Lako, come!"

"Malu, come!"

"Come quickly! We have struck a rock. We can dig no farther."

Every man and boy ran to the post hole from where the shouting had originated. There was more yelling and pushing. Each one was trying to see. Each was asking questions or telling others what to do.

"See! They have struck a rock."

"Dig it out!"

"We can't. Don't you see how we have dug around on every side? This rock is very large."

"Then move the post hole."

"That can't be done. This is the hole for a corner post. It must be here at the corner of the platform."

"That is true," said Malu. "This spot was chosen by the *kahuna*. The corner post must stand here."

Lako quieted the shouting. "All will be well," he said. "One corner post must be cut shorter than the others. We shall wedge it in the hole with stones. It will stand firm."

The men understood and went back to their own work.

Soon the four corner posts were in place. Ropes of braided *'ie'ie* rootlets were tied about the posts at top and bottom. "Now dig the other post holes," Lako commanded. "These ropes will help you to keep the holes in line."

When the tall end posts had been firmly set, Lako again called Malu. The two climbed the tall posts. The ridgepole was passed up. While Malu held one end, Lako scratched a mark to show where the pole must be cut.

Soon the ridgepole was tied firmly in its place with strong cord, or sennit, of *niu* fiber.

When all the posts were set in their holes the rafters were measured, cut and pointed. A rafter notch was fitted onto the point Malu had made in the upper end of every post. Each rafter was tied firmly with sennit to the post and to the ridgepole. These rafters made the slope of the roof.

Malu watched Lako as he wound the sennit around the wood and made it fast. "O Lako," he said, "the sennit makes a beautiful pattern. I wish I could do it. I try to see how it is done but your fingers move so fast! The lashing is finished before I know it."

By this time the sun was high in the sky. Now and then an old man would stretch out in the shade to rest. Now and then a boy would run to the ocean for a short swim or a few would stop for some *poi* and fish and then back to work.

This was fun, building a house for two young people—young people they knew and liked. As they worked the men joked, laughed and sang.

The ropes of *'ie'ie* had held the posts firmly. "Take them off now," called Lako. "Take off the ropes. The rafters are all tied and the house stands firm."

"Next are the long slender poles to hold the thatch," he added. Men began tying these along the roof and sides.

When this was done everyone stood back to admire and a glad shout went up. "A good job finished!" someone said.

"Not finished," Lako answered. "Be here early tomorrow for the thatching."

As the men went to their homes Malu heard his name called. He turned and saw an old blind man and a young woman sitting under a tree not far away. It was the old man who had called him.

Malu went toward them. He spoke to the old man, "*Aloha,* Grandfather."

While he spoke his eyes were on the young woman. He was thinking of words from stories he had heard: "Back straight as a cliff," "Hair black as the feathers of the 'ō'ō bird," "Beauty as of a flower of the mountain." None of these words seemed good enough to tell of the beauty of Keao, the young woman Malu was to marry.

It was not the custom for young people to be much together before marriage. So Malu spoke to the old man. "I wish you could see the frame of our sleeping house, Grandfather."

"I do see it with the eyes of my mind," the old man answered. "I see it with the eyes of my grandchild here. Post by post and rafter by rafter she has told me of the building."

"Tomorrow you thatch," he added. "This may be needed," and the old man held out a ball of sennit.

Malu took it, wondering that a blind man could braid *niu* fiber so evenly. For a moment he held the old hand in his young, strong one. "Thank you, Grandfather," he said, "much sennit will be needed to tie the thatch."

The old man's face was happy as he answered, "I thank the gods who have let me have a small part in building a house for my youngest grandchild."

Thatching

Next morning Lako was the first one to reach the new house. As the others came they saw him walk about the house frame. He examined every part. "It is strong," he said, "Now for the thatch."

"Start at this corner," he commanded two men.

One of the two took a large handful of *pili* grass. He held it roots up and spread it across the corner. The ends rested on the ground. As he tied it firmly, the other man worked from inside.

The two moved along one side of the house, adding one bunch after another. Their fingers moved swiftly. The sennit was tied firmly and neatly. As they worked they chanted:

> "Tie it outside,
> Trim it inside,
> Lay it smooth.
> Rain must never
> Find its way
> Through this thatch."

Soon other men were tying another row of thatch above the first. The upper row lapped over the lower. When rain came it would run off the thatch onto the ground and those asleep inside the house would be dry and comfortable.

Round and round went the thatch, higher and higher. The men worked as they had yesterday. Now they kept time to a chant. Soon they broke off to joke and laugh. One would lie in the shade for a short rest while another took a quick swim.

Still the work went on. The walls were covered except for the doorway at one side. Soon the thatch climbed up the roof until it reached the ridgepole.

Now came the time for skillful and careful work. The thatch from the two sides of the roof must be joined. If this were not done well, rain would come in. This was work that only old Lako could do.

He scrambled up. *Pili* grass was passed to him and the old man fastened a bunch at each side of the ridgepole. Then he prayed. Lako knew that all work must have help from the gods. Everyone knew this. Only then would the work be good.

More grass was passed up. Lako took grass from each side of the roof and began to braid. The grass from one

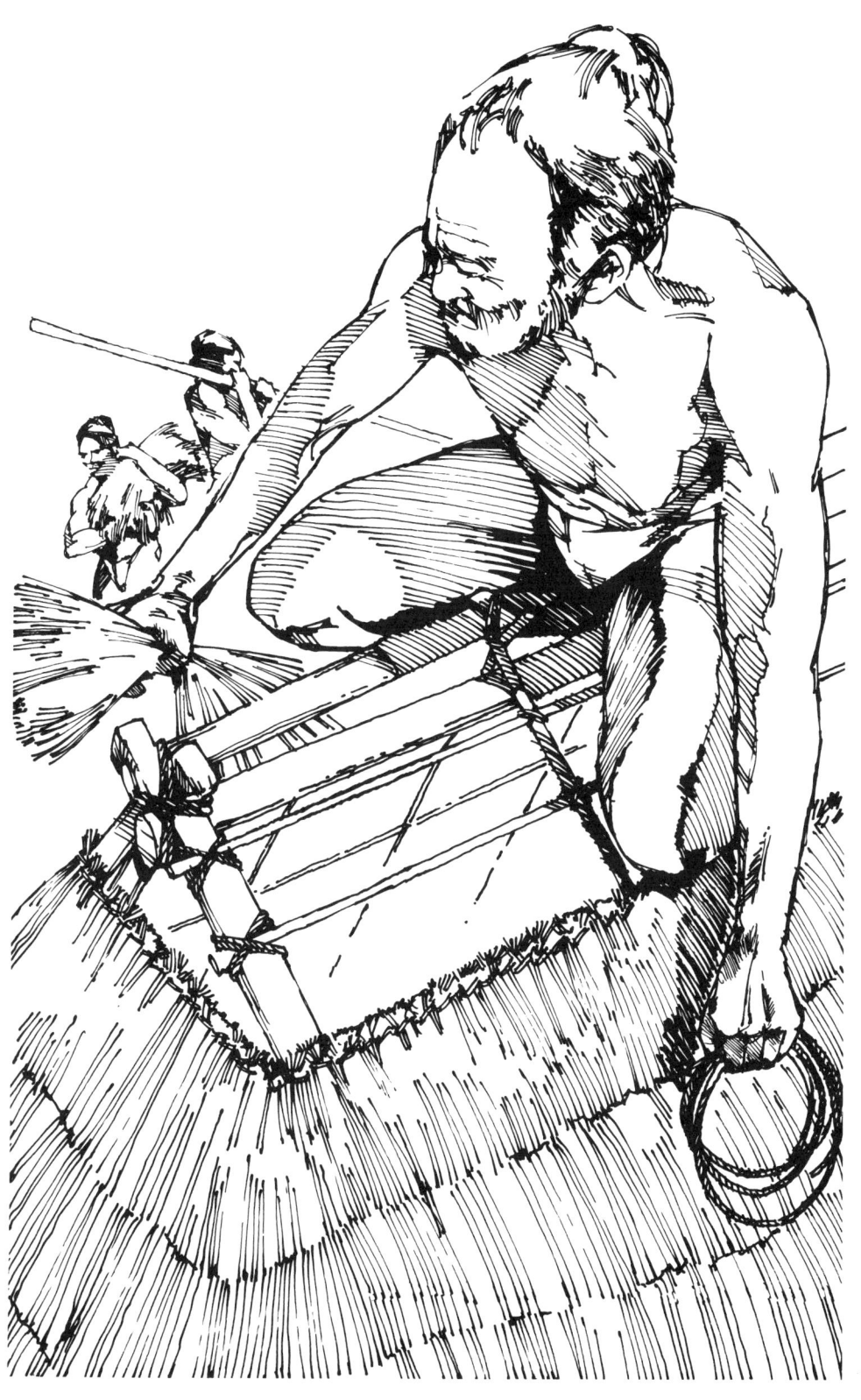

side made one part of the braid, the grass from the other side a second part, the grass just passed to Lako made the third. Over and under, over and under. Soon a wide, smooth braid lay along the ridgepole. Rain would not soak through that, but would slide down the thatch and reach the ground outside the house.

Lako scrambled down and held out his hands for more grass. Using this he made a braid around the doorway while everyone watched quietly. How smooth and neat the old man made that braid! A wisp of the braid framing the door hung over the low doorway. This was the *piko*. The cutting of the *piko* would come later.

"Now the net!" he said, turning to Malu. The net was ready. Long fishnets had been knotted together to make a square. This was spread carefully over the house to hold the thatch in place for three days. This would train the thatch to lie flat and ensure a trim, smooth covering.

The house was finished! Malu thanked each man as he left. "We shall be back for the feast," laughed Pūpū. "The feast and dedication and…" He stopped, looked at Malu and laughed again.

Lako did not leave with the others, but stayed for a few words with Keao's family. Ana, the girl's mother, stood beside the blind grandfather. Puakō and Lako joined them. "This is a glad time," Lako said. "When sons marry they leave home and parents. Sometimes to go to another district. But a daughter you may keep."

He turned to the grandfather. "The gods have blessed you," he said. "You are old like a yellow *hala* leaf yet you will see the marriage of this grandchild whom you love. Before the year is over may you hear the cry of her little one in this new house."

Gifts

"Oh Mother, I wish I could make *kapa* as beautiful as yours!" Keao was looking at a bed *kapa,* her mother's gift. Four sheets of white *kapa* had been sewn together at the end. Over them was the cover in dull red with a design in black.

"The *kapa* you make is smoother than mine was when I married your father," Ana answered. "Day by day your skill will grow as Malu's does."

"He is already a good fisherman," Keao said quickly. "Some say that when 'Aukai is old, Malu will be our chief's head fisherman."

They were interrupted by voices calling, "Ana! Keao! Come! They are taking off the net!" Yes, the net which had covered the house was off. Yet every straw of the thatch lay in its place as if the net still held it.

Gifts were coming and food for the feast had been prepared. Relatives came with calabashes, *kapa* and mats for the new house. There were calls of greeting, talk and laughter. Keao went about among her guests admiring the gifts. "What a beautiful mat, Hīnano! I can make a coarse mat to cover an *imu* but I cannot do fine plaiting such as this."

Hīnano's face lighted with a smile but before she could answer Kahana had come with a *kapa* beater. Keao examined the patterns carved on it. "Why these are the patterns which belong to my mother's family!" she cried. "I have longed for such a beater. Where is Malu? I want him to see this gift."

Malu too had gifts. His were nets and other fishing gear. Those were collected in the special house where he and his companions made ready for fishing, for Malu was one of the chief's fishermen.

Now he came to find Keao, his eyes bright with happiness. "Keao!" he exclaimed.

"Malu, see my *kapa* beater. This is…"

Both were so happy they could not wait to tell the other. They stopped and laughed. "Tell me, Malu," Keao said at last. "Then I'll show you my special gift."

Malu spoke quietly now. His voice was low and reverent. "'Aukai has given me this *aku* hook. It has been long in his family, for it is a sacred hook. And he is giving it to me! Think what it means, Keao. The head fisherman of our chief is giving me this hook."

"He has no son," said Keao, "and you are a relative."

"That is true. Still it is a great thing that he should give it to me. He says a story goes with the hook and later he will tell it."

Now many relatives had gathered. Grandfather's face was shining as he sat between old friends. People from the upland were happy to join cousins who lived beside the sea. Children were skipping stones on the surface of a tidal pool. Babies slept in the shade or climbed over grandparents and older sisters. Keao and Malu put aside their own happiness for a moment to watch the happy crowd.

The Dedication

"The dedication! Come! The *kahuna* will dedicate the new house now." The word passed quickly through the crowd. Children left their games. Shouts were quieted. Old people were led to a shady spot near the new house while others stood behind them. Grown people held little ones, hushing talk or cries.

The *kahuna* took his place before the new house. Everyone was still, for all but the smallest children understood that this was a sacred time. No sound must interrupt the prayer or blessing by the *kahuna* for the new house. All was silent except the whisper of wind in the trees and the lap of waves on the sand. In the stillness Malu laid a white *kapa* and a red fish between the door posts. This was an offering to the gods.

The people were silent as they watched the *kahuna*. In his left hand was a block of wood, in his right a sharp stone adze. He slipped the block under the *piko,* the braid of thatch that hung over the doorway. With his adze he struck, cutting the *piko,* and as he struck he chanted. His chant kept time to the blows which cut the braid of thatch.

This was his prayer:

> "O Kāne, O Kū, O Lono,
> O Kū'ula, god of this fisherman,
> I am cutting the *piko* of this house.
> The house is offered to you.
> Its wealth is offered to you.
> Take care of your children.
> As the house shelters against the rain,
>   the wind, the cold, the heat of the sun,
> So may you gods shelter us from all misfortune."

The quiet lasted a little while. Then came happy talk and laughter as gifts were taken into the new house. Floor mats were spread over the pebbles. These mats were large and coarsely plaited. Sleeping mats were piled one on another to make a comfortable bed. A large covered calabash held the bed *kapa.* While some spread mats others decorated the house with many *lei* of vines and flowers. The house had been offered to the gods and must be made beautiful for them.

Meanwhile the *imu* had been opened. Boys laid *kī* leaves over the food mats and helped the men bring food.

Children sniffed hungrily. "Is it time to eat?" a small boy whispered.

"Not yet," his sister told him. "See! The *kahuna* wants us to come to the new house again. Keao and Malu are there. This is their marriage."

Once more everyone was quiet. They watched and listened as the *kahuna* spoke to the two young people. This too was important. The voice of the *kahuna* was deep and earnest as he said, "You two will live together for many years. There will be good times—times of fun and feasting. Remember each other then. There will be bad times—times of hunger and sickness. Help each other, be true. And may the gods give you long life together. May children bless your home. May you live till you are bent with age and your eyes grow dim."

Keao and Malu looked into each other's eyes. Each saw the other's love. Keao took her husband's hand and led him to her grandfather.

The old man was very happy. "Those were good words," he said. "May the gods bless you as they have blessed me through long years with Keao's grandmother. May the day come when you will see your grandchildren enter their new home as I see you today. Then you will know the joy I feel."

Now came the feast. Men and boys gathered round the food mat shaded by *niu* palms. Fish, pork so tender it was falling apart, *mai'a*, *'uala* bursting their skins and much, much more!

Women, girls and small children sat around the mat spread under a *kamani* tree. Chicken, fish, *limu, poi, 'ulu!* Women did not have certain kinds of food, but their food mat was as well filled as the food mat of the men.

Oh, how good it smelled! How hungry they all were! Yet no boy or girl, no little child, reached out to touch the food. They waited for the prayer.

The *kahuna* was sitting among the men. He took a cup of *'awa* drink in his hands and prayed:

"Here is food, O gods,
 Food for the blessing of this marriage.
 Come, drink and eat with us."

He drank a little of the *'awa*. The spirit of the feast was shared with the gods. The people ate and drank.

The crowd was gay in their new *kapa* and many fresh *lei* and the feast was merry. When the first hunger had been satisfied there was time for jokes and laughter. One of Malu's friends danced a *hula*, telling how Malu had overslept one day and had to swim after the canoe. Then a father rose to chant how Malu had saved a little one from drowning.

Keao had never heard of that brave act and looked proudly at her husband. Malu did not seem to hear, for he was busy putting choice bits of food before Grandfather and 'Aukai, his special guests.

"No more!" 'Aukai said at last. "I can eat no more of this good food." He rose and went to join the old men who were already gathered near the ocean where the wind blew cool. Malu followed. Even active boys stretched out, too well-fed to play.

"A story would be good," said one.

Malu turned to his master. "You said that you would tell the story of the pearl-shell *aku* hook. Is this the time?"

"This is the time," 'Aukai answered. People moved close to listen. All were still. "You have heard the story of the first pearl-shell hook," the head fisherman began. "Listen once more. I tell the story as my father told it to me."

Legend of the First Pearl-Shell Hook

"Ka'eha was a fisherman of Kona on Hawai'i. He stood beside his dying father, his heart heavy with sorrow. The old man opened his eyes and spoke: 'Do not be sad, my son. I have lived long and my time has come to die. Throw my bones into the sea and the gods will give you a good gift.'

"Ka'eha obeyed his father's dying words. When he returned to the place where he had thrown the bones he found them gone. He looked carefully for the gift his father had promised and found the shell of a pearl oyster. He took it up and looked long at its beauty. Then he separated the halves and tossed one to the sea. From the other he carved an *aku* hook.

"That was the first pearl-shell *aku* hook and it proved a good gift indeed. It was a sacred hook which seemed to call these fish. With it Ka'eha became a great fisherman and his fame went all about these islands.

"One day when he was fishing, a great *aku* leaped from the sea. It took the hook and Ka'eha pulled with all his strength, eager to land that great fish. But his line broke and the *aku* swam away carrying the sacred hook.

"For days Ka'eha was filled with sadness. Then hope came. Perhaps some other fisherman had caught that fish and found the hook! He journeyed all about Hawai'i but heard nothing of the hook that he had lost.

"Finally he went to other islands but had no news until he came to windward O'ahu. There, as he paddled near the shore, he saw white-capped terns dipping and circling over a house just as they dip and circle over a school of *aku*. My hook is there! he thought, and beached his canoe.

"'These are the houses of a chief,' he was told.

"Then I shall visit him, Ka'eha thought, for he too was of chiefly family.

"He was made welcome and stayed for many days. Always the white-capped birds circled and dipped above the house where fishing gear was kept. But nothing was said of *aku* fishing. Ka'eha heard nothing of a sacred hook. Perhaps the chief does not know its power, he thought. If only he would go *aku* fishing!

"But something very different happened. Ka'eha married the chief's daughter and settled down as son-in-law of the chief. Had he forgotten the pearl-shell hook? Much time passed.

"Then one day the chief said, 'Tomorrow, O Ka'eha, my men go *aku* fishing with Kāneiki, my son. I have heard that you too are a fisherman. Will you go?'

"All the young man's longing for his sacred hook returned but he only answered quietly, 'Yes, I will go.'

"'Good!' said the chief. 'Then tomorrow you shall be head fisherman. Be ready at the rising of the morning star.'

"But Kaʻeha thought, I must make sure that we take the sacred hook. He did not rise before dawn but lay upon his mats, waiting.

"'Kaʻeha!' He heard the voice of Kāneiki outside his sleeping house. His brother-in-law was ready to start. He had a hook. That Kaʻeha knew. Kaʻeha knew also that this was not the sacred hook so he lay as if still sleeping.

"'Kaʻeha!' The call came again. Kāneiki was angry that the young man was not ready and chanted:

> 'The paddles make a rattling sound
> And the bails of the fishermen too,
> O Crab Claws!'

"The name Crab Claws angered Kaʻeha, for it meant one who talks much and does nothing. However, he did not show his anger but chanted quietly:

> 'A white shell is the hook of Kāneiki,
> A lifeless thing, a lifeless thing to use.
> Where is the many-colored hook?
> Take that worthless hook back to your
>   father, Kāneiki.'

"The brother-in-law looked at the white shell in his hand. Kaʻeha lies in his sleeping house, he thought. How does he know what shell I have? He must be very wise. And Kāneiki went to get another hook.

"'Come now!' Kaʻeha heard the call once more. 'I have a good hook for you.'

"But Kaʻeha knew that this still was not his sacred hook. 'It is useless!' he called in answer. 'Only the many-colored hook will catch *aku* today.'

"Again and again this happened. Kāneiki could find no hook that pleased his brother-in-law and at last the chief's hook bowl was empty. What should he do? Suddenly he remembered a hook found some time ago in the stomach of a big fish. The chief had stuck that hook in the thatch of the house where fishing gear was kept. 'It is an old and useless hook,' he had said.

"That is the only hook left, Kāneiki thought. I shall take it.

"Ka'eha met him at the door of his sleeping house. 'That is the one!' he cried, taking the hook. Tears came to his eyes as he looked at this gift from his father and the gods. He put it carefully into a small gourd box which he wore on a cord about his neck. 'Today we shall have good fortune in our fishing,' he said. 'Let us go.'

"They reached the landing place. 'Remember, I am head fisherman,' Ka'eha said. 'We shall take this double-hulled canoe and the paddlers must be strong men able to save it if it swamps.'

"The men listened with wonder. Of course they were good paddlers! But the sky was clear and there was no sign of storm. Soon the canoe was launched and the men paddled fast. Others had gone *aku* fishing when first the morning star arose. Those early ones must not get all the fish!

"'Look!' someone cried. 'There are the other canoes! There the birds circle and dip. Let us paddle swiftly! Any moment the great fish may sound!' They paddled with all their might.

"'Here!' called Kāneiki. 'We are among the *aku*.'

"'Paddle farther,' Ka'eha commanded, and the men turned to stare at him.

"'The fish are here,' repeated Kāneiki.

"'Today, I am head fisherman,' Ka'eha reminded him. 'Paddle farther out.'

"Wondering greatly, the men obeyed. On and on they paddled until Oʻahu was only a dim gray line upon the ocean. 'This is the place,' Kaʻeha said at last.

"The others looked about. No white-capped birds! No *aku*! Again they stared at Kaʻeha. What was he thinking of?

"'Listen to my commands,' the young man said. 'Turn the canoe and paddle toward the shore. Paddle with all your might. Do not once look back. When I shout, leap into the sea.'

"Wondering greatly, the men obeyed. They did not see Kaʻeha take the sacred fishhook from his gourd, but they heard the rush of *aku* following the canoe. They felt them splash into it. They felt the canoe sinking beneath the weight of fish. 'Leap overboard!' They heard Kaʻeha's shout and leaped into the ocean, just as the canoe filled and swamped.

"The paddlers were strong men, at home in the sea. They splashed the water from the canoe and bailed. Wondering greatly, they scrambled in once more. They had no fish, for Kaʻeha had put the sacred hook back into its box and the *aku* had all swum away. Silently the men paddled toward the shore.

"As they came near Oʻahu and could see the breaking surf, Kaʻeha repeated his commands; 'Paddle toward shore with all your strength. Do not once look back. When I shout, be ready to leap into the sea.' Again the rush and splash of *aku*! Again, the men leaped from the swamping boat. Again they emptied the canoe, then paddled toward the reef.

"When they were over the reef, Kaʻeha spoke once more. 'Paddle steadily,' he said. 'Here I shall fish.'

"Again the men stared in wonder and Kāneiki said, 'It is useless to fish here. It is true that small fish swim over the reef, but not the great *aku*. To fish for *aku* here is useless, O Kaʻeha.'

"'Today I am head fisherman,' the young man told them once again. 'Paddle over the reef without looking back. Be ready to leap when I call to you.' He took out his sacred hook and watched as the *aku* came rushing through the shallow water to splash into the canoe. 'Leap quickly!' he shouted to the men as he put away his hook.

"The paddlers leaped into the water just in time to prevent their boat's sinking to the coral. They waded to the beach, pushing the full canoe. Along with the chief came a great crowd of attendants and common people. All stared in wonder at the huge, silvery fish. 'Never have I seen such a catch!' the chief exclaimed.

"'Let these fish be shared,' Ka'eha said. 'This is my last command. Let the chief feast and let common men feast also. This is a great day, for my sacred *aku* hook has returned to me.' He took just two fish—one for his wife and one to offer in the *heiau* to the spirit of his father."

A long moment of silence told the master the deep interest of those who listened. At last Malu took out the pearl-shell hook which 'Aukai had given him. He took it from an inner fold of his *malo* where he had kept it close to his body and very safe. "What of this, O master?" he asked.

"Ka'eha found a pearl shell. Do you remember? One part he returned to the sea. From that came many hooks. This is one. This hook has been in my family for years. It brings good fortune in *aku* fishing. I have no son and give the hook to you, O Malu. Someday you will be head fisherman."

Malu did not speak but 'Aukai knew his joy in the gift.

The good time went on—games, *hula,* riddles. When at last the guests went home, no one was empty-handed. Each had a bundle of food as well as some other gift. This had been a day of sharing, a happy memory for everyone and, especially for Keao and Malu, a time never to be forgotten.

Kapa-Making

In the Upland

"O gods of *kapa*-making,
 Be our guides,
 That we may find bark,
 That we may find roots
 To dye our *kapa*."

A group of women stood in reverent silence while Laua'e laid an offering on a little shrine at the edge of the forest. Their hearts joined in her prayer. They had come to get bark and roots for *kapa* dyeing and needed help from the gods. The women thought of the many gods who lived in the forest. They must never speak or laugh loudly here for forest gods did not like noise.

Last of the women came Keao and Pua. Pua laid a hand on her friend's arm. "Look!" she whispered.

The two turned to look down the mountainside toward homes beside the beach. At the ocean's edge women and children waded as they searched for shellfish or seaweed. Over the many-colored sea canoes paddled—fishermen perhaps. While the two watched, a light rain came over the ocean. It hid the canoes and sent women and children running for shelter. As it reached the houses it was touched by sunshine.

"A rainbow!" Keao and Pua whispered in excitement. "A rainbow over the houses of our chief!" The next moment there was a clap of thunder.

"The child has come," said Pua. "Our chiefess has a baby!"

"Oh, I hope it is a girl!" Keao exclaimed. "The district chief has sons and every family wants a girl!"

The rain swept up the mountainside and reached the forest. Without a word the two young women ran along the trail. Already trees and bushes were dripping and wet vines reached out to trip the two. Pua fell. As she scrambled to her feet Keao said, "The cave! This way!"

Soon they reached a cave where the women had already taken shelter. "What happened?" Ana asked. "Did you lose the trail? Here, Keao, put on this dry shoulder cape."

"We have asked Laua'e to tell the legend of *wauke.*" This was a story every woman knew and loved. Everyone listened quietly. Rain pattered outside their cave then swept farther up the mountain.

"Long ago, in Nu'uanu Valley on O'ahu, lived a farmer named Maikoha. He raised *kalo* and *'uala* to feed his two daughters and himself. He made offerings to the gods and prayed. He loved his upland garden. He loved the clouds that rested on the mountains and the stream splashing among the rocks. He loved the winds that swept down the valley swirling rain about him as he worked. His *malo* and shoulder cape of leaves would be wet but soon dried in the sunshine.

"When Maikoha grew old he no longer loved the wind and rain. He came shivering to his home. 'Leaves do not make good clothing,' he told his daughters, 'there should be something else.' The daughters listened, wondering. What other clothing could there be? Leaves plaited into *malo, pa'u* or shoulder cape—that was the only clothing people had.

"Cold and tired, Maikoha lay upon a bed of grass and fern leaves. He lay shivering and pulled the leaves about him for warmth but shivered still. 'There should be bed covers,' he said, 'something soft and warm to comfort tired people.' Again the daughters wondered. A soft, warm cover? They had never heard of such a thing.

"Their father lay quietly and seemed to sleep. Suddenly he opened his eyes and the daughters saw an eager light in them.

"'There is a way!' he said. 'People shall have good clothing and soft, warm covers for their beds. Listen to my words.' His voice was low but firm. 'My time has come to die, but through my death the gods will send a good gift to you and to all people.'

"'You shall bury me beside the stream I love. From my burial place a tree will grow. Peel off its bark and beat it till it is thin and soft. Those strips of bark will be *"kapa,"* the "beaten thing." Make clothing from it and warm bed covers to shelter old and sick and tired folk.'

"That was Maikoha's last command and the two obeyed. They buried his body beside the Nuʻuanu Stream and in the evening when their work was done they sat near the place. They talked about their father's words and wondered.

"One evening they found a tiny plant peeping from the earth. Day by day they watched it grow. They watched it as it shot up, formed leaves and sent out branches. 'This is our father's gift,' they said. 'It is a new plant such as we have never seen before.' They called it *wauke*.

"Time passed and the tree grew tall. The two women cut young limbs, peeled off the bark and beat till they had long, thin strips. They learned to make beautiful clothing from them and soft, warm covers for a bed.

"Meanwhile shoots from the *wauke* plant had floated down the stream, landed on its banks and taken root. Other shoots had been carried to gardens all about Oʻahu and to other islands. Lauhuki and Laʻahana, the daughters of Maikoha, taught the arts of *kapa* beating, of dyeing and of printing. Throughout Hawaiʻi women made good clothing and soft, warm covers for their beds.

"That is why, when men plant *wauke* or go to gather young saplings for bark, they make an offering of flowers, leaves or fruit to Maikoha. That is why *kapa*-makers offer gifts of food and pray to the two daughters. These are the gods of *kapa*-making."

The rain was gone. Bright sunshine lit the forest as the women started to gather bark and roots for dye. At last, tired with their work, they turned toward home. As they reached the forest edge Pua and Keao remembered the rainbow. "The child has come!" the women exclaimed joyfully.

"We heard the thunder," Laua'e recalled, "and wondered what it meant. Rainbow and thunder often tell of the birth of a chief."

"Perhaps it is a girl," said Ana. "Our chiefess longs for a daughter. Let us hurry home for news."

Wauke *Bark*

"A little chiefess!" The news spread quickly through the village. Next morning the women were talking of it as they worked in Laua'e's *kapa* yard. "Will she be as beautiful as her mother?" some wondered. "What name will they give her?" No one had heard.

There was talk of their own babies, of sickness and of cure, of cunning baby ways.

While they talked their hands were busy. *Wauke* slips had been planted two years before under the direction of the overseer. The growing shrubs had been trimmed so that saplings should be long and straight with no side branches. Yesterday men and older boys had cut these saplings. Now came the stripping.

With a sharp-edged shell a woman slit the bark the whole length of a sapling. She peeled it off, then rolled it, inside out, to flatten it.

"Wrap each bundle of bark in *kī* leaves. When all the bark is ready we shall carry it to a sea pool to soak for many days."

"I know!" Keao exclaimed. "I have seen it soaking."

"I have too," Pua added, "but I never thought about it. Why does the bark need to soak?"

"So we can scrape off the brown outside part," Keao explained.

"Women put stones on the bundles to keep them from floating away. I remember now," Pua added. "What are you looking at, Keao?"

"Some of this is very fine. I was thinking—"

"What?"

"From this finest bark some woman might make a *kapa* for the baby."

"You might!" Pua cried. "Here is Laua'e. Let us tell her."

"The bark is fine enough," Laua'e said thoughtfully, "but, has Keao skill to make *kapa* for a chiefess?"

"She is the best *kapa* beater among us younger women."

"Your mother is the best *kapa*-maker in our district, Keao," Laua'e said at last. "With her as teacher you may try. If your *kapa* is well done it shall be given to the baby."

Some days later Ana and Keao were preparing materials for work in Ana's *kapa* yard. After soaking and scraping, the fine bark was ready to be beaten. Keao laid an offering of mullet on the shrine and prayed:

> "O Lauhuki,
> O La'ahana,
> Bless my work.
> Give me skill
> To beat *kapa*
> For the little chiefess."

She put her *kapa* log on a mat at the shady end of the yard. This log was of *kāwaʻu* wood and had been hollowed on the under side. Its top was smooth and rounded. Near the log the young woman placed a calabash of water and a round beater.

She laid a strip of fine, cream-white bark on the log. Still praying, she began to beat. Down, down, down came the beater and the log rang with a sound as beautiful as the beat of a *hula* drum.

> "My *kapa* shall be clear as the light
> of the moon,
> White as the snow on the mountain,"

Keao chanted softly as she worked.

Beat, beat, beat! Now and then the young woman stopped to sprinkle the bark with water from her calabash. When the strip grew thin she folded the ends together, then beat until the strip was thin once more. Ana looked up from her own work. "Is it not time to fold the bark lengthwise?" she asked.

"Yes." Keao folded the long edges together, sprinkled and went on beating. The sticky sap in the bark held the fibers to each other as Keao folded and beat.

When one strip was finished she started another. Later she beat a number of these together until she had a piece wide as the length of her arm and long enough to make a wrapping for the baby. She worked steadily, happily. As she worked she half heard the music of other *kapa* logs. Each had a different tone, one high and clear, another deep and booming. Though Keao and her mother each worked alone, the music of many logs gave them companionship. Every woman up and down the beach must be pounding *kapa*.

The last beating was put off until next day. For that Keao planned to use the beater carved with designs used by women of her mother's family. One side bore a diamond-shaped design. That I shall use, the young woman thought.

Again she made an offering and prayed. She prayed as she worked, for this beating would leave the design in the *kapa*. It must be even over the whole piece.

At last she called her mother. Ana came at once and, without a word, took an end to help hold the *kapa* so that light could shine through. Both looked long and carefully. At last Ana said, "It is good."

"But here is an uneven place and in that corner figures cross each other."

"It is always so," her mother answered. "The whole is even and beautiful. More than that, this final beating makes the *kapa* soft and flexible so that it can be wrapped easily around Kehaulani."

"Kehaulani, Dew-of-heaven! Is that the name the baby is to have? How beautiful! If only I can dye it well my *kapa* shall be given to Kehaulani."

Dyeing and Printing

"Laua'e has sent for workers," Ana said next morning. "She has *kapa* to dye for our chiefess. You must help."

Keao loved to work with others in Laua'e's *kapa* yard, but today she had her own plans. "I thought you could help me dye my *kapa*, Ana."

"If you work with Laua'e for a few days you will not need my help. She is more skillful in dyeing and printing than anyone I know."

"Laua'e says you are the best *kapa*-maker in the district."

"I have some skill in beating perhaps," the mother answered, "but Laua'e knows more about dyeing and printing. Go, Keao."

It was fun to join the women in Lauaʻe's yard. Pua and ʻIlima were there and others of her own age. Lauaʻe set each one to work. "Here is your task, Keao," she said. "Crushing root bark is tiresome. I have chosen you because you are a steady worker. You will go on working until every bit is turned to powder."

Keao got a stone bowl and a pestle which was like a small *poi* pounder. She seated herself on a mat in a corner of the yard. Her task was slow and tiresome, but Lauaʻe's words of praise helped. So did the chants, the talk and laughter of those about her.

Once she stopped to join the others as they crowded around an attendant of the chiefess. "Tell us about the baby," everyone was asking.

"She is beautiful. From the top of her head to the soles of her feet she is perfect—our Kehaulani."

"Dew-of-heaven!" Keao went back to work with the name ringing in her ears. Dew waters plants that they may grow, she was thinking. "Dew gives life to the land. O gods," she prayed, "guard this little one from evil. May she be a wise chiefess who will give life to our district."

At last Keao had crushed all the root bark. Most of the other women had finished their tasks and had left. "You have done well," Lauaʻe praised her. "Tomorrow we shall dye."

"My arm and neck ache," Keao told her mother. "I crushed bark the whole time and did not learn a thing!"

The next day was different. Keao added water to the powdered bark in a large calabash. With Lauaʻe's help she dipped one of the chiefess' *kapa*. When that was dyed she had time to watch the work of others. ʻIlima and Pua were dipping *kapa* in dye made from crushed leaves and stems. One woman was grinding charcoal to make black dye for printing.

"I have learned much," Keao told Ana when the dyeing and printing were finished. "I think I am ready for work on my own *kapa*. I want it yellow."

Her mother raised her brows for "yes." "A chiefly color," she said.

"Leave the dyeing until tomorrow," her mother advised. "Do it when you are rested and the day is young."

When tomorrow came Keao added water to the powdered root bark and took out fibers. Then Ana helped her dip her *kapa*. "O gods," the young woman prayed, "let the color be even and lovely."

"That is enough," she told her mother when they had dipped several times. "That is just the soft yellow that I want."

"Think, Keao," Ana said. "When the *kapa* dries, will it still be this color?"

The young woman thought of the work in Laua'e's yard. "I remember *kapa* dipped in deep red," she said slowly. "When it dried it was pale pink. You are right, Ana. Let us dip more."

At last even Ana thought the color strong enough. "Are the *kī* leaves ready?" she asked.

"Yes. In the shade."

When the *kapa* had been spread to dry Keao still prayed, "O gods, give help that the yellow shall be even and smooth."

While the *kapa* was drying she pounded charcoal. *Kukui* nuts burned to charcoal made a good black for printing. Printing *kapa* seemed to her the most difficult part of the work, "except the last beating," she added in her mind.

She moistened the powdered charcoal and made ready the little bamboo printing sticks. She examined her *kapa* as it lay on the *kī* leaves. It was dry. And the color was

KAPA-*MAKING*

even! It was just the soft yellow she had wanted. Keao placed a smooth piece of wood under one edge of the yellow *kapa* to keep it smooth and firm for printing. Everything was ready.

Once more she laid an offering on the little shrine and prayed:

> "O Lauhuki, O Laʻahana,
> I thank you for your help in dyeing.
> Give me wisdom and skill
> To print my *kapa*."

Then her work began. The young woman dipped a three-pronged bamboo liner in the dye and pressed it near the edge of the *kapa*. She held the liner in her mouth by its clean end while she dipped a printing stick. She laid this just inside the lines and pressed it with her left hand. When she saw the pattern the two had made she drew a quick breath of joy. This printing is a sacred thing, she thought. O gods, make all the pattern clear.

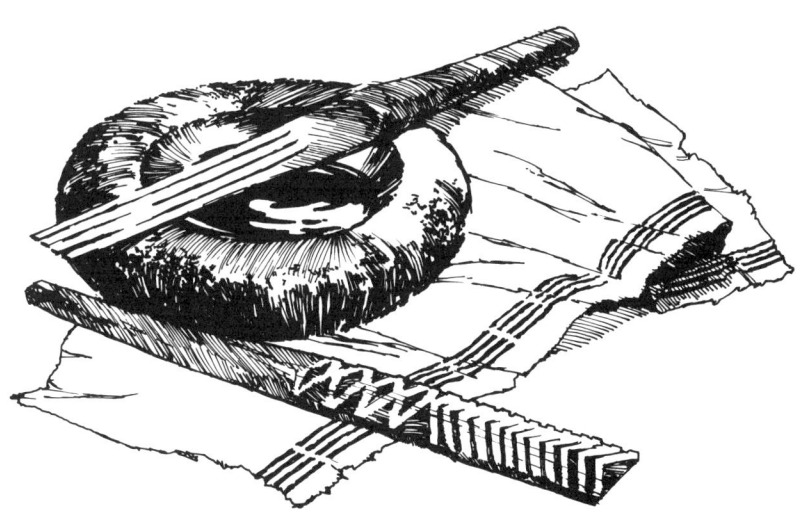

Again she dipped and pressed, dipped and pressed. Soon she must move her smooth wood farther along. She must add more lines, then dip and press the pattern. It is like waves breaking on the reef, she thought happily. O gods, help me to keep it even and beautiful.

Keao did not know how tired her arm and back had grown. She thought of nothing but the delicate black pattern growing on the yellow *kapa*.

The sun which had been low in the east was now overhead. Tiny beams crept between leaves of the *kukui* tree and touched the young woman as she rose at last from her work. She walked slowly about her *kapa* examining every part. Was it perfect? No. Here lines did not quite join. The pattern was not as clear and black as she had thought.

"It is lovely," Ana said.

"But not perfect."

"No work is perfect," the mother answered. "It is the work of a woman, not a god. The place where lines do not quite join shows how earnestly the woman tried."

"*Aloha!*" The two turned quickly to greet Laua'e. "I came to see whether Keao had dyed her *kapa*." Ana led the visitor into the yard. "Printed?" Laua'e exclaimed. "O, Keao, it is lovely! Did you do it all yourself?"

"With the help of the gods of *kapa*-making," the young woman answered.

Laua'e said quietly, "All work needs help from the gods. Put your lovely little *kapa* in a calabash with fragrant *maile* leaves. When Makahiki comes you shall give it to the baby chiefess."

A Morning on the Reef

Keao spread her sleeping mats over bushes and branches where wind and early sun could reach them. Suddenly 'Ilima stood beside her—'Ilima, wearing a *pā'ū* of vines and with her long hair coiled about her head. In one hand she carried a small net and in the other the stiff end of a *niu* leaf. Keao knew what these things meant. "You are going wandering," she said.

'Ilima raised her brows for "yes." "Will you come?"

"As soon as I take in the mats I have been airing."

"You had better change your *pā'ū*," 'Ilima suggested. "That one is too good to be torn by thorns and branches in the upland."

Keao chuckled softly as she piled her sleeping mats. This talk of thorns and branches amused her, for she knew 'Ilima was not going to the upland but out on the reef for fish. One never talked about one's fishing plans. Some bad spirit might hear and disturb or even warn the fish.

A few days ago 'Ilima told me no fish came to the *umu* of her family, Keao was thinking as she put on an old *pā'ū*. Then why the leaf and net? However she did not ask, but followed her friend to the water's edge.

There each picked up a bit of seaweed. With her left hand she tossed it into the waves praying:

"O Kū'ula,
  Keep us safe from harm from the sea,
  Safe from all evil."

More seaweed was tossed onto the sand, this time with the right hand. The young women prayed:

"O Hina,
  Keep us safe from harm from the land,
  Safe from all evil."

The two waded out in a sandy place. Keao loved the feel of wet sand between her toes and the wash of little waves about her ankles. She loved the pattern of moving sunlight through the waves. The young women were on coral now, stepping carefully. In spite of her care Keao slipped into a hole. What a splash! she thought as she climbed out. That upland pool was deep, she chuckled, but she did not speak or laugh aloud.

They reached the *umu,* a little underwater house of stones. It was loosely built so that water could flow through. At each end was an opening. Over one of these 'Ilima fitted her net, then raised her brows as a sign that she was ready.

Keao shook the stiff leaf at the other end, though she thought the *umu* was empty. She was surprised to see little fish dart into her friend's net.

A moment later 'Ilima rose holding up the net to show that it held many fish. The girls waded ashore and climbed to the shrine on the rocks. 'Ilima laid two of her fish on the shrine, thanking the gods for her good catch.

"I thought you said no fish came to that *umu*," Keao told her friend, "yet today there were many."

"My brother found that an eel was in the *umu* and small fish feared to hide there. He speared the unwanted visitor and took him home to broil for a meal. Soon the little fish came there to hide just as they hide among the rocks."

When her friend had gone Keao got a calabash. I shall gather seaweed for my family while I am dressed for the upland, she thought.

For a short time she stood on the sand listening and watching. Seabirds made shrill cries as they darted down for fish but the people she watched were quiet. Women made soft splashing sounds as they waded, searching in holes for fish or gathering *limu.* The cry of a child pinched by a crab was quickly hushed. An old woman left the ocean with a dip net in one hand and a well-filled calabash in the other. Keao saw her climb to the shrine to make an offering.

Still the young woman waited on the sand. Her eyes were searching among the many who worked over the reef. Where is Malu? she wondered. I have not seen the canoes go out. That man near the outer edge of the reef—can that be my husband? Yes, but what is he doing?

As Malu bent over, Keao saw a flash of sunlight on the cowrie shell he lowered on a short line. He is after *heʻe,* she thought with a shiver. Keao loved *heʻe,* octopus, as food—dried and salted or cooked in the *imu.* But she did not like to touch a live one.

Malu told me that in one district a man reaches his arm right into the hiding place of the *heʻe.* When the animal has twined itself about him he pulls it out. *Ē!* I'm glad Malu fishes with line and hook.

Though she could not see clearly what her husband was doing, her mind followed him. He was bending over, lowering hook and shell before a hole where a *heʻe* was hiding. A stone sinker tied to the cowrie carried it down. Now the animal was trying to get the shell with one of its long arms, for a live cowrie was food. The *heʻe* tried to pull it into its hole, but Malu held his line firm. Out came another arm and another. As the *heʻe* could not pull the cowrie into its hole it reached out with more arms until its whole body hugged the shell. With a quick jerk Malu straightened up. This was the part Keao did not like. What if those slimy arms should get hold of Malu! His neck! His head!

But Malu had already bitten the animal between the eyes. It was dead. He dropped it into the bag fastened to his *malo.* Keao was almost glad to see her husband wade farther off where she could not watch him.

I am silly to worry about Malu, she told herself. He is skillful and quicker than any *heʻe.* With this thought she drove away her worry and waded out to find her family's favorite kinds of *limu.*

A Morning on the Deep Blue Sea

What was that? Malu woke with a start and lay listening. He heard again the scratching that had awakened him. A rat in a gourd! Why? he wondered sleepily. Never before have I heard a rat in our new sleeping house.

Suddenly Malu was wide awake. He was not at home! He was in 'Aukai's house, near the shrine. 'Aukai was going deep-sea fishing. And he will take me! the young man thought excitedly. Nothing had been said of this, lest the fish should hear and be wary, but Malu was sure that 'Aukai wanted Malu to go with him.

Like a flash yesterday's happenings went through Malu's mind. He had found the head fisherman tying hooks to the bamboos of his deep-sea line. "Get what we shall need," 'Aukai had said.

Malu went for *he'e,* for its arms can be cut in pieces and used as bait. When night was near 'Aukai's other helpers had been sent away but a gesture had commanded Malu to share the master's meal. 'Aukai had prayed earnestly as he made an offering of *'awa* and *lū'au.*

When the meal was cleared away the head fisherman spread mats near the shrine. He always slept near the shrine before a day of important fishing. Malu turned to leave but was called back by a sign. 'Aukai wanted him to share his mats!

The young man lay down beside his master, too excited to sleep. Deep-sea fishing was secret fishing and the master never took any of his helpers to the secret fishing grounds. True, Hepa paddled, but Hepa was a stupid fellow. He was too stupid to even wonder where they went.

How could 'Aukai himself tell where to find his fishing ground? By landmarks, yes. But how?

Again that scratching noise—louder this time. 'Aukai wakened. "The gourds are calling," he said in a low voice. "Come." He rose from his mats.

Malu was up at once. He almost laughed as he thought of the sound which had awakened him. I thought it was a rat, he told himself, but it was the gourds in their net outside the door, rattled by the early wind. 'Aukai knew that they would wake him.

The master lit a candle of *kukui* nuts. He made an offering and the two ate quickly. Carrying a calabash of fishing gear they went to the canoe. Malu took off the canoe covering and the canoe was launched. The two stepped in. Malu paddled while the master steered.

The young man was strong and paddled fast. The morning star dimmed and sky and sea were softly colored by the coming sun.

'Aukai was looking toward their island and Malu's gaze followed his. They had come so far that, while the mountain peaks were clear, they could no longer see the lowlands. The young man noticed how two of these peaks looked to be in line. The nearer one seemed like a hill on the slope of the other. To the right another peak rose higher still.

'Aukai signaled Malu to paddle gently. Again the master gazed earnestly toward the island. Malu knew that he too must look. Now all three peaks were in line. That was the landmark!

But that is not enough, the young man thought. One might paddle far and keep those peaks in line. The master's eye caught Malu's. Then he gazed toward the east. Malu turned and also gazed eastward. The sun was just rising behind the peak of another island. That was the other landmark! They had reached the fishing ground.

'Aukai signaled that Malu was to hold the canoe in this place while he fished. The master took out his deep-sea line. The day before he had tied a bone hook to each of five bamboos near the end of this line. He had left threads above each hook. Now, with these threads, he tied on bits of *heʻe*. He fastened the end of the line around a chunk of lava rock. Malu understood that this was a weight to carry hooks and bait deep into the ocean.

A current was trying to pull the canoe away. Only by steady gentle paddling could Malu keep the landmarks where they should be.

ʻAukai paid out his line. When the lava rock touched bottom he gave a quick jerk to free it then raised his hooks just a little off the bottom. Almost at once he started to pull in his line, coiling it so that it should not tangle. How long it took! The ocean must be very deep in this place. Suddenly the hooks appeared. On three were fish, red-gold beauties from deep ocean.

Malu paddled steadily to keep the canoe in place. Yet he watched every move his master made. ʻAukai baited the hooks again, put on another weight and let out his line once more. This time he caught five fish.

To Malu's surprise ʻAukai passed the line to him. While the master paddled Malu tied on bait and lava rock. He worked quietly but under his quiet was great excitement. He let out the line. Out and out it ran. Would it never reach the ocean floor? Perhaps it had! How could he tell?

He knew! Through the long line he felt a bump as the rock touched bottom. With a jerk he loosened it then raised the hooks a little as ʻAukai had done. He waited. If a fish took the bait how should he know?

He felt a tiny tug. Was that a fish? As quickly as he could he pulled in his line, coiling it carefully. *Ē!* The line was so long. If he ever had a fish it must be gone by now. At last the hooks came up. No fish but only four hooks were baited! With a smile ʻAukai signed that a fish had taken bait from one. He showed Malu how to tie the bits of *heʻe* more firmly.

Another weight was tied on and Malu let out his line again. He remembered that his master had once told how he knew when deep-sea fish were on his hooks. "Their tug is like the tug of little pigs nursing and resting," he had said.

Suddenly the young man felt a tiny tug at the end of that long line! This time he had a fish. If only he did not lose it! It took so long to draw up the line.

The hooks at last! On three were fish! Malu put the largest at the prow. His first fish must be in a safe and honorable place, for it would be an offering to the gods.

The two fished until the sun was high, taking turns. Once Malu had a fish on every hook—five more red-gold beauties. 'Aukai was pleased and Malu was filled with joy.

"We have enough," the master said at last. "Paddle west."

West was not toward home. Malu wondered but he obeyed without even a questioning look. The sun was hot, the young man was tired and knew himself to be paddling away from home. Yet he was happy—happy and excited.

"Now toward shore," the master said. Malu obeyed. 'Aukai was steering and the canoe rounded a point of land. Waves were breaking on a reef. There was their landing place. As they came in sight of it the master spoke in a low earnest voice. "Today, O Malu, we have fished at the chief's own fishing ground where rocks rise from the bottom of the sea and make a hiding place for fish. No one knows how to reach that place except our district chief and his head fisherman. I have no son and pass the secret on to you. Someday you will be head fisherman."

Malu said nothing but his look told 'Aukai that he understood the meaning of the secret.

"You know the landmarks?" Malu raised his brows. Clear in his mind were the three peaks in line while the sun rose behind the island to the east.

'Aukai went on, "Never paddle straight to the fishing ground or straight home from it." Again Malu made a sign for "yes." That was why he had been told to paddle west, then circle toward the landing place. No curious watcher would guess where their fish were caught.

"A good ground such as this is like a parent or grandparent who gives food to a child," the master said earnestly. "This fishing ground gives food for our chief and for his attendants. A man should give up life itself rather than give up the secret of such a place."

No more was said. After the canoe was beached each took his first fish for an offering to the gods of fishing. Then they carried their good catch to the home of the district chief and gave all but a share for themselves to the attendants in charge of food.

As Malu turned toward home he seemed to hear again the master's words: "A man should give up life itself rather than give up the secret of a fishing ground."

Upland Gardens

A Visit of the Overseer

"The overseer is coming! The overseer is coming!" It was Kaiki, the son of Keao's oldest brother, who burst into the *kapa* yard with the news.

"Be careful where you step, Grandson," Ana warned gently. "Dirty footmarks on damp *kapa* strips will not be a good sight for our overseer."

"He is talking to Nāwai, the netmaker," the boy told them eagerly. "Nāwai has not one finished net. The overseer said that he had hands like those of a wooden image."

"Kaiki!" Ana spoke sternly. "It is not for a boy to repeat criticism of an older man. Wait until you yourself do more than play before you carry tales about the work of others. Be off now to carry news of the overseer's visit. Tell everyone you see, Grandson, and do not stop to listen to words not meant for your ears."

The boy raced eagerly away. Soon the overseer himself appeared. People called him a stern hard man. But Ana, and Puakō her husband, respected him. "He is hard only to those who do not work," Puakō had said. "Many would spend their time in idleness. Their gifts would not be ready for the Makahiki. Their families would go hungry. Better a hard overseer than starvation!"

But the overseer did not seem a hard man as he looked at Ana's work. He said little but his face showed pleasure. When Ana brought out the *kapa* striped with pink and gray the overseer examined it with care. "You made it?" he asked. "I have never seen a *kapa* like this. You must offer this to Lono at the Makahiki season. Such work is fit for our high chief."

"That is my Makahiki gift," Ana replied. "Also, I am making a white *kapa* to be carried with Father Lono when he goes around our island. Lono's *kahuna* sent a runner asking that I make it. The *kapa* that goes with Lono was torn last year by a sudden wind."

The overseer was pleased. "You have done much," he said, then turned suddenly to Keao. "Have you no Makahiki gift?" he asked. "Has all your time been given to making *kapa* for yourself and Malu? Then you are no true daughter of your mother!"

"I made a *kapa* for the little chiefess," Keao told him. "Her mother was pleased with it and said that it can be my Makahiki gift."

"That is well," the overseer answered. "You are learning from Ana who is always beforehand with her work and from your grandfather. *E,* old man!" The overseer spoke loudly as though Grandfather were deaf. "Are all these balls of cord your work? If the young men worked as you do, this district would never know starvation."

"Where is Puakō?" he added, turning again to Ana.

"In the *kalo* patch, fixing a broken wall."

Kaiki had finished his errand, announcing the coming of the overseer, and now, with other children, followed him to the *kalo* patch. A number of men were mending a broken wall. They had built up stones and were packing earth firmly about them. They joined the overseer and followed him respectfully as he walked along the banks. He examined the *kalo*—some well-weeded patches of young shoots, some strong mature plants ready for pulling. He examined the *kī, kō* and *maiʻa*. "These are good ponds," he said at last, "but they are too small."

"The stream is small," Lako explained. "It will not water more ponds."

"That is true. But what of the upland? There the rainfall is heavy. There you should have much land planted with *kalo.*"

"We have *'uala,* sweet potatoes, up there now and they do not grow well," Pakī objected. "Why plant *kalo?*"

The overseer spoke angrily. "Why *should* they grow well?" he asked. "Have you prayed? Have you worked? Of course your *'uala* are small and poor. You give them no more thought than you would give to wild sweet potatoes. I have talked with our district chief about this matter." The overseer was speaking more quietly. "Two days from now we shall get *hau* and *kukui* twigs to cover the potato patch. We shall pray. Then we shall prepare land for a large new *kalo* patch. Be ready for many days of work in the upland. This is our chief's command."

The men were silent as the overseer walked away but when he was out of hearing they began to talk. "He has gone to tell other men," said Pakī. "Nāwai won't be pleased. 'Make more nets,' the overseer tells him. Then a little later, 'Get *hau* twigs for the *'uala.*'"

"This is a poor time for upland work," grumbled another man. "The trail is long when the sun beats down. Why not wait for rain?"

"The overseer is right," Puakō said. "We must get the *hau* and *kukui.* We must clear land for *kalo.* Then we shall be ready for the rain."

"Yes." It was old Lako speaking. "A time of drought will come if our small stream should cease to flow. Then we shall be glad of sturdy plants in the upland. Let us finish this wall and sharpen our tools for cutting *hau* and *kukui.*"

The 'Uala *Field*

"O Keao, what a beautiful *lei!* Who is to wear it?" Kaiki had come in from surfing with other boys of his age. Now he stopped beside the group of girls and women who were braiding *lei.*

"This is for Father," Keao answered. "Tomorrow the men are going to get *hau* branches. Everyone must wear a *lei*. Such a sign of plenty is pleasing to the gods."

Kaiki ran off for a dry *malo,* then looked for his grandfather. He found him sharpening adzes on a hard rock by the stream. The boy watched quietly. When the work was finished he spoke: "Grandfather, I want to go with you tomorrow to work in the upland."

Puakō's eyes twinkled. "You want to wear a *lei?*" he asked. "And go with a company of men and boys? The way will be long and hot."

"I am almost a man, Grandfather."

Puakō looked at the well-built little figure before him. "You are strong, Kaiki," he answered. "But have you patience? Can you take a long trail without complaint? And can you work and pray? If you go tomorrow you do not go to race about and shout. You do not go to play with the little ones. You go to work."

"Yes, Grandfather," Kaiki spoke seriously, "I will work."

"Then be ready at dawn," Puakō told him and the boy raced away to gather *kou* blossoms to make himself a *lei*.

"I am going to work in the upland," he shouted to Noe, his best friend.

"So am I," Noe answered. "My father says boys are needed to climb the trees and break off leafy twigs."

Kaiki had hoped to be the only boy with the company of men. But when he took the trail in the chill of early morning he was glad of the companionship of Noe and the other boys. Men and boys wore fresh *lei* and carried backloads of food and tools. Most were happy to be going up the trail in a company. But all were quiet, for shouting and loud laughter would not please the gods of the upland.

The way was long. Part of it led over rough lava rock. Here the men stopped to put on sandals made of dry *maiʻa* leaves or *wauke* bark. Some of the boys had made sandals for themselves but neither Kaiki nor Noe had thought of this protection. They looked at each other, a little ashamed of their thoughtlessness. Then each squared his shoulders. Their feet were tough! They did not need sandals! But the two were walking very carefully before the rough stretch was past. Their feet were scratched in spite of their toughness but neither boy complained. Nor did they complain of the dusty stretch where the sun beat down upon them. They had fallen a little behind the others. They had taken many drinks from their water gourds so that now both gourds were empty. Still neither boy complained.

They were very glad, however, to reach the edge of the forest. Men and boys stopped to rest in a green and shady spot beside a spring. "Don't drink too much," Puakō warned his grandson. "Fill your gourd but drink only a few swallows." Kaiki obeyed though he longed to drink all that his gourd could hold.

Now the men separated, some following the stream to gather *hau* twigs and others entering small gulches. Kaiki went with his grandfather. Kaiki climbed *kukui* trees and broke off leafy twigs. He dropped these to Puakō who bound them in bundles. Each carried a backload of *kukui* leaves and twigs as they made their way to the sweet-potato field.

All were gathering there. Kaiki saw the need for prayer and work. The *ʻuala* vines were weak and yellowing. Now, under the overseer's direction, the patch was thickly covered with leafy twigs. In one corner Lako thrust the leafy end of a *hau* branch into the ground. The stalk stood upright but the leaves were deeply buried in the earth. "Is he planting it?" Kaiki whispered to Puakō.

"No. It is a testing branch," his grandfather answered. "After a time Lako will pull it out. If the leaves have not rotted he will put it back and wait. When the leaves of that branch have rotted, we shall know that all our covering of leaves has rotted also. We shall know that they have given their power to the earth so that it is ready for the planting of new slips. As wild trees and plants grow abundantly in the forest so will our *'uala* grow abundantly. It is for that we pray.

As the men prayed Kaiki listened reverently. He saw that Noe was praying with the others. Noe knew the prayers! I must learn them too, thought Kaiki as he listened. The men prayed to Lono to come in his cloud form and watch over their garden:

> "O great black cloud,
> Watch over this field.
> It belongs to you and to us.
> O great black cloud,
> Bring rain to our field
> That it may grow
> And bear abundantly."

They prayed to the great god, Kāne, asking him to come in his pig form to root in the field, to loosen the earth and bring good growth to the *'uala:*

> "O Kānepua'a,
> Root from this corner to that corner,
> From that border to this border,
> To increase the root,
> To increase the stem,
> To increase the branches,
> To increase the creeping roots.
> Preserve our field for the life of our families,
> For those belonging to our houses,
> And for strangers turning into our houses.
> The plants are growing and increasing for
>   Kānepua'a."

Kaiki felt deeply happy. He had worked with the men. He had shared work with the gods. Today he understood for the first time that men and gods work together to bring life to the land. Kaiki followed Grandfather to a cave where they were to spend the night. "Remember that our sweet-potato field is *kapu* now," Grandfather said. "No stone or stick may be thrown there. The great god, Kāne, will come in his pig form to root in our field. You will not see him, but he will be there. You must not anger him."

"I will remember," the boy promised earnestly.

The Kalo *Patch*

Mats laid on fern leaves made a comfortable bed and Kaiki was warm beneath the *kapa* covers he had brought from home. Next morning, while it was still dark, the boy awakened. Puakō was crawling from his place beside him. "Grandfather," Kaiki whispered, "I want to go with you. Remember how hard I worked in the *'uala* field?"

"Come then," Puakō answered, "since you are awake. We are going to cut digging sticks to use in clearing land for our new *kalo* patch." He took the covered food containers from the ledge where he had placed them. He made an offering to the gods and ate. "Here is dried fish and *poi*," he said to Kaiki.

"I am not hungry," the boy replied.

"Then take this cooked *mai'a*. By and by you will want to eat."

Outside dawn had come and clouds were already touched with pink. The trail led beside the *'awa* patch. In the growing light Kaiki could see *'awa* bushes. They were green and sturdy, not pale and sick like the *'uala* vines. That is good, thought Kaiki, for we must have *'awa* as an offering to the gods. I suppose the spirit of the *'awa* gives rest to the gods just as the drink gives rest to tired men. Also, the chiefs want much.

They passed the garden and came to the *kauila* grove. Here they were joined by other men. Puakō had brought *'awa* drink and as he offered this to the forest gods to whom the trees belonged, he prayed:

> "O Kū who spreads green over the uplands,
> Watch over the hewing of the *'ō'ō*.
> O Kū, take the *'awa*
> And give success to this work of ours."

Puakō drank a little of the *'awa* which was shared with the god and the men began cutting long *kauila* limbs for *'ō'ō*, or digging sticks. "In some districts short digging sticks are used," Grandfather explained to Kaiki. "The digging goes well with those but a man must work stooped over. His back gets very tired."

When the men had cut and sharpened all the sticks needed they returned to the others who had started clearing land for *kalo* planting. They were cutting down tree ferns and bushes and uprooting vines. Moving about among them, the overseer directed the work.

Kaiki found his friend. The sun was high by now and Noe was wet with perspiration. "This is hard work," he said as he stopped to wipe his face.

As Kaiki looked at Noe he burst out laughing. "Why are you laughing at me?" Noe asked crossly.

"I am not laughing at you," Kaiki explained. "It's just the mud on your face where you've wiped it with dirty hands."

"I wish the field were muddy!" Noe exclaimed. "My father says we should have waited for a rainy time. Here, Kaiki, help me pull."

The two boys tugged at the vine. "Let's dig around it to get it loose," Kaiki suggested. "Now! Let us pull together." A long strong pull and suddenly the boys sat down with the vine in their arms.

Several smaller boys had come to the upland with their fathers. These little fellows were very busy about something at the edge of the forest. "Let's go and see what they are doing," Noe suggested.

"No," answered Kaiki, "I promised Grandfather that I would work. I am almost a man," and he went on digging and pulling.

Noe was tired and sat on the ground watching his friend. "Don't throw those plants away," he warned. "When the rain comes they must all be tramped into the ground to give food to the *kalo*. The gods don't want anything wasted."

For a long time Kaiki worked with short rests between. How slowly the sun goes! he thought. I wish the ocean were here so we could wash and cool off! But he did not speak his thought even to his friend.

"Noe! Kaiki!" The smaller boys were calling them.

"They need us," Noe said. "Let us see what they want."

"Yes, we shall see what they want. Then we shall work again," Kaiki answered. He was tired and glad of an excuse to stop.

The small boys had dug a little *imu*. They had lined it with stones and had piled bits of dry wood on them. "Help us make a fire," they begged.

"Those stones aren't the right kind," Noe told them. "We have to get stones that will hold the heat," and in a moment he and Kaiki had joined the play. They dug the *imu* deeper and lined it with stones which would hold heat and would not burst when heated.

"I know just how to pile the wood so it will burn," said Kaiki, stooping over the *imu*. "You get the fire-making sticks, Noe."

Noe started off then stopped to look about. "I wish we hadn't made the *imu* so close to the forest," he said. "I don't think Father will let me start a fire here. Oh look, Kaiki!" he added. "Lako is talking to your grandfather. Now they are walking off. I think they are going home."

"Not without me!" exclaimed Kaiki. "Come!" And the two raced away, leaving the smaller boys no better off then when they had joined the play.

The two men stood talking beside the trail as the boys came panting up to them. Kaiki was eager to know where Puakō was going. He was eager to go with him but he controlled his impatience and waited quietly until Grandfather noticed him.

"Oh, here you are!" Puakō said at last. "The overseer is sending Lako and me to get *kalo* slips for planting. I had better take you home. This work is too heavy for small boys."

A bath in the ocean! Kaiki thought happily. Then he remembered his friend. "May Noe go with us?" he asked.

"Yes. Tell your father, Noe, while Kaiki and I get our things."

Kalo *Slips*

Early next morning the two boys were racing along the beach. Now and then they stopped to throw a stick into the bay that Noe's dog might swim for it. "Look!" Kaiki suddenly exclaimed. "Grandfather is uncovering his canoe!"

A moment later the boys joined Puakō. "Let us help," Kaiki offered and lifted off the last coarse mat. Each took his place behind one of the crosspieces, or *'iako,* which join outrigger to canoe, and grasped it with both hands. At a signal they lifted the heavy canoe and slowly carried it into the waves. Then they stood looking up eagerly at Grandfather.

He understood the question in their faces. "Lako and I are going to the next village for *kalo* slips," he told them. "That district has fine upland gardens. Our relatives who live there will give us slips for planting." At that moment Lako appeared. "Shall we take these boys?" Grandfather asked him and Kaiki and Noe held their breath as they waited for an answer.

"Can you keep still?" Lako asked. "Children who chatter in the presence of their elders are ill-mannered and disturbing. Those who watch quietly can learn. Can you two be still if you go with us?" he asked the boys.

Eagerly each made the sign for "yes," a quick lift of the eyebrows. Lako saw their eagerness. "Let them come," he said as he stepped into the canoe.

Puakō called to a passerby, leaving word that the boys were safe with him, and they were off. Oh, the joy of the early morning paddle into the wind! Then the canoe rounded a point and changed its course. The triangular sail of *lau hala* was raised and the canoe raced through the waves. *Mālolo,* flying fish, darted into the air before them, gleaming silver in the sunshine. One splashed into Kaiki's lap and the boy gave a small cry of surprise, then grasped the fish and held it firmly.

A few moments later they reached the village. "There is the shrine," Grandfather said and pointed to a high point near the sea. Kaiki's heart gave a sudden leap. This was his first fish! He must offer it to Kū'ula! The four climbed to the shrine. On a pile of rocks stood one special stone. No person had carved it yet it looked a little like a man. Before that stone Kaiki laid his fish.

While Grandfather prayed the boy looked earnestly at the strange rock. He felt that Kūʻula himself had sent it. Puakō prayed:

> "O Kūʻula,
> The boy has brought his first fish.
> He offers it to you
> That you may bless him.
> One day this boy will be a man.
> Give him success
> That he may provide food for his people."

Kaiki walked behind the rest as the men and boys went down into the village. In his mind were the thoughts of the strange stone, his own first fish and Grandfather's prayer. He was indeed almost a man!

As they passed through the village, Lako and Puakō stopped now and then to chat with friends. Feeling strange and shy the boys looked about.

Puakō's cousin, a white-haired man, was sitting on a mat in the shade and twisting *olonā* fibers into cord. "Slips for planting?" he repeated when Grandfather had explained their errand. "Yes. We have two kinds. Yesterday my son pulled *kalo lehua* to make delicious pink *poi* for the chiefs. We saved the slips. Also we have slips of *wehiwa*, a quick-growing kind. Come with me to get them."

The boys followed, remembering Lako's words about keeping still. Puakō's cousin led them to his *kalo* patch. From the moist bank he pulled a bundle of slips bound together with morning-glory vine. "Why, they are just the tops cut from the *kalo* that we cook," Noe whispered softly, but the old man heard. "See these tiny buds," he said, showing the slips. "They are root buds. From them strong roots will grow. We have good *kalo* and always save the cuttings for relatives and friends who want to plant.

You carry these," he added, laying the bundle in Noe's arms, "and my young cousin, here, can carry the *wehiwa*."

"Take the cuttings to the canoe," Puakō directed.

As they turned to obey the boys heard the cousin say, "In ten days or so our long-leafed *kalo* will be ready. You must have slips of that for it is the kind the *kahuna* offers to the gods. Why don't you send your new son-in-law to get those cuttings, Puakō? Then we may get to know him."

The boys returned to the beach, laid their bundles of slips in the shady end of the canoe, then looked about. "There's something I never saw before," remarked Kaiki, motioning to a pole firmly planted in the sand at the water's edge and leaning seaward. "What do you suppose it's for?"

"For some sort of fishing," Noe answered. "There is a line attached to the top, running to the bottom and then out to sea."

Just at that moment the line began to shake violently and caused a rattling sound at the pole's top. "It's a fish!" Noe was jumping up and down in excitement. "A big fish is caught! What shall we do, Kaiki?"

Before Kaiki could think, a young man came running, summoned by the rattling sound. He seized the line and pulled. The fish pulled mightily and the boys watched the struggle in great excitement. At last the fish was tired and the young man pulled it in—a large *ulua*. "Good!" both boys shouted as he landed it.

The young man baited his hook and threw it far out once more. As he picked up his *ulua,* he turned toward the eager boys. "This is a good scheme," he remarked. "You see I'm a woodcarver. My master's work yard is right over there. I attach my line to that gourd partly filled with shells at the top of the pole. When a fish is caught it rattles the shells to call me." He laughed. "This is the fourth today! One for Kū'ula, two for my master, this one for my family. I need one more for my wife's parents."

As the young man returned to his woodcarving, Lako and Puakō reached the canoe and the four paddled home. Noe and Kaiki exchanged looks. Each knew the other was thinking, keeping still and watching has been fun!

Back in their own village the boys helped to carry the canoe onto the beach and spread mats over it to protect it from the hot sunshine. Then they ran to the lowland *kalo* patch where Puakō was putting the bundles of slips into the moist bank. "So they will keep damp," Kaiki remarked.

"Yes," his grandfather replied, "and the root buds will grow. We always keep slips for planting bundled together, for so they keep the power of growth the gods have given them."

Toward nightfall the other men returned from the upland. "The *kalo* land is cleared," they said. "Now if the gods send rain, we can soon plant."

Rain

That night the rain began. Kaiki was wakened by its whisper on the thatch of the sleeping house. He sniffed the odors which the rain brought out. It must be raining in the upland, he told himself drowsily. Then he was roused again, this time by a roar. The gentle rain had become a downpour. This will soak the upland *kalo* patch, he thought. He pulled the *kapa* about him and, dry and warm, slept once more.

The rain continued for a week. Reef fishing was spoiled by muddy water, sleeping houses were moist and cooking places too wet to use. Food supplies were giving out, families were chilly, wet and tired of staying in damp crowded houses. But no one complained for complaint might anger Lono. Instead they rejoiced that the new *kalo* patch would be ready for planting!

The rainy days were good for ocean fishing but men returned at the day's end as wet as the fish that filled their canoes. Keao saw Malu coming and ran from the *kapa* house to meet him. "You are shivering," she said as she handed him a dry *malo*. "Here! Put on your shoulder *kapa*."

"Get a dry one for yourself, sweetheart," Malu advised. "We all need *kī*-leaf rain capes such as the men wear in the upland."

"Let us ask Nāwai to make a net cape for you," said Keao quickly. "Then I'll tie on the *kī* leaves. Every fisherman needs such a cape."

"Good!" her husband answered. "'Aukai has one. It helps to keep a man dry and warm on a day like this. I have thought much about you, Keao," he added. "The *kapa* house must be a dark place to work, these days."

"Oh, we can see to beat *wauke*," Keao answered bravely. "Dyeing and printing can wait till sunny days. The rain is worse for men. Poor Father! He can neither farm nor cook!"

"But he has a good time!" Malu answered. "I saw a crowd of men in Lako's house as I came by. Puakō was there with Grandfather. Some were playing games or telling stories, others were listening while they twisted *olonā* cords. The rain is a vacation time for them. Why don't you join your friends for a friendly talk?"

"Not while my husband fishes!" replied Keao quickly. "Let's wrap in a *kapa*," she added. "We are both shivering still."

"Food is ready, Keao!" Puakō's voice sounded through the storm. "Has Malu returned from fishing?"

The two ran swiftly to the eating houses. Their *kapa* capes were damp before they could reach shelter. "It is good that you salted much fish," Malu said to Puakō as the meal began. "Some in this village have no food left."

"The *poi* is almost gone," answered the older man, "but I think of how our crops will flourish after this good rain!" Hungrily men and boys began their meal.

As they were finishing, voices called outside: "*E*, Puakō! May we come in? We want a game of *no'a*."

"It is Lako!" Malu exclaimed, jumping up to push aside the door board. The chilly eating house, smoky from the *kukui*-nut candles, became suddenly a happy place. Puakō and Kaiki gathered up *niu* shell bowls and put away the food mat while Malu ran to get the pieces of *kapa* used in playing *no'a*.

He found Ana and Keao in Ana's sleeping house. It was dimly lighted by a lamp which gave out a pungent odor. Malu saw that the house was filled with girls and women. Keao brought him the *kapa* he wanted. As he darted back through the rain Malu heard the women chanting. Now I can enjoy the game, he thought, knowing that Keao, too, is happy.

When he returned to the men's eating house he found the players already arranged. They sat on the floor mat in two lines facing each other. There were five on one side and four on the other. Kahana, Malu's special friend, beckoned him to join the four. Between the two lines of players Puakō arranged the *kapa* pieces. There were five of these, of different colors. Each was folded in a loose bundle and they were laid in line, touching. A player could put his arm under the *kapa* at one end and slip his hand back and forth under the five pieces. As he did this, he left a small stone under one. Under which one? That was for the other side to guess.

Lako was on the side opposite Malu. He held the pebble for he was to have first turn to hide. To a player on Malu's side Puakō gave a polished wooden rod with a bit of *kī* leaf tucked in the tip end. The rod was longer than a man's arm and one end was slit a little to hold the leaf. "You are to have first turn to guess," Kahana said to Malu.

"Oh, no!" Malu replied. "I am not lucky at this game."

"It is not luck," said Keao's grandfather. "Watch the muscles of the arm that has the stone. By the movement of those muscles one who sees can tell when the hand lets go the stone."

"I can't!" Malu insisted. "You be first on our side, Grandfather. You show where the stone is hidden."

The old man was nearly blind, but he loved the game and took his turn eagerly. Lako put his hand and arm up to the elbow under the end *kapa*. He moved it under all five pieces, back and forth several times. At last he drew out his hand and sat with his head bowed and his eyes fixed on his lap.

Malu's side began to point, first at one piece of *kapa* and then at another. They were not guessing yet. They were watching Lako, thinking his face would show when they pointed to the *kapa* under which the stone was hidden. But Lako's head was down and his eyes looked only at his hands resting in his lap. He did not show that he knew the men were pointing. They could learn nothing that way. They turned to the old grandfather. "The middle *kapa*," he said in a low voice. Kahana directed the blind man's hand and he struck the middle *kapa* sharply with the rod.

Puakō lifted the *kapa* and there lay the stone! "*Ē! Ē!* Good for the blind man!" his companions exclaimed. They had won their first point and all were pleased.

How did he know? wondered Malu. Perhaps his guardian spirit told him where the pebble lay.

Another man took the stone. Again Malu tried to see when the hider dropped the stone but he could not. Again Malu's side began to point. When someone pointed to the blue *kapa* the hider's face grew troubled. Kahana had

first turn to guess. He struck the blue *kapa* and there lay the stone.

The other side hid five times. When Malu had first turn to guess he struck the middle *kapa*. It was lifted. There was nothing there. I was just guessing, he told himself and watched the man next to him. He had no better luck. That round Malu's side missed four times. Lucky for them their other scores were good.

The game went on. Each side hid five times. Malu's side was one point ahead. After a time they changed the rule. Now instead of trying to strike the *kapa* under which the stone was hidden, they tried not to strike the right one. That time Lako's side won by two points.

The candles of *kukui* nuts had been renewed several times during the game. As Puakō got up to look for more he noticed that the rain had stopped. The men crowded through the low doorway and out into the yard. The stars were shining. "Tomorrow we must rise early," Lako said. "After a long rain there is much to be done. Let us go to our mats."

Kaiki had watched the game for a long time, wishing he could play. The men were deeply interested in their guessing, no one paid attention to the little boy. Kaiki grew tired. Finally he slipped off through the rain to the sleeping house. The visiting women and girls had returned to their homes and Ana and Keao were alone. They were sitting, cuddled together for warmth, wrapped in *kapa* and talking in low tones.

"O Ana," Kaiki said, "I am tired of rain!"

"Grandson," Ana spoke sternly, "that is something you must never say, something you must not even think. Rain is the good gift of the great god Lono. It fills our streams and springs and feeds our plants. Without it we should die. Rain, sunshine, winds—these are life-giving. Never find fault with them. Remember always, Kaiki."

The boy looked up at Ana with solemn eyes. "I will never forget," he promised.

"In some districts," said Keao gently, "there is not rain enough. Men pray for water and sometimes the gods answer their prayers in strange ways. Do you know about the cave of Mākālei?"

"No. Tell me, Keao."

"Mākālei was a boy about your age. He went with his parents and sisters to live in Kona on the island of Hawai'i. His father was a farmer and as soon as the family reached their new home he set about planting. 'It's no use to plant here,' a neighbor told him. 'There is very little rain. It is hard enough to get water for yourself. There is none for your crops.' The father found this to be true and was much discouraged. His family would starve! Though he prayed earnestly, no rain fell.

"One day Mākālei was out behind the house. He felt a gust of wind that seemed to come up out of the ground. The boy searched and found a small hole from which the wind was blowing. He called his father. 'This is a strange thing,' the father said and broke away rock until they could look down into a cave. In the cave they heard a dripping sound. Water! 'Tonight we shall make a larger hole,' the father added. 'We shall take *kukui*-nut torches and examine it. Now let us cover the hole with grass and sticks and keep it secret.'

"After dark they pushed off the grass and sticks and the father pounded on the rock until he had made a larger opening. He lowered Mākālei into the cave and followed him. They lighted torches and looked around. The cave was large. They could stand and walk about. There was not a stream in the cave, but its walls were wet. Water dripped steadily. 'Tomorrow we shall get logs,' the father said, 'and hollow them to catch the water.'

"And so they did. They took logs into the cave the next night and hollowed them as a canoe is hollowed. When they came again their logs were filled with water. Each night Mākālei and his father dipped water from their cave and watered their garden. When they left the cave they pulled grass and sticks over the entrance to hide their secret.

"No other vegetables in that part of Kona grew so well as those of Mākālei's father. People stopped to admire his fine sturdy *kalo* and *'uala*. 'The gods are very good to this man,' they said. It was many years before they knew about the cave of Mākālei."

"Mother," Keao whispered, "Kaiki has gone to sleep." She slipped from under the *kapa* and stooped to look out the doorway. "The rain is over," she called softly, "and stars are bright. The men are going home," she added and ran to meet her husband. Together they gave thanks for rain and clearing weather.

After the Rain

The village was up at dawn. Puakō went at once to a cave where he stored driftwood. Even in this dry cave the wood had become damp. He brought backloads of the damp wood and spread it out where the morning sun could dry it.

During the heavy rain his *imu* had filled with water. This had drained away but the pit and stones were still damp. Puakō took out the stones and laid them in a sunny spot. Sunshine poured down drying them and the *imu*.

While wood, stones and *imu* dried, Puakō pulled *kalo* and washed it in the *'auwai,* the ditch which brought water to the *kalo* patch. Besides his carrying net, heavy with *kalo,* he brought *mai'a* leaves and some stalks of juicy *kō*. From a pit he got ripe *mai'a*. Before the rain he had put a bunch of green *mai'a* into his pit, lined and covered with dry *mai'a* leaves and covered with a layer of earth. Now the fruit was ripe.

Just as Puakō started to build his fire a relative came by. "Here are *'ulu,*" his relative said. "My boy and I went up to the grove and gathered more than we can cook."

"One more kind of food for my *imu!*" Puakō exclaimed. "We are all hungry so much food must be made ready. If I am to work in the upland I must leave food for the women of my family. I give thanks for the *'ulu,* my cousin."

Now for their fire! There was an *imu* for men's food and a separate one for women's. Puakō lined each with dry stones. On them he laid twigs, warm from the sunshine, and small bits of wood, then larger pieces. He stacked these carefully so that air could come among them to make the fire burn. Over the wood Puakō laid rounded stones, selected to hold the heat in this kind of underground oven. When all was ready he brought his fire sticks which he had kept dry in a gourd with a tight-fitting

cover. He held the piece of *hau* wood with his feet, then rubbed a stick of *hau* back and forth to form a groove in the larger piece. Soon powder formed. Puakō rubbed faster and faster. The powder grew hot. It smoked! Puakō saw glowing sparks. He blew on them gently through a bamboo pipe then caught the fire on a bit of *kapa*. When this was blazing he lighted the dry leaves of the men's *imu*. The wood caught and fire flashed up till all was burning. He started a blaze in the women's *imu*, then crushed out the fire that was in his *kapa* and put away the fire-making tools. With a long stick he pushed stones close to the blazing wood so that all should heat, then set about wrapping food in *kī* leaves.

"Sit here, Father. Already these stones are dry." Ana led her father to a sunny place where he could rest his back against a tree.

"The sunshine is good," he said. "Old bones need the sun. Where are the *niu* fibers, Daughter?"

"Here," Ana set a wooden bowl filled with fibers where her father's hand could touch it. "Keao and I shall be working near if you should want more fibers." A moment later the two women were spreading mats on the grass and hanging bed *kapa* on low branches.

"Look, Mother!" Keao exclaimed. "Our houses seem to be on fire." The two women smiled at the clouds of steam which rose from the thatch as the sun warmed it.

"It is good that our houses face the east," Ana said. "The sun's rays are coming through the doorway to dry them inside. You must put your big containers of gourd and wood out in the sunshine, Daughter. Even though covered, some have become damp."

Malu, too, was busy. He and other fishermen were spreading damp nets and lines on the grass. They worked reverently and quietly, never forgetting that all their gear must be kept clean and treated with great respect. No girl or woman might come near. No one might step over the gear as it dried, for fish come only to lines and nets well cared for.

Kaiki was the only member of the family not at work. He had wakened with a shout, "The sun is shining! The rain has stopped!" And he had run straight to the beach. For a long moment he stood looking at the bay. He was not thinking of the busy workers about the reef. He thought instead of the blue sparkling water and the white line of breaking surf. The bay was calling him. The next moment he plunged in and swam out to the point. He scrambled onto warm rocks and sat there enjoying the sunshine.

For a little while he rested, happy in wind and sun, then looked about him. Here was driftwood. Wind and waves had brought it and during the rainy days no one had gathered it. Grandfather would want some of this wood. The boy picked up several pieces, but he could not scramble over rocks with his arms full of wood. Laying his small load where he could find it, he ran to the sand for beach morning-glory vines. He saw Noe just going home with a gourd full of seaweed. "Noe!" he called. "Come and help me. I want to load myself with wood."

"Yes," his friend answered, "we shall both get wood. I'll come as soon as I have taken home my *limu*."

The two scurried along the beach carrying morning-glory vines. They gathered wood then each helped to load the other, binding the wood on the other's back with cords of morning glory. "That is all that I can carry," Noe said. "Now I'll fix your load, Kaiki. You have enough for three trips."

"I can carry it in two," Kaiki insisted. "Put on more, Noe. I am strong."

"Very well," his friend told him, tying the wood firmly. "You will see!" Then Noe started for home, leaping and scrambling quickly over slippery rocks.

Kaiki followed slowly. His load was heavy and he must keep his balance. Something shining caught his eye. His foot slipped and down he went. "Noe! O, Noe, help!"

Noe heard his friend's smothered cry when Noe was half way home. I told him he'd find that load too heavy, Noe thought as he went on. He had almost reached the sand.

"Noe! Oh, help me!" He heard the cry again and turned. Kaiki had fallen among rocks where Noe could not see him. Noe must help but what a bother! The next moment he was scrambling and leaping back to his friend. "I can't get up!" said Kaiki.

"Of course you can't! I told you that was too big a load."

Noe unbound the wood and Kaiki scrambled to his feet. "Look what I found," he said.

"A red cowrie shell! O Kaiki! That is the most beautiful cowrie I ever saw!"

"Yes," Kaiki answered proudly, "I shall give it to Malu. He said he needed another cowrie for catching *he'e*. Tie my wood once more, Noe, about half of it. I'll come back for the rest."

"Good boy, Kaiki!" Puakō exclaimed when his grandson brought the wood. "Spread it in the sunshine near our cave. I was wishing I had time to go for driftwood." Puakō was wrapping food in *kī* leaves. Kaiki longed to watch him put the bundles into the *imu* to steam but there was too much to do. A man could not stand idle!

The *imu* stones were glowing with heat. Puakō pushed out the bits of half-burned wood with his long stick or pulled them out with quick fingers, for wood left in the *imu* would smoke and spoil the food. He brushed the stones clean with a small leafy branch. Then he laid his bundles of *kalo, mai'a* and *'ulu* among the hot stones of each *imu* and pushed the stones close to the bundles with his stick so that all would be cooked. He covered stones and food with a thick layer of *mai'a* leaves. These would give moisture to steam the food. Over the leaves he laid coarse mats then covered the mats with earth.

Now Puakō had time to bring out mats from the men's eating house. He spread these to dry just as Ana and Keao had done. He set the food containers in the sun. Even though they had been washed carefully they needed sun and air. Food put in damp and musty bowls would not taste good.

"*E, Kaiki!*" he exclaimed as the boy returned from spreading a third load of driftwood on the grass beside the cave. "That is enough. The driftwood belongs to all the village. You have taken our share. Now help me get drinking nuts." Kaiki got strong cord of *niu* fiber and the two went to the nearby grove. Others were there before them but there were nuts for all. "Climb this tree," said Grandfather.

But Kaiki's hand made the sign for "no." "That one!" He gazed upward. "The nuts are just right."

The tree Kaiki had chosen was a tall one—too tall, Puakō thought. But he looked at the eager boy and raised his brows for "yes." Up Kaiki went, climbing with toes and fingers, agile as a lizard. The cord was tied about his waist. When he reached the nuts the boy stopped to wave to his grandfather. He balanced his body firmly among the leaves and tied an end of his cord to the big bunch of nuts. Then he broke off the bunch and lowered it carefully. A boy could throw down mature nuts but not the young green ones. Thrown from a tree top, green nuts would break and their milk be lost.

When Kaiki had climbed safely down he and his grandfather divided the nuts between them to carry home. "I can take half," the boy insisted.

"Very well," Puakō answered and helped Kaiki sling his share over his back with the cord. "That was the tallest tree I ever saw you climb," he said. "You are sharing a man's work, Kaiki." As they walked home, he was pleased to see that his grandson carried the nuts with ease.

But when they reached their houses Kaiki sounded like a small boy as he said, "I am so hungry, Grandfather! I feel as if I should die of hunger! Isn't there anything to eat?"

"Milk from one of these *niu* will help," Puakō replied, "and here is *kō*. As soon as I have opened the *imu* we shall eat." Kaiki made a hole in a green *niu*, drank the milk and scraped out the soft delicious meat. Then he broke off a piece of *kō,* peeled it with his teeth and chewed the juicy fibers.

Meanwhile he was watching grandfather push the earth from the *imu* where the women's food had cooked. Puakō carefully lifted mat and leaves, trying not to let any earth fall among the steaming bundles of food. He dipped his hand in a gourd bowl of water and lifted out a hot stone. More water and other stones. Then came the hot food bundles. These he laid on green *mai'a* leaves. Working fast and dipping his hands in water, Puakō did not burn himself.

Keao came with a bowl full of seaweed which she would wash and pound for a relish. She too watched as her father unwrapped *'ulu* and *mai'a*. "I am just as hungry as you are, Kaiki," she said. "The hot food smells very good. We had nothing but salt fish this morning."

"I didn't have anything," Kaiki said, "I forgot to eat. Oh, here is Malu!" he shouted and ran eagerly to meet his uncle. As he ran he was struggling with something tucked in an inner fold of his *malo* for safekeeping. He pulled it out. "Look, Malu!"

"*E,* Kaiki! What a beautiful cowrie shell. It is red as an *'ōhi'a 'ai* ripened in the shade. This is the color the *he'e* love at noon time of a sunny day. Where did it come from?"

"I found it," Kaiki answered. "It is yours, Malu."

"You have given me a good gift," the young man said, "for I have no shell like it. I pray Kū'ula to send many *he'e* to this cowrie," and he put it carefully in the fold of his own *malo*. "Come," he added, "the food is ready and you and I are hungry!"

Meanwhile Puakō had taken food to the women's eating house. Then he had opened the second *imu*, unwrapped the food and carried it to the men's eating house. Malu led Ana's father to his place beside the food mat. The men and boy seated themselves sideways on the mat, for to sit crosslegged was a sign of undue pride. They listened reverently while Puakō prayed:

> "O spirits of the four corners of the earth,
>   behold,
> Here is food for you.
> Kāne, Kū, Lono, grant life."

Then they ate. The food, fresh from the *imu*, was hot and, oh, how good! The four talked and laughed together as they ate, for eating was a pleasant time—never a time to discuss the day's work.

After they finished Malu said, "I can help with the *kalo*. 'Aukai is working near where the nets are spread and he is watching them. Later I must go to help him take them in but now I can work here."

"And I can help," offered Kaiki.

"Good!" Puakō looked at the boy with love and pride. Never until the last few days had his grandson shown such willingness. "Lead Great-grandfather to his place under the *kamani* tree. Clear away the leaves on which our food has rested and give the scraps to the chickens. Wash the *niu* bowls in the pool where food dishes are washed. Wash the food mat too and hang it in the sun to dry. When *'ulu* and *mai'a* are cool, put them in covered gourds. These must be hung in the food net out of reach of animals. Is that work enough?"

"Oh no," the boy replied. "I'll clean the yard. And then may I pound *poi?*"

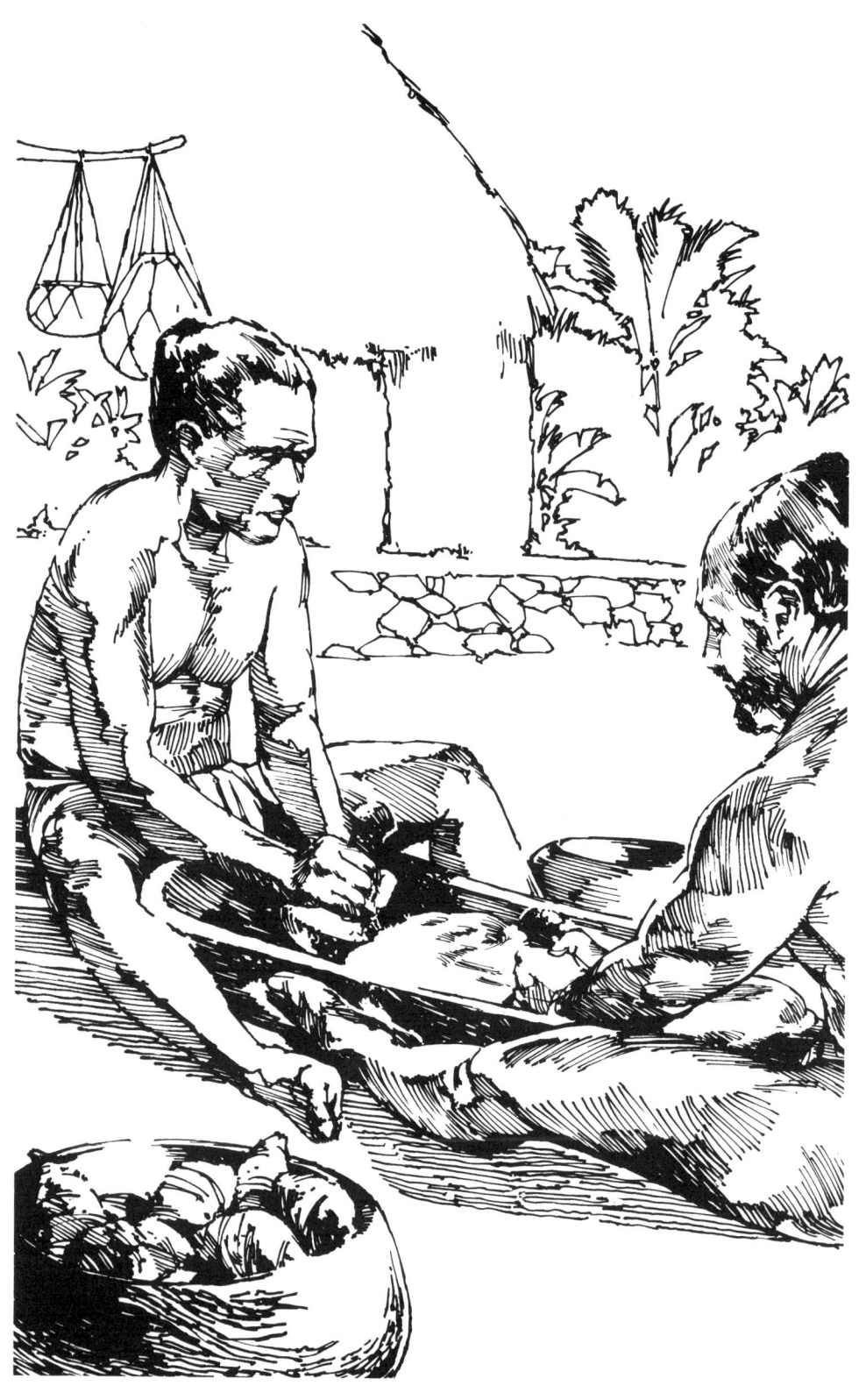

Puakō smiled as he signed "yes." "It is good to have three men to pound *poi*," he said. "After one more day we must return to our upland field to plant the *kalo* slips. There is much to do before we go."

He made ready the long *poi* board. With *'opihi* shells he and Malu peeled the *kalo* from the women's *imu* and laid them on the board. Then the pounding began. The men sat on a mat, one at each end of the long board. Beside each was a gourd of water. First, the wet pounder was pressed against the slippery root to flatten it. Without this the *kalo* might slide from the board when struck by the pounding stone. As each man took the stone pounder in his right hand, he dipped his left in water. For an instant the pounder rested on the wet hand. Then it was raised high and came down on the soft *kalo* with a "squish." Again it was wet, lifted and brought down. Squish! Squish! Squish! Soon the men were chanting and their pounders kept time with the chant.

"*Ē!*" Puakō stopped with a sudden exclamation. "Where did that lizard drop from? It's lucky for him he did not fall into the *poi!*"

"A lizard dropping in front of one is a sign of a present," Malu remarked.

"And here is the present," a new voice added. The two men turned to greet Kekoa who had set down a basket and was lifting out fish with large colorful scales and great round eyes.

"*Uhu!*" Puakō exclaimed. "Is this a free time for *uhu?*"

"Yes. The *kapu* was lifted some days ago but I could not go fishing until today. You know the fish I told you of? My decoy *uhu?* It has grown very tame and comes to me for food. Today it helped me to catch these."

Kaiki left his yard cleaning to see the fish and hear the story of their capture. Old Kekoa was happy to find listeners and seated himself comfortably to tell of his fishing. "We paddled out, the fish and I. With my right hand

I paddled gently, with my left I held the cord fastened to my *uhu*. The fish came willingly. It knows and loves me. When I had paddled far enough, I chewed *kukui* nut and spat out oil. Looking into the quiet, oil-covered water, I saw a little beauty. Down went my net with the tame one on it. The strange *uhu* swam in curiously. Quick as the lift of your *poi* pounder, up came my net. I dropped the strange fish into my basket and paddled on. I got ten fours of fish in a short time! Think of that! It is my tame *uhu* that brings such luck. That fish the gods have sent to me. Here, Puakō, you are my relative and I share my fish with you."

The old man went on his way to give fish to others. "Your turn has come to pound," Puakō told Kaiki, "while I clean the fish. Raw *uhu* will taste very good. For weeks they have been *kapu*."

Kaiki washed his hands, then settled himself with water gourd and pounder. He had tried *poi* pounding before, just a few strokes. But this was different. Now he was taking his turn at the work as a man does. He was sitting opposite Malu and trying to keep time with him, trying to make his *poi* as smooth as Malu's. All too soon arm and back grew tired. "Let us chant," Kaiki suggested.

"Yes," his uncle agreed, "chanting helps this work. I'll teach you a chant about *uhu*." Kaiki learned quickly and forgot some of his tiredness as he chanted:

> "*Uhu,* the shy and timid fish,
> The fish that swim proudly,
> The fish that gather to watch,
> The fish that touch and dash away,
> The fish that kiss each other,
> The reddish *uhu*."

Planting

"Kaiki!" The little boy snuggled sleepily under his *kapa*. "Kaiki!" The call came again. "I promised to wake you early." It was Puakō's voice that spoke.

Suddenly the boy sat up. "This is the day!" he exclaimed. "The day for *kalo* planting! I'm not sleepy, Grandfather!" A moment later he was outside. It was dark and chilly. The boy shivered. But he was going with the men! He got his *kapa* shoulder cape and sandals, for this time he and Noe had made sandals for themselves.

Meanwhile Puakō had lighted a candle of *kukui* nuts and set food on the eating mat. "Come!" he called from the doorway of the eating house.

"I'm not hungry," answered Kaiki shivering.

"All men must eat," Grandfather replied. "As we eat abundantly on the day of planting so will the *kalo* plants bear abundantly. They will give life to the land." Kaiki came then to take his place beside the food mat but was too excited to choke down much of the cold food. He hoped the *kalo* would not bear less abundantly because he had not eaten much.

The women of the village were out to see their men and boys off to the upland. Kaiki had persuaded Grandfather to let him carry food bundles since Puakō had a load of *kalo* slips. When Keao twined a fern *lei* about his head the boy forgot cold and darkness and rejoiced to be starting off with the older men.

Daylight brightened as the men and boys wound their way up the trail in a long line. Gray clouds became many-colored and, by the time the party reached the upland, the sun was shining. "This is as it should be," Lako said. "The shadows are long so our *kalo* plants will grow well and cast long shadows."

No time was wasted. Under the direction of the overseer all went to work at once. The new field had been well soaked by days of rain. Bushes and weeds, cut or pulled, had already begun to rot. Now they must be trampled into the earth to give their power of growth to *kalo* plants. Kaiki and Noe had once helped to trample the wetland *kalo* patch near their homes. They had been splashed with mud but they had had great fun. Men and boys had laughed and shouted. Some had even danced a *hula*, trampling all the time. But this was different. Here all worked quietly lest they anger the forest gods.

As soon as one end of the field had been trampled the overseer commanded some of the men to begin planting, while others trampled farther on. Kaiki and Noe came to watch the planting. Each man took slips in his left hand and his digging stick in his right. He thrust the stick into the soft moist earth and wiggled it around to make a good-sized hole. Then he dropped in two *kalo* slips and went on to make another hole. "They are making slanting holes," Kaiki said wonderingly to his friend. "I thought holes for planting always went straight down."

"I understand that," Noe answered proudly. "Wind and rain usually come this way." He waved an arm. "The holes are slanted so rain will not drive into them and fill them. The kinds of *kalo* that we plant in the upland do not like to stand in water, Father says. Water would rot them."

"First the slip must root," said a voice just behind the boys. They turned and saw the overseer. "After the slips are all well rooted, we will return to pack the earth about them. Raising food requires much work." He seemed pleased at the eager curiosity of the boys. "You will be good farmers," he told them, "but today all must work. Go, you two, and gather *kī* leaves. We shall need many."

The boys found that the planting did indeed require much hard work. After the ground was planted they scattered *kī* leaves thickly over it to keep in moisture. All the work was done with prayer. Only as the gods worked with them could the labor of men succeed.

The planting took several days. The *kalo* slips brought by Puakō and Lako were planted. Later Malu paddled again to his cousin's home for the promised cuttings. These slips were of the long-leafed *kalo* used as offerings in the *heiau*. They were planted at one end of the big field. At the other end was *kalo lehua* which made the *poi* most enjoyed by the chiefs. Between these two the larger part of the field was planted with *kalo* for the people of the village. Some was the quick-growing *wehiwa* that Puakō had brought. The slower-growing kind was a gift from Kahana's cousin. It would be ready for pulling after the quick-growing kind had all been used. This slow-growing variety kept well and could feed people in a hungry time.

On the borders of the field the men planted *kī, kō, maiʻa* and, finally, *wauke*.

The men had waited for the right day, for *maiʻa* planted when the moon was nearly three weeks old would grow sturdily and bear well. Noe's father and five other men had gone to the village for *maiʻa* sprouts. They brought good sturdy plants which had grown on the east side of mature plants, warmed by the morning sun. Now the six men came bearing the sprouts. They walked, two by two, backs weighted down by plants fastened to carrying poles. The boys watched every heavy, labored step. They understood that the young plants were not really so heavy. But the men were thinking of the great bunches of fruit these plants would bear and walked heavily to show the gods how they would someday carry the *maiʻa*.

Large holes had been made ready at the border of the field. A plant was laid beside each hole. It was almost noon, the best time for *maiʻa* planting. If *maiʻa* were planted early or late in the day, when shadows are long, those *maiʻa* plants would grow tall.

Farmers do not care for tall, spindly plants. What they want are short, sturdy plants loaded with fruit. Noon is the time for planting, when the sun shines down on a man's head and his shadow disappears into his body.

Each of the workers had brought food to the field. Now they spread green *kī* leaves like a food mat and laid the food ready for a feast. They seated themselves and waited reverently while the overseer prayed. He asked the gods to bless these young shoots that they might grow into sturdy plants bearing great bunches of *mai'a*. Then the men ate. They were hungry after a morning's work and ate heartily. Such eating would please the gods. It was like an added prayer for abundant fruit.

At noon, with the sun overhead, the men planted the sprouts. They strained, as if the plants were almost too heavy to lift. All together men and boys chanted:

> "The great *mai'a*!
> The great *mai'a*!
> It will yield many hands!
> The bunch will feed many people.
> It will take two men
> To carry it with difficulty."

After the sprouts were placed in the holes the men packed earth firmly about them.

Then boys and men gathered up their things and filed down the trail toward the village. Kaiki's heart was full of happiness. Life! he was thinking. Our work with the gods gives life to the land. Then the land will give life to the people. It was a great thought, born of prayer, rain, sunshine and work. Kaiki was growing up.

Matmaking

"O Ana, come! Come quickly! My mother is hurt!" Piko rushed into Ana's *kapa* yard. The little girl leaped over strips of *kapa* spread to dry, though she seemed not to be looking where she stepped. "O Ana, come quickly!" she repeated.

Ana rose from her *kapa* beating and laid firm, gentle hands on the child's shoulders. "You must tell me, Piko, what has happened," she said. "Where is Hīnano? How is she hurt?"

"Up near our cave." The child answered. "Our matmaking cave. O Ana, Mother called me to come with her and I didn't come!"

"You can tell me about that later. Now I must know what happened. How is your mother hurt?"

"I don't know, Ana. It is her leg. She just lies on the ground and holds her leg and moans. Oh, I am so frightened!"

"You must be brave, Piko," Ana told her. "I shall go to your mother at once. You go to the beach for Keao. She is gathering shellfish. Tell her where Hīnano is and ask her to come also."

The child dashed away while Ana hurried up the trail, then left it to cross open rocky ground toward Hīnano's cave. She heard the woman groaning and went quickly to her.

When Hīnano saw her friend she tried to smother the groans. "O Ana, I am glad that you have come!" she said. "I tripped over something and fell on the stones. My leg is broken."

With gentle hands Ana felt the injured leg. "Yes, it is broken," she said. "Both bones. But they are not out of place. They have not torn muscle and flesh."

"Where is Piko?" Hīnano asked. "That child is never here when needed. She could run for 'Ēwe, the *kahuna*, to set the bone."

At that moment Piko and Keao reached them, panting from their hurried climb. Ana explained to Keao what had happened. "Stay with Hīnano, daughter," she said. "Rub her hands and the well foot and leg, for she is cold. Piko will bring a *kapa* to tuck around her. Do not move the broken leg, either of you. I shall get upland morning glory. Then I shall set the bones. Come with me, Piko."

The little girl was standing near, sobbing helplessly. Ana took her hand. "Come, child," she repeated. "You must help Mother."

Piko came at once. "It was all my fault!" she sobbed.

"Tell me later when we have more time," said Ana. "I must get some roots of the upland morning glory. Your mother is cold. Run to your sleeping house and get a bed *kapa* to tuck about her. Then come and help me make a poultice to heal her leg."

Ana quickly found the vine she wanted. She mashed the roots in a hollowed stone and mixed salt with them, praying as she worked. When Piko returned Ana sent her for a strip of clean *kapa* to bind the leg. Together they went to the injured woman.

Hīnano was warmer now and not so frightened as she had been at first. Piko had stopped crying and watched with deep interest everything that Ana did. Hardly moving the broken leg Ana wrapped a soft *kī* leaf about it, then put on the poultice she had made. Last she bound on the *kapa* strip. "The *kī* leaf keeps the poultice from burning your leg," she explained to Hīnano. "The root of the upland morning glory mixed with salt helps the break to heal quickly while the *kapa* holds the bones in place. A break like this will not take long to knit."

"But I can't lie here!" exclaimed Hīnano.

"The ground is dry," Ana replied. "Piko can get big leaves and make a shelter to keep off the sun when it grows hot. At noon the men are to plant *mai'a* in the upland. When that is done they will return. Then your husband and Puakō can carry you home."

"Why not to the cave?" Hīnano asked. She was feeling better and thinking of her work. "I am making a fine mat for my Makahiki gift and I have two others started. I need to work."

"Oh yes, you can work," Ana agreed, "but that cave is too damp. The dampness is good on a hot dry day, for it keeps the *lau hala* from growing dry and brittle. But the cave is too damp to stay in at night. Piko can bring your mats to you at home so you can work during early morning and when the day is damp. Then when the sun grows hot she can carry them back to the cave. You want to do this for Mother, Piko?"

"Oh yes!" the child answered eagerly.

"Go now," Ana directed, "and get big *niu* leaves. Mother will show you how to plait them to make a shelter for her when the day grows hot." As the child ran down the slope, Ana turned to Hīnano. "You must let Piko help," she told her. "She can gather *lau hala* and run errands for you. She is a dear child."

"Yes," the mother assented, "Piko is loving, but so heedless! I'm afraid she won't be much help."

Ana smiled wisely. "Wait and see," she advised.

The next morning Keao was awake long before day. She knew that Malu was going fishing for he had slept in 'Aukai's house. A fisherman's wife must be quiet and reverent while her husband fishes. Loud talk or idle visiting with neighbors might bring bad luck. But I can help Hīnano, Keao thought. I shall go to the *hala* grove to get leaves for matmaking.

She found Piko there before her. The child ran to Keao, threw her arms about her and began to cry. "O Keao," she sobbed, "do you think it was my fault that Mother broke her leg? I couldn't sleep all night for thinking of it. She called me yesterday to come with her. But I was getting smooth pebbles for a game of *kimo*. I had almost enough and I didn't go when Mother called me. When I had all my pebbles I took them to the sleeping house and put them in the covered bowl with my treasures. Then I walked slowly up the trail. All at once I heard Mother groaning. O Keao, if I had gone with her she would not have fallen!"

"I don't think that would have made any difference," Keao told the little girl. "I remember falling once when Malu was beside me. Don't worry about yesterday. There is much to do today. Your mother will need *lau hala*. You are her legs for a little while. You must collect leaves and take them to her and you must stay with her, for you can help in many ways."

"Oh yes, that's what I want to do, Keao! See, I have a pile already."

"But, Piko, you must choose the leaves more carefully. This one is rotten. This is broken. Sort them for length. Cut off the hard base of each leaf. Did you bring a bamboo knife?"

"Yes, I know how, Keao, only I have been so worried I forgot. Can you stay with me a little while? You make me happier."

So Keao got a sharp shell for cutting off the prickly edge of each long leaf. Piko worked carefully and happily. "Thank you," she said at last. "Now I have two big bundles. Mother will be glad."

"I shall carry one," Keao told her.

Hinano had slept well and was eager to get to work at her half-plaited mat. "Where have you been, Piko?" she asked impatiently. "Why child," she added in a happier tone, "you have your arms full of *lau hala!* Let me see. All sorted as to size! Good leaves and the prickly edges cut away! Dear little daughter." She took Piko in her arms and held her close while Keao slipped away unnoticed.

"I shall stay with you all day and help," Piko told her. She brought the half-finished mat from the cave and listened quietly while her mother prayed for help in plaiting. For a time she watched the pattern grow in the fine mat, then asked, "What shall I do?"

"Some of this *lau hala* you have brought must be spread in the sun to bleach," her mother answered, "while the rest dries more slowly in the cave so that it will be a darker color. Dark and light together make a good design."

When that work was finished Piko brought from the cave a bundle of leaves that had been picked some time before and were ready for use. "Now shall I slit them?" she asked.

Hīnano looked at her in surprise. Several times she had set Piko at the task of slitting leaves into long straight strips. But making many strips of even width is not easy and soon Piko had tired and run off to play. Today, however, she worked patiently and well until her mother stopped her. "The sun grows hot," Hīnano said. "Take the mat and the leaves back to the cave. I shall stretch out and sleep a little while you go and play. This afternoon rain may come. Then we can work again."

Piko rolled the fine mat carefully, for the long unplaited strips must not be tangled. She stayed near her mother much of the day and it was she who noticed the darkening sky. "I think it's going to rain," she said. "Shall I run and get *lau hala* from the cave?"

That afternoon Hīnano beat *hala* leaves with an old *kapa* beater to make them soft and pliable. Piko rolled them over her hand to flatten them. When all were beaten and rolled Piko asked, "Shall I get more *lau hala* from the cave?"

"No, it is raining hard," her mother answered. "Would you like to make a mat?"

"Oh, I want to!" the child exclaimed eagerly, "but I don't know how. Am I old enough to learn?"

"You are nearly as old as I was when I began to plait," her mother answered. "You can start with a small mat. Split wider strips than those that I am using. Then the plaiting will go faster."

"But, Mother, this is your *lau hala*. You gathered and flattened it and you will need it for your mat. I must not waste it."

"*Lau hala* used in learning is not wasted," her mother told her, "and you have prepared more. Here, let me show you how to start. Let this first mat be a small one."

Over one, under one! Having often watched her mother and others, Piko quickly got the feel of actually plaiting herself. Hīnano showed her how a new strip could be started. "Slip the end under so it does not show. And you must learn prayers to the gods of *lau hala* workers. No work can be well done without help from the gods."

Hīnano let her own mat lie on her lap while she rested and watched Piko. After a time the child glanced up at her. "Where did it come from, Mother?" she asked. "The *hala*?"

"I have heard that Pele gave it to Hawai'i," Hīnano answered. "You know the legend of Pele's quarrel with her sister. As the goddess fled from the angry one she was caught by prickly *hala* leaves. She struggled but could not free herself. 'O Brother,' she shouted, 'I am in trouble!' Her brother came and poured sea water over the *hala*. The salt water wilted the leaves so that they let go their hold. Angry because the thorns had caught her, Pele seized *hala* seeds and threw them far and wide. Some landed here, took root and spread throughout our islands."

Piko's first mat bent and twisted because she pulled the strips too tight. "I tried too hard," she said and plaited the next so loosely that it seemed ready to fall apart. But she was learning. By the time the bones of Hīnano's leg had knit, Piko had made a smooth firm mat. "I want to make a large one now," she told her mother. "I'm going to be a matmaker—a very good matmaker like you."

Hīnano looked at the eager child and at her own finished mat. "Good things came of my broken leg," she whispered.

Capturing a Tiger Shark

Tomorrow we shall catch a tiger shark! That exciting thought kept Malu awake. The chief's fishermen lay in the house beside 'Aukai's shrine. The others slept. How could they sleep, Malu wondered.

Only twice had the young man gone out to catch this fierce fish. Tiger-shark fishing was a sport for chiefs, but tomorrow…! Malu tried not to think of the part he was to have. What if he failed? O gods of fishing, he prayed silently, give me skill. Give me courage.

Everything was ready. Spoiled pork—very bad-smelling—had been wrapped in *kī*-leaf bundles with shells of *kukui* nuts. That had been a most unpleasant job. Malu hoped the smell would bring a shark. Again his mind was planning—planning and praying. Would he never sleep?

Suddenly he sat up. He had slept and a wonderful dream had come—a dream of kite-flying. His *kapa* kite was large yet he pitched it easily into the air. The wind caught and lifted it. In his dream Malu was running and shouting as he paid out the cord. He felt the pull of the kite as it rose. It went higher and higher until it was out of sight above the clouds.

Then he had wakened and remembered. The men around him were rising from their mats. This was the day! He was to have an important part in catching a tiger shark and the gods had sent a good dream. A kite, flying high, meant success!

The fishermen were quiet as they gathered before the shrine. 'Aukai made an offering and prayed. He spoke quietly as he always did, yet Malu heard excitement in his voice.

The morning star was rising as the men carried the chief's double-hulled canoe into the water. A strong pole had been tied to the *'iako* which held the two hulls together. To this pole Malu tied the bundle of bad-smelling pork. As he worked he prayed.

Meanwhile other men made fast bailers and extra paddles. They laid the sail ready in the canoe then stood holding their own paddles, waiting.

Out of the darkness came three more—the chief and his two half-grown sons. They took their places in the canoe and the fishermen stepped in. 'Aukai raised the sail while the men paddled. The canoe flew through the starlit waves fast as a flying fish.

The morning star climbed high in the sky. That was the ruler. He and the other stars had watched over the ancestors of chiefs and men. Silently Malu prayed. He knew that all were praying.

Dawn came. At a sign from the master, Malu rose to pierce the *kī*-leaf bundles with a pointed stick. This freed the strong-smelling grease from the pork. The smell should attract a shark. The canoe sailed steadily.

When 'Aukai lowered the sail Malu turned to look back. They had come so far he could no longer see the lowland of their island, only mountains dark against bright sky.

What was that among the waves? A fin? Suddenly a shark rose for a moment, then plunged after the canoe. Malu could see the fierce eyes gleam. He could see the cruel mouth open to swallow grease-covered water. That was good. If the shark filled himself with sea water he would be easier to kill.

The double-hulled canoe was moving slowly and the shark swam close, eager for the pork grease. Malu laid down his paddle and took up a noose of strong *hau* rope. This noose was held open by a forked stick. The young man watched the wicked head come closer—right between the two hulls.

Now was the time! At a signal from 'Aukai, Malu slipped his noose over the shark's head. He glanced back. Another noose had been slipped over the tail. Malu raised

his arm and the watching men tightened ropes fastened to the nooses. They were pulling the head back and the tail forward. The great fish fought fiercely but the ropes did not break.

The chief was ready, spear raised. Now he struck and struck again. "Our enemy is dead!" he cried. "Thanks to our fish god Kūʻula."

The two boys shouted and the men joined the shout, "$\bar{E}$! The chief has killed a tiger shark. Thanks to the gods of fishing."

At a signal from the master the canoe headed toward home. They had come far and wind could not help them now. But success filled the men's hearts with joy and paddles dipped strongly in time to a chant.

When they at last reached their landing place the chief took part of the shark as a thanks offering to the gods of fishing. The heart was cooked, for that was food—food to give fierce courage to the chiefs. Part of the skin would be cured to use as drum heads and the teeth saved for carving tools. The flesh of the shark was cut into strips, salted and dried. Later it was cooked in the *imu* for food for those families who were permitted to use shark flesh.

Malu was eager to tell his wife the day's adventure. She shivered when he told of slipping the noose over the wicked head. "It frightens me," she said, "yet I am glad. Because of this victory you will always be victorious—will always win. Someday you will be the head fisherman."

Lū'au and Salt

Lū'au

Once again the men were in the upland. The sun had risen when they reached the *kalo* patch and they had stopped, all together, and stood silent beside their field.

Why do we stop? Kaiki asked himself. And then he knew, for he saw the beauty of the field. Green shoots had grown from every slip. The leaves were unrolling and gleaming in the morning sun. They threw long shadows across the field and the air was full of the good smell of moist earth and growing plants. The boy thought of prayers, of offerings and hard work. The gods have blessed us, he said to himself. This field has life.

And now there was more work. While some men cut young leaves for offerings and food, others straightened the seedlings and packed fern leaves and earth firmly about their roots. They pressed an earth bowl around each plant to hold the rain. "You boys gather *kī* leaves," the overseer commanded. "Many will be needed."

"What are the *kī* leaves for?" Kaiki asked Noe as the two worked together, pulling off leaves and carrying them to the *kalo* patch. But Noe did not know.

"Now that the first *kalo* leaves have been cut and earth packed about the slips," said the overseer, "it is time for you boys to cover the ground with your *kī* leaves. Spread them so that all the moist earth is covered, but do not cover the young plants. They need sunshine."

Noe's father came by and stopped a moment to watch the work. "That is good," he said. "The *kī* leaves will keep the ground moist for the growing plants. When

Lono sends dark rain clouds we must hurry up here to remove the mulch of *kī* leaves so that rain may soak the ground. When the rain is over the *kī* leaves must be spread once more."

Nāwai, the lazy netmaker, also stopped to chat. "These upland fields are too much work!" he grumbled. "We tramp up here to clear the ground. After the rain we tramp up here again to plant. Then mulch. Then remove mulch. Weed. Mulch again. Remove mulch and put it back again. Tramp! Tramp! An upland field takes too much time from other work."

Noe's father laughed. "Tomorrow when we eat the *lū'au* we shall forget the work." he said. "Next year when all our district has food enough, we shall thank the gods and rejoice in all our labor. Come, my friend, we are needed to pack fern and earth about the slips of *kalo lehua*. Our chiefs too must have food."

The next day men and boys returned to the village. There the *kalo* were cooked. Puakō heated stones red-hot as for an *imu*. These he dropped into a calabash containing the *lū'au* and water then covered the calabash. When the greens were partly cooked he removed the stones, sprinkled the *lū'au* with salt and dropped in more red-hot stones. *Lū'au* must be well cooked or it scratches the mouth and throat.

Meanwhile he had cooked fish over the coals of the fire which had heated his stones. When all was ready he made a special offering and prayed:

> "Here is a prayer for your favor,
> O god, O Kāne,
> O Kāne of the living waters.
> Here are the first leaves of our *kalo*,
> O god, grant us food,
> Food for the family,
> Food for the pigs,

Food for the dogs.
Grant success to us, your children,
In farming, in fishing, in house building,
Until we are bent with age,
Old as yellowed *hala* leaves."

Kaiki listened reverently to the prayer and thought about its words. As the feast began he tasted first the cooked *kalo* leaves, the *lū'au*. He ate slowly, took another mouthful and again ate slowly. "This is good," he said. "I think it is the best *lū'au* we ever grew."

Keao's grandfather turned toward him. "You are right," he said. "A farmer cares for his garden lovingly. The young plants are like children. The food they give is sweet to his taste. It is life-giving. This is *lū'au* you helped to raise, O Kaiki. Puakō has told me of your work. My prayers are answered for I have lived to eat food raised by a great-grandson."

After eating the boy carried food to the chickens, dogs and pigs. "We prayed for food for all," Puakō told him. "Kāne will be pleased when he sees us share with our animals. He will bless our *kalo* patch."

Salt

Later that day Puakō called his grandson. "I am going to the salt pans," he said. "Do you and Noe want to help me?"

The boys hesitated. It would mean a long hot walk for the trail circled a marsh. But when Puakō added, "I am going by canoe," both boys were eager to join him.

There was no beach near the salt pool. Puakō tied the canoe by slipping its rope through a hole carved in a rock which stood above the reef. The out-going tide would carry the canoe away from the rock so that it would not bump and be damaged. As the three waded ashore, Noe stepped in a deep hole. "Oh! Oh!" he cried. "I've hurt my leg!"

The others came at once to help him. "Is it broken?" asked Kaiki anxiously.

Puakō lifted the sobbing boy. "Just a bad scratch," he said. Searching over the reef, he found a healing *limu*. He crushed this with a stone and squeezed its juice onto the cut. "That will make it well," he said to Noe. "Rest here in the shade and chew this juicy stalk of *kō*. I brought a piece for each of you. Kaiki and I will not be far away."

Meanwhile Kaiki was examining the salt pool. Long ago men had cut a narrow trench to carry seawater to a large shallow pool in the rocks. As water evaporated, salt crystals formed around the edges of this pool. Kaiki gathered a few and tasted them for he was very fond of salt.

Then he went a little farther inland to the salt pans. These were shallow places, hollowed out of the earth and lined with *kī* leaves to keep the water clean. The water in them was very salty with little gleaming islands of salt showing above the surface.

Puakō had tucked a cord in his *malo*. "We shall need *kī* leaves," he said, starting for the gulch once more.

"We use *kī* leaves for everything!" his grandson exclaimed.

"Yes, *kī* is a gift of the gods," Puakō answered reverently. He showed Kaiki how to lap the leaves and tie them at each end.

"Why, I've made a little canoe!" the boy laughed.

"Yes," his grandfather replied, "a salt canoe."

Carrying a number of small "canoes" the two returned to the salt pans and found Noe fast asleep. They filled their *kī*-leaf canoes with the very salty water from the pans and set them on the rocks nearby. "The sun will soon drink up the water and leave only salt," Grandfather explained.

"I see," Kaiki said thoughtfully. "Here are canoes with salt on sides and bottom. It is almost dry. Shall we take these back with us?"

"No. Those belong to someone else. Perhaps tomorrow he will come. He will carry home his salt and spread it on a clean coarse mat laid in a sunny spot. Someone will watch the drying salt, for chickens and pigs and even children must be kept away. Nothing must step on it. Later it will be pounded fine and stored carefully in a covered wooden bowl.

"Come, Kaiki," he added. "We must refill the salt pans, so that the next comers will find much salty water." With wooden bowls, which Puakō had brought, the two dipped water from the pool to fill the leaf-lined pans.

Noe awakened and, with help, managed to wade back to the canoe. "The saltwater hurts my leg," he said, proud that he was bravely bearing pain.

The food, that night, seemed especially good. There was *poi* and *lu'au* with a relish of seaweed and salt fish cooked over hot coals.

"I like salt fish!" Kaiki exclaimed. "But getting salt is work. Everything is work!"

"And work is good," his great-grandfather remarked.

"Yes, work is good!" Malu repeated. "And some work is fun!" And he told of the capture of the tiger shark.

The *Hula* School

Laka, Goddess of the Hula

Keao and ʻIlima were watching children playing in the sand. Suddenly ʻIlima spoke. "I was playing in the sand that way when I heard the call of the drums. It was long ago and I was very small, but the call of the drums drew me as a fisherman draws in fish. I ran. People were crowded together watching something. I slipped through the crowd to see. You know how a child can slip in where there seems to be no room.

"It was a *hula*. Men and women were dancing to the beat of drums. There was my grandmother—my own dear grandmother. Perhaps I had seen the *hula* before. I do not know. But this one I remember: the dancers with moving arms and swirling *pāʻū,* the shine of sunlight on their many *lei* and bracelets, the tinkle of anklets and Grandmother softly tapping the drum with her fingertips.

"That night I crawled into her lap. 'Teach me, Grandmother,' I said. 'I want to be a dancer.'

"She did teach me in the years that followed. There is much a child can learn. She said, 'I am too old and heavy to dance and gesture,' but she was not. To me she was beautiful.

"'What are you seeing, Grandmother?' I asked one day. She was looking beyond me and I turned to look. I saw only *ʻulu* trees touched by the wind. 'What are you seeing?' I asked again.

"'Laka, my goddess.'

"'Where?' My eyes searched the *ʻulu* grove.

"'In my mind, Grandchild. I see her as I once saw her in the forest.' Then Grandmother told me about Laka, goddess of the *hula*. 'She is also the goddess of the wild plants that grow in the forest.'

"'She is my goddess,' I said. Everyday I prayed to her. Whenever women went to the forest I went with them. I looked for Laka everywhere.

"'Someday you will see her,' Grandmother told me.

"One day I was in the lower forest helping women who were gathering berries to make dye. Rain came and the women ran into a cave but I stayed to watch the rain. It was only a light misty rain. Sunshine sparkled on it and made a rainbow. Then I saw her!" 'Ilima's voice was almost a whisper and Keao leaned close to listen. "Her *pā'ū* was swirling mist. Her anklets were shiny raindrops. She was dancing a *hula* I did not know. Oh, Keao, I cannot tell you how lovely she was, how graceful!

"Then the misty rain was gone and the women called me to gather berries. Laka was gone too—but the memory of her is still clear in my mind.

"That night I told Grandmother. 'She has chosen you, 'Ilima,' Grandmother said earnestly. 'You are to be a *hula* dancer.' After that I worked harder than ever to learn the chants and gestures.

"'When can I train with a *hula* group?' I asked.

"'We shall ask Wahi.'

"But Wahi, the *hula* master, said I was too young. 'The training of the *hālau* is very hard. You know that,' he said to Grandmother. 'Wait until your grandchild is older and stronger.'

"We have waited. It is three years since Wahi taught the *hula* in this district. Grandmother has heard that he will come this year. If only he will take me!" Keao saw the longing in her friend's eyes. She heard the longing in her voice. She did not answer but in her heart she prayed.

Chosen

A few days passed. Then 'Ilima found Keao making ready to beat *kapa*. Keao jumped up when she saw her friend for 'Ilima's eyes were shining. "Wahi has chosen you!" she cried. "I knew he would. I prayed."

"Can you come, Keao? I have something for you to see."

Keao looked at the bark and *kapa* beater. She did not like to leave her work. But Ana, her mother, said, "Go, Keao. This is a great day for 'Ilima. When she enters the *hālau* you two cannot be together. Go with her today."

'Ilima took her friend's hand and urged her along the beach to the place where an old woman sitting under a *hau* tree was braiding sennit. Her hair was white and her face wrinkled but shining with happiness. "'Ilima has told you," she said.

"I didn't have to tell," 'Ilima answered. "She knew by just looking at me. May I show her—you know what—Grandmother?"

The old woman took a *kapa*-wrapped bundle from the top of her *pā'ū*. The girls were on their knees beside her as 'Ilima unwrapped the bundle. "Shells!" Keao exclaimed. "Such beautiful red-striped shells and all the same size! I have never seen shells like those, 'Ilima."

"They are anklets. See. They are strung on *niu* fiber. Tell Keao about them, Grandmother."

"You know that I was a *hula* dancer, Keao," the old woman began. "Once the troupe I was in danced before a visiting chiefess. I danced one *hula* alone to the rhythm of sharkskin drums. When I finished, the chiefess said, 'That is a *hula* dear to my heart, for it is like sunshine on rippling water. Here is something for you to wear next time you dance it,' and she gave me these rare shells.

"They were my dearest treasure and I wore them many times. When I was too old and heavy to dance and gesture I learned to play the instruments. Now I am very old.

"Yesterday Wahi said, 'The grandchild should have bracelets or anklets that have been used before. Have you something you have worn, something that will give her the blessing of our goddess?'

"So I brought out these shells. They are 'Ilima's now for she is my dearest treasure."

The two young women looked thoughtfully at the anklets and Keao said, "The sunlight shines on them as it shines on a *lei* of feathers. The color glows."

Grandmother put the shells away. "Until tomorrow," 'Ilima whispered. The she added, "Tell us about the *hālau*, Grandmother. Tell us what Kanoe is doing."

"An altar will be built in the *hālau*," the grandmother explained, "an altar to Laka. Kanoe was the one chosen to get branches for the altar as well as vines and flowers to trim it. He went into the forest at dawn and as he went he prayed. His work is sacred. It must be done in silence and with prayer.

"Tell Keao what he must gather, Grandchild."

"He is getting *koa* branches." 'Ilima was speaking now. Her eyes seemed to be looking into the dark *koa* forest as she went on. "'*Koa*' means 'unafraid.' The *koa* branches are a prayer that we shall never be afraid even when we dance before a crowd."

"What else must he gather?" the grandmother asked.

"*Lehua* in the lower forest, *halapepe*, *'ie'ie*, sweet smelling *maile* and *palai* fern," 'Ilima answered. "He must repeat a special prayer for each. And *pili* grass," she added quickly. "That is very important for '*pili*' means to 'cling.' The *pili* grass is a prayer that chants and gestures may cling to us through all our lives.

"You tell what happens next, Grandmother."

"When Kanoe comes back to the *hālau* Wahi will sprinkle the vines and branches with purifying water. He and Kanoe will build an altar to Laka, an altar made of the sacred branches and trimmed with vines and flowers.

They will pray Laka to send her spirit into that altar. If you and the others try earnestly Laka will be pleased. Her spirit will stay in the altar and vines and branches will be green and full of life."

There was a long silence. Keao was thinking, tomorrow 'Ilima will be there. She will see. O Laka, she prayed silently, bless my friend. Help her to be a good *hula* dancer.

Then 'Ilima spoke, "And tonight, Grandmother? Tell Keao about that."

"Tonight Wahi will stay alone in the *hālau*. He will pray Laka will bless his teaching. He will pray that he may remember every chant and gesture, that he may teach with patience and with wisdom. He will pray for all his pupils—that you may work earnestly and remember, that your voices may be rich and true, your bodies graceful, your hearts reverent and unafraid.

"Wahi will also pray for new wisdom. He will ask the goddess to come to him in a dream and teach him a *hula* he did not know or call to mind one he had forgotten."

Again the three were silent, thinking. Perhaps all three were praying. There was no movement but the sunlight dancing through *hau* leaves.

At last the old woman picked up the *niu* fibers which had fallen in her lap. Keao watched her quick fingers as she braided. Though she was old her hands were not stiff, but beautiful in movement. Her voice too is strong and sweet, the young woman thought. It is because of her *hula* training.

Aloud she said, "I think our district has the best dancers on this island."

"That is something we must never think," the old woman told her. "Chants and gestures taught in one *hula* school are always different from those of another school, though sometimes different only in little ways. But each is good. I still remember the words of my master, 'Never find fault with the teaching of another school. All knowledge does not come from one source.'"

"That is what my mother said about *kapa*-making," Keao offered. "Patterns and dyes may be different, but all work done with prayer and skill is good."

Then she asked, "Do you know any stories about the *hula*?"

"I was taught the art was brought from far Kahiki by our ancestors," the old woman told her. "Girls of Hawai'i instructed Hi'iaka in the dances and she and other sisters of Pele danced in the fire pit. Then La'a came. Do you know that story, Keao?"

"I have heard it—but tell it once more so we shall be sure to remember it."

"La'a was a son of Mo'ikeha, the voyager," Grandmother began, "He came from far Kahiki. As his canoe sailed along the coast of Hawai'i by night La'a softly beat his drum.

"The sound was new and beautiful.

"'What is it?' people asked. Others answered, 'It is the great god, Kū.' At daybreak they paddled out with offerings of food for the god.

"Sometimes La'a stopped at a landing place. Then *hula* teachers gathered, for they had heard the voice of La'a's drum. He taught them *hula*. Though he beat the drum he kept it hidden. 'What is it?' they asked each other. 'Its tone is rich and beautiful. If only we could make drums like that!'

"A *hula* master on O'ahu followed the canoe. That drum's voice is most beautiful! he thought. I have nothing with such a deep tone. I must see the drum! So he ran, following the canoe. Sometimes he ran along the beach. Sometimes the trail was on the cliff above.

"As the *hula* teacher ran he listened to the rhythms of the drum. They were new to him and he knew he must learn them. So he beat each one with his hands on his chest until it was fixed in his mind.

"When at last the canoe landed the *hula* master was there to greet La'a. 'I heard your drum,' the *hula* master said. 'It sounds like one of mine. I wonder whether they are the same.'

"La'a brought out his drum. The *hula* master saw it was larger than any he had known before. It was made from a section of an *'ulu* log, hollowed and covered with sharkskin. The sharkskin was laced on with sennit. 'Yes,' said the hula master, 'as I thought, it is much like mine.'

"Soon these words became true, for the *hula* master made a drum just like that of La'a. On it he played the rhythms he had practiced pounding on his chest to learn. Since those days the sharkskin drum has been used with the *hula* through all Hawai'i."

In the Hālau

As 'Ilima came to the *hālau,* the house where the *hula* dancers were to be trained, she felt chilled with nervous anticipation. She joined others who had been chosen for training. Some were older men and women who had been dancers and would now be trained to play the rhythm instruments. Some were young men and women of 'Ilima's own age. All were people she knew—but today they seemed strangers.

At the door of the *hālau* Wahi, the *hula* master, sprinkled them with purifying water. Once inside 'Ilima looked about. The *hālau* was larger than a sleeping house but smaller than she had expected.

On the east side was the altar. 'Ilima knew it must be on the side of the rising sun. Placing the altar on the east was a prayer for health and life and for growth in dancing. In the center of the altar stood a block of *lama* wood draped with soft yellow *kapa.* On it vines and flowers were banked. It was beautiful—more than beautiful—for 'Ilima knew that Laka, her goddess, was in that altar. Laka would watch the work of the *hālau.* Her spirit would enter every earnest dancer.

Pupils gathered around the food mat where a feast was ready. Wahi prayed. Then, as he divided the pig, he gave some of the brain to each pupil. 'Ilima had wondered what it would be like to eat pork. Usually that meat was forbidden to women. Now she did not even remember that it was food she had never tasted. She thought only that it was food shared with Laka. It was a prayer that Laka's power might be in her and in all the pupils.

After the feast was finished work began. Again Wahi prayed. Then he chanted and the pupils repeated the chant. Learning the words was easy for 'Ilima but two or three others found it hard. "They are frightened," the young woman told herself. "How patient Wahi is, going over and over a chant until all have learned it!"

Then the *hula* master chose one pupil to chant while he showed the gestures that must go with the words. 'Ilima had learned *hula* gestures from the time she was small. This was what she loved. But Wahi's movements were so perfect that she felt discouraged. How could she get every part of her body to move in harmony with a sacred chant? It seemed impossible. Over and over the chant rang out. Over and over the pupils tried to gesture as the master did. When at last Wahi gave the word to stop 'Ilima was exhausted.

Morning came too soon. 'Ilima longed to stay on her mats but one dip in the pool near the *hālau* brought her wide awake. The pool was fed by a cool spring and gave new life to those who bathed there. Each dancer found fresh garments and a *lei* hanging on a bush or tree near the pool. These had been brought by some relative, for everyone must be clean and pure in the presence of Laka.

Dressing was a ceremony. 'Ilima soon learned the chants which went with each part of her clothing. All stooped together to put on anklets.

"Bind on the anklets, bind," they chanted. 'Ilima thought of her grandmother who had worn these beautiful red-striped shells in many dances.

> "Gird on the *pā'ū*.
> Great the toil and care to make the *pā'ū*."

The *pā'ū*, or skirt, was indeed a beautiful piece of work. It was made of five strips of *kapa* wide enough to reach below the knees. It must be pleated at the waist so that it would swirl around the dancer.

The *kapa* cape, or *kīhei*, passed under the right arm and was tied with a knot on the left shoulder. Last of all the *lei*. This morning hers was of the yellow *'ilima* flowers, whose name she bore.

Then work began. Each pupil must learn to control his breath, for tones must be strong and beautiful. There were many chants to be learned. Some honored the gods, others honored chiefs. Each had its own beauty of music and gesture. Always the tone of voice and instruments must be suited to the chant.

The musicians sat or knelt. They used drums, rattles, pebbles, sticks—each with its own tone. Over and over each *hula* was repeated until beat, voice and gesture fitted perfectly.

'Ilima had never worked as she did now, from early morning far into the night. Yet she had never been so happy. Laka's spirit is in me, she thought. It is in us all. That is why gestures are easier to learn than at first. That is why we do not confuse the chants. That is why we forget we are tired or hungry.

There was time for short rests and for food but not for games and idleness. The pupils could never forget that they were in the presence of their goddess. They could never be careless in speech or act.

Food was brought to the door by relatives. These people did not enter the *hālau,* for it was sacred. Certain kinds of food were *kapu* to those who learned the *hula* and these were never brought. The name of one *limu* meant "to hide." It was *kapu,* for eating it might make the memory of chant or gesture hide from those who tried to learn.

One morning as the pupils came from the bathing pool they noticed the master's face. It shines like the sun, 'Ilima thought.

"Wahi has had a dream," someone whispered. And it was so. The master told them that he had tried for many months to remember a certain *hula* learned in childhood. "But it had flown," he said. "Last night, as I slept, I saw our goddess, Laka. She danced the *hula* I longed for. Every gesture, every word was clear."

As 'Ilima learned that *hula* she seemed to see the goddess dancing. Laka is in me, the young woman thought again, and danced and chanted easily. That *hula* was indeed a sacred thing.

Graduation

One morning Wahi said, "Soon our district chief will send for this *hula* troupe to dance before his household. That is your graduation. Before we go I have asked Kaipo, a great *hula* master, to watch your work and tell us how it can be made better. Yesterday a message came from him. I think he will be with us today."

Many had heard of Kaipo. It would be an honor to have him watch their work. There was excitement in the *hālau* and in 'Ilima's heart a little fear.

Just as the pupils were taking their places for a dance they heard a voice chanting the password. Wahi's face lighted with joy. The drums were hushed and everyone listened eagerly as Wahi chanted the reply, giving permission to enter.

Kaipo was old and white haired, but straight and handsome. Wahi sprinkled him with purifying water. The old man went to the altar and lifted his voice in prayer. How strong and rich his tones!

> "Thy blessing, O Laka,
> On me, the stranger,
> And on these within the *hālau,*
> Teacher and pupils.
> O Laka, bless the dancers
> When they come before the people."

Then Wahi took Kaipo in his arms. Their faces touched and their eyes filled with tears of joy. But they did not wail aloud, for they were in the presence of the goddess.

Wahi seated the old master on a mat to watch. Kaipo did not interrupt a dance but after each told how it could be improved. "In this place your breathing was not right," he might say. "Fill your lungs and do not stop for breath until the phrase is finished." After another chant, "Your tone is not that of the bamboo rattles. Listen!" He struck a rattle. "Do you hear the light song of wind blowing through reeds in a marshy place? The music of your voices must be as light as the note of the bamboo."

That night 'Ilima went to her mats tired with the effort of the day, yet happy. The old man's words had made the *hula* even more full of beauty and worship than before.

Kaipo stayed for several days while pupils worked their hardest on dance and chant. At last he said, "It is well." That was all but, coming from the master, it was praise enough. 'Ilima knew—everyone knew—the troupe was ready for graduation. A few days later came the chief's command to dance before his household. The time had come!

Just after midnight, when no one was about, the pupils went to the ocean to bathe. Oh, how good to feel its waves once more! At the door of the *hālau* Wahi sprinkled each one with purifying water as he had done every time they entered. Then he himself went to bathe. When he returned they danced and chanted then slept a little while.

At daybreak the pupils were wakened by their teacher's tapping on the sharkskin drum. 'Ilima was wide awake at once. This was the day!

All bathed in the pool just as they had each morning. They chanted as they dressed, but the *pā'ū* each put on was new and beautiful. They gathered about the altar and chanted prayers to Laka.

A long ceremony of prayers and chants followed the morning meal. The pupils watched as vines and branches were taken from the altar and replaced with fresh ones. They listened as Wahi talked to them. "Be true to what you have learned in this *hālau*," he said. "Then the chants will be yours through all your lives."

And now, for the first time since entering the *hālau*, the pupils visited their homes. The men might shave. Everyone might trim hair and nails. They were all given many fresh *lei* made by their families. For a moment 'Ilima held her grandmother in her arms. Each knew that understanding and love had grown between them.

The time at home was short. Soon all returned to the *hālau* to be sprinkled once more with purifying water and to chant reverently:

> "Laka sits in her shady grove.
> An offering we give to you.
> O Laka, let it be well,
> Well with us all,
> O giver of all things."

As the chant ended the pupils crowded to the altar and heaped all their *lei* upon the block of *lama* wood where the spirit of Laka rested.

The many prayers were answered. Quietly the *hula* troupe went to the chief's home. The audience was there, sitting or lying about the large mat made ready for the dancers. The program was long. Chants and instruments changed but always the voices carried the tone of instruments used—drums, gourd rattles, sticks, small stones. It seemed to 'Ilima that the spirit of Laka had driven fear from everyone. The praise which followed the program was not praise for the dancers and musicians. It was not praise for Wahi but for Laka, their goddess.

That night when graduation was over Wahi took all the sacred things to Kanoe's canoe. He took the branches which had made the altar, the vines and every *pā'ū* and *lei* worn by a dancer, even bits of food from the feast shared with the goddess. Wahi and Kanoe paddled to deep ocean and reverently dropped everything into the starlit waves. Wahi prayed and the two watched the sacred things disappear. They were safe. No careless hands could touch them, no careless feet step on them.

As she lay in the sleeping house 'Ilima heard the dip of a paddle. Perhaps it is Wahi and Kanoe returning, she told herself. Our training is finished. There was a bit of sadness in the thought. Then came another. Soon Makahiki will begin. Our *hula* troupe will dance in this district and in others. With a thankful prayer to Laka the young woman fell asleep.

Kahana and His Master

Woodcarving

Swish, swish, swish! The fine sand made a soft scratching sound as Kahana rubbed it back and forth on the *kapa* log. I have polished this four hundred times four hundred! the young man thought crossly. I have polished it with coral rock, with sharkskin and now with sand. Why did I choose Māmane for a master? "It is not smooth enough." That is all he ever says! Kahana brushed away the powder that his polisher had left, he ran his hand along the log. It felt smooth—so smooth! But it felt smooth to me days ago, he thought. Always Māmane finds a rough place. He dipped the moist *niu* husk into fine sand and continued to polish the log.

Kahana remembered how eager and confident he had been when he came to work for Māmane. He had watched the tool of the master as he carved delicate patterns on a *kapa* beater. The work had looked easy. That is what I shall do, Kahana had told himself and asked Māmane to take him as a pupil. That was long ago, he thought, and what have I done? Learned the first rough cutting of a *kapa* beater! Cut bamboo for printing sticks! Pressed oil from *kukui* nuts! Laid blocks of wood in the thick mud of the *kalo* patch to soak and darken for the making of a bowl or a platter!

Then he told me I could make a *kapa* log. I was so happy! At last I am a woodworker, I thought. *Kāwaʻu* wood is hard. The adzes dulled and chipped. Māmane sent me to the stream to grind new edges on my tools. There, on the polishing stone at the water's edge, I worked until my back ached. I cut three logs before my master was satisfied. Oh, why did I choose Māmane as a teacher?

The young man stopped sanding and glanced at his master who sat bent over the beater he was carving. He carves fine patterns and gives no thought to me, Kahana told himself. Slowly he went to work again. Swish, swish, swish!

"Let me see your log." Kahana was startled to find Māmane beside him. The master ran his hand over the surface of the log, then turned it and felt the hollow of the underside. "It is ready for the oil."

That was all he said but Kahana could have shouted with joy. The young man wiped the sand from his log with a bit of *kapa*, then rubbed on the oil which he had prepared. Rub, rub, rub! The motion was the same as he had just been using but now, because he was finishing his work, the young man did not feel the ache of arms and back. At last he put the log on a shelf of Māmane's work house along with finished bowls, platters and *kapa* beaters made by his master. "Tomorrow take it to Leimomi," the master said. "She saw your work and asked to have that very log." Kahana's heart leaped with joy. Leimomi was one of the best *kapa*-makers in the village and she had liked his work! Besides, she might give him fine *kapa* in return.

"What shall I do next, Māmane? Sharpen adzes? Split bamboo?" Kahana was so happy, now, no job would tire him.

"You are ready to learn the carving of a beater," the master said. "Here is one to practice on."

Kahana took the beater. "This is a good one," he said, "and I lack skill. I must not spoil this beater, O my master."

"I have already spoiled it," Māmane said. He turned the beater in Kahana's hands. One side was carved with delicate wavy lines, but on the second side a crack had somehow formed. Kahana looked at the wasted work, then raised his eyes to glance at his master, already bending over another piece of carving. Even a man of skill—the best woodcarver in the district—even *he* had accidents! To do all that delicate carving and only then find a bad place in the wood! Or let a tool slip, making a deep cut! Kahana's heart went out to Māmane with new understanding.

"O gods of woodcarving," he prayed,
"Give me patience.
 Teach me
 That I may have success."

Often Kahana had watched his master and so he knew what tools to use. He chose a straight piece of split bamboo and a shark's tooth pegged into a wooden handle. With his left hand he held the bamboo ruler firmly on a polished side of the beater. Then he drew a line with the shark's tooth. His line hardly showed. When he had watched Māmane the work had looked so easy that Kahana had not known how much strength he must put behind his tool. Again and again he went over the line, until it was deep enough. Once ruler and tool slipped. Suppose three sides were already well carved! Perhaps that wrong cut would spoil the whole. He rubbed it with a bit of sharkskin, proving to himself that a small mistake could be erased. Then he drew more lines. Now lines must go the other way, making tiny squares.

He was so intent upon his work that he did not notice his friend, Malu, standing beside him watching. Māmane had glanced up at Malu with a small grunt of welcome, then returned to his carving.

The squares finished, Kahana stopped for a deep breath. "Why Malu," he exclaimed. "I did not hear you!"

At the sign from Māmane, Kahana brought his work to show the master. "It is not even," he admitted.

Māmane grunted. "All skill is not learned in a day!" was his reply.

Tattooing

"I have put fish in the net which hangs beside your eating house," said Malu, "and Kaiki brought drinking nuts."

"My relatives are good to supply me with food," the woodcarver replied. "How may I serve you, Malu?"

"Have you ever done tattooing?" Malu asked. "You know how my uncle is tattooed. Half his face and body are covered with fine squares. My grandfather has wavy lines on chest and forehead. I longed to be tattooed but Grandfather said, 'Wait.' Well, I have waited. Can you do this work, Māmane?"

"It is some time since I have done it," the master answered, "but I have the tools. Let us plan, then I shall do a little at a time for it is painful."

"Does it hurt much?" Kahana asked eagerly. "I'd like to be tattooed. Two of the young men who are learning the *hula* have tattooed bracelets and anklets. Did you see them?"

"That is not real tattooing," Māmane told him. "Men cut designs from leaves of a mountain plant and bind them on. These leave a pattern that lasts a year or so. If one likes it, he can have it done in real tattooing."

"I know," said Malu. "That is what Keao did. She had lizards on her wrists and ankles and on her chest as well. I didn't like them. Time passed and now the marks are gone. But I want real tattooing." Malu went into the work house and looked at the finished *kapa* beaters. He brought one outside where Māmane and Kahana had been working. "Can I have this design?" he asked. "Can you make this, O master?"

"The *hala* fruit? That is a good design. Where do you want it?"

"On my chest first. Later on my arms, cheeks and legs. I want as much as my uncle has. I think no one in our village looks so fine. Yet I want mine to be different."

Māmane brought out a wooden bowl with a close-fitting cover and with it a smaller covered gourd. He opened the bowl and showed the young men his tools. "This punctures the skin."

"What a thin slice of bone!" Malu exclaimed, taking it in his hand. "A bird bone?"

"A section of the leg bone of our largest seabird," the master answered. "My father had several of these. I have tied on new handles. See! I hold the bone needle by this handle." He held it over Malu's arm to illustrate. "Then I strike it with this little wooden mallet. You see the edge of the bone has been filed into tiny points. Those puncture the skin."

"I don't see how you get the pattern."

"You will see." Māmane opened the small gourd. "Here is *kukui*-nut charcoal," he said. "Moku, the feather-gatherer, prepared this very carefully when he was in the upper forest. Sometimes I use the charcoal of sugarcane. Split one of the drinking nuts, Kahana. We shall need a little of its milk."

The young men watched eagerly as Māmane mixed some of the charcoal with *niu* milk in a *niu* shell cup. On Malu's chest he ruled lines with a delicately pointed stick dipped in the black mixture. "These are guidelines," he said. "After I have used them, they can be washed off." Between the lines he drew *hala* fruit. Malu lay on his back and Māmane knelt beside him as he worked.

At last the master said, "Now the tattooing!" He dipped the bone tool in a black dye, placed it at the point of a *hala* fruit and struck quick light blows with his mallet, driving the sharp bone points into the skin.

"Does it hurt?" asked Kahana curiously.

"I hardly feel it," whispered Malu, afraid to draw a deep breath lest he interrupt the work.

For a long time Māmane worked, following the *hala* pattern he had drawn. At last he straightened up. "The sun has gone to his resting place," he said. "The light grows too dim for work but one area is done. Can you come tomorrow so that I can continue?"

"I think so," Malu answered. "But O Māmane, this hardly shows at all!"

"Wait!" replied the master with a smile. "Come to me tomorrow when the light grows strong."

"How does it feel?" asked Kahana eagerly when Malu came next morning. "Did it hurt you in the night? Why, the tattooed place isn't swollen much, Malu!"

"It smarted a little," Malu admitted. "Last night it was swollen and red but now it is just a little pink. It hardly shows at all, Māmane."

The master raised his brows in a quick sign of assent. "Wait!" he repeated. He brought out a certain leaf, full of sap. He rubbed this firmly over the tattooed place, squeezing the sap into the punctured skin. "How is that?" he asked at last.

"$\bar{E}$, Māmane!" Malu shouted in his pleasure. "It is just what I wanted! Now my *hala* fruit is the beautiful blue-black of my uncle's squares. I must go now to help in caring for the fishing gear. May I come again this afternoon?"

"Yes. Many hours of work will be needed to cover you with *hala* fruit!" The master smiled. "How about you, Kahana?" he asked as the two settled to their carving. "Do you too long to be a handsome man?"

"I had not thought about it," Kahana answered. "Can I get the root you spoke of and try a design?"

"That is a good idea," Māmane agreed. "Let us each do that."

Later, while the master worked on Malu's chest, Kahana hiked for the plant whose leaves were needed. He washed them, then cut thin slices. These he carved into the form of stars and circles. When a section of Malu's chest was finished, the master laid stars and circles, alternately along his pupil's forehead and bound them firmly with a strip of *kapa*. "Darkness comes," he said, "tomorrow we can put on more."

Next morning Kahana removed the strip of *kapa* that held the leaf patterns in place. He ran to Malu's house. "O Keao," he called, "may I use your mirror?"

Keao came out with a wooden bowl. "The mirror is in this," she said, "but our water gourds are empty."

"O Kahana," she added, "how fine you look! Pua ought to see you!"

The young man hurried to the pool, knelt beside it and dipped up a little water in Keao's bowl, then set it on the ground. In the bottom lay a circular piece of polished lava stone. Covered with water this became a mirror in which Kahana saw himself quite clearly. Oh, I do look fine! he told himself with pride. I'll just walk by Pua's house, he added.

Malu's *hala* fruit designs were now a deep, dark blue. All the family gathered to admire. "He's going to have it all over him!" said Keao proudly. "Malu, you will be the handsomest man in our district. I'm going to have some too," she added watching for her family's approval. "Just a little *hala* fruit, so people will know I'm Malu's wife."

"Yes," Ana answered, "but wait a while. After your baby comes will be a better time."

Malu's tattooing caused much admiration. A number of older men and women of the district had been tattooed. Now a wave of enthusiasm for this decoration seized the young people. Māmane put aside his carving, for a time, and Kahana was busy preparing charcoal. Carefully he burned *kukui* nuts in a stone dish with clean pebbles resting on the nuts. As the nuts burned, soot collected on the pebbles. This Kahana brushed carefully into the master's gourd.

Then Kahana decided to join the other young people and have his body decorated with a little real tattooing. "We shall be a handsome village!" he chuckled proudly.

With the Birdcatchers

The Baby is Named

"**M**oku!" Grandfather took the baby in his arms and looked at him lovingly. Then he told the parents, "As I slept my god Mokuhāli'i stood beside my mats. He told me that you have another son. 'Let this boy bear my name,' he said."

"Moku," the father repeated, "our family has always worshiped the forest gods. The name is good."

The baby grew to be a healthy active child but he was silent. He made no baby sounds. He learned to understand what others said and sometimes his mother saw him move his lips as if to talk—but no sound came. Tears filled the mother's eyes. "Our boy cannot talk," she said sadly.

Now and then Grandfather came from the far-away village where he lived. He played with the baby, carrying him about. When the child was larger he rode on Grandfather's shoulders, holding on by hair or ear. As Moku walked beside the old man or sat on his knee the child listened to talk of life in the forest.

After a time Grandfather paddled away to his distant home. Moku will forget him, Mother thought. Months later when the old man came again the child ran to him. He had not forgotten.

The two played together. Mother watched as Grandfather swung the boy in his arms, then tossed him up and caught him. "Is Moku riding a canoe in rough waves?" she asked.

"No," Grandfather told her. "He is in a tall tree shaken by the wind."

This time when the old man left, the child stood watching sadly. "He will come back," Mother promised.

As Moku grew he came to understand that Grandfather was a birdcatcher. He listened to stories of the deep forest where many gods live. He heard how birds were caught and feathers gathered so that chiefs might have capes of red, yellow and black. As long as Grandfather's visit lasted the boy was with him—except in the eating house. Moku was still a little fellow who ate with his mother and other women.

Kūpā, his older brother, ate with the men. One day Kūpā ran from the eating house to tell Moku, "I am going to be a birdcatcher like Grandfather. Soon I shall go to live with him."

Moku did not wait for Grandfather that day but took the trail leading to a cave where he often played. The boy sat in the dark cave while tears ran down his cheeks. He knew that older brothers could do things a small boy could not. Kūpā ate with men and told of eating pork. He went fishing with bigger boys and was learning to paddle a canoe.

But I am the one named for a forest god, Moku thought. I am the one to live with Grandfather and be a birdcatcher. Not Kūpā. For a long time the child stayed in the cave. When he went back to the beach Grandfather was gone.

In the weeks that followed Moku thought often of Kūpā's words. It must be so, he told himself. Older brothers have everything. Kūpā will go to live with Grandfather. He will learn to be a birdcatcher. I cannot talk. I am no use to anyone.

The Consecration

Then Grandfather came again. Moku ran to him at once, held his hand and listened as the old man talked to Father and Mother. "Mokuhāli'i spoke to me again," Grandfather said. "These were his words, 'Take my namesake and train him. The silent child pleases the forest gods.' O my son, O my daughter-in-law, we must obey."

Mother was troubled. "You cannot take a little boy into the forest," she said. "Who will care for him while you are gone?"

"Ana, my relative. You know it is the custom for a boy to live with the parents of his father. Because my wife is dead I have not asked for your boys. Now our god has spoken and we must obey."

"We shall obey." Moku's father spoke slowly. "Moku shall be a birdcatcher. Today he shall be consecrated."

That afternoon Moku went to the men's eating house. On the shrine stood a wooden image of Lono, the great god. The boy watched as Father put an offering before the image—a cup of *'awa* drink and *'awa* root, *mai'a, niu* and cooked pig's head. A gourd hung from a cord around Lono's neck. Father cut an ear from the cooked pig and put it in the gourd. All the men and boys watched reverently. Why did he do that? Moku wondered.

Then Father prayed:

"Here is the pig, *niu* and *'awa,*
O ye gods,
Kū, Lono, Kāne and Kanaloa."

The prayer was long. Moku could not understand all but one thing he did understand. As the pig's ear was shut away in the gourd by the cover so were Moku's sins shut away. Every bad thought he had had was gone. He was clean. His life as a man was beginning.

The next day when Grandfather paddled to his own village Moku was with him.

Life in the strange village did not trouble the child for he was with Grandfather. Ana was kind. At first the children thought Moku odd because he did not speak. Soon they learned his sign talk and liked him. "He is good at crabbing," they said, "because he is quiet and quick. When we go for shrimps he sees them on the undersides of water grasses and quickly knocks them into our baskets. He never shouts and argues as we do."

Moku paddled the canoe when Grandfather fished. He helped plant *kalo* and weed. He learned to make fire and cook food.

And Moku listened as the old man talked of the *lehua* forest and the work of birdcatching. Perhaps he will take me this year, the boy thought, and let his nails grow long like claws as birdcatchers do.

Grandfather saw the fingernails and the longing in the boy's eyes. "Not this year," he said. "The trail is long and the work hard. You are still a little boy."

Moku helped Grandfather and the other birdcatchers with their backloads of food and watched them take the trail. Next year I shall be strong enough, he thought. He worked alone in Grandfather's garden. He went with the men to cut *olonā* or *wauke* saplings. He helped to bring *kauila* wood for posts for a new house. If I do much work I shall be strong, he told himself again and again.

Soon after the birdcatchers returned to the village the Makahiki festival began. Moku loved the months of gift giving, games and feasting. This year he listened more eagerly than ever before to stories of the forest. He knew that many gods lived there and that they loved and cared for every living thing.

"In the fall birds molt," Grandfather said. "Old feathers are loose because new ones are growing. That is the time we may take feathers. It is also the blossoming time of *lehua* high on the mountain slopes. The little honey-sucking birds come to the *lehua* and at that time the gods let us catch the birds and take a few feathers from each one."

When Makahiki was over it was time to begin many kinds of work—fishing over the reef, gathering salt, planting *'uala*. Later *'ulu* and *'ōhi'a 'ai* must be gathered.

It was also time for the feathergatherers to make ready for the forest. Moku tied fresh *kī* leaves to the net of *olonā* fiber which made Grandfather's raincoat. This is a thatch of *kī* leaves to keep Grandfather dry, thought the boy as he carefully tied one row of leaves above another.

He salted fish and pounded *poi*. It is almost time for the men to start, Moku was thinking. Tomorrow I must gather *'ulu* gum and then...

Sap had come from places on an *'ulu* trunk cut by a sharp stone. The sap had hardened into balls of gum. It was while Moku was gathering these that he heard Grandfather call. Grandfather sounded excited. Moku ran.

On the Way

"Let us see if this fits." The old man was holding up his raincoat of *kī* leaves. No, it was not his raincoat, but a new one which he threw over the boy's shoulders. "It is just right," he said. "You will need this for the rain is heavy in the upland."

Then Moku knew! He was going with the birdcatchers!

That night he prayed earnestly. He could not pray aloud, but Grandfather had often told him to pray in his mind. "The gods will understand." So Moku prayed:

> "O Kāne,
> O Kanaloa,
> Give me power,

Give me wisdom,
Give me great success.
Oh, climb to the wooded mountains,
Climb to the mountain ridges,
Gather the birds.
Bring them to my gum to be held fast."

Before dawn the men made offerings to the gods and prayed once more. Then they were off. The trail was dark but they knew it well and walked quickly in the cool of early morning.

The sun had risen when they passed the gardens. Now the trail was steep and rough. At last they reached the forest and stopped beside a spring to drink and rest. Moku had been here before but today it seemed different because he was with the birdcatchers. The moss about the spring was like tiny ferns, vines crawled along the ground and tree ferns stood taller than the men.

Taller still, *lehua* trees reached for the sunlight. These trees had already lost their blossoms. Moku knew that the birdcatchers were going to the higher forest where flowers came in the molting season.

Vines and mossy logs tried to trip men and boy. Once the four waded through a marshy place where their feet grew heavy with mud. Once they climbed up a waterfall, passing their bundles from one to another to keep them dry. Then along a narrow ridge. Cliffs dropped steeply on each side but Moku was not afraid. Grandfather was leading and Grandfather knew the way. Perhaps the men grew tired but the boy was too excited and happy to think of rest.

It was growing dark when they reached their house. Moku had heard of this forest house ever since he was a little boy but now it seemed a cave of darkness. Then one of the men kindled a fire. Smoke at first, then dancing flames.

Moku hugged himself with joy. He liked the cozy fire inside a sleeping house. The fire was in a trench lined with stones. Near it a log walled in the sleeping place filled with fern leaves. As the fire burned brightly Moku saw rolls of mats on a shelf and on the other side of the small house large gourds which he knew held *kapa* covers.

While Moku looked about, Līhau unpacked food. The four ate beside a little shelter where cooking could be done in time of rain. The boy was hungry yet he hardly tasted the fish and *poi*. He was listening to forest sounds— the wind in the trees, the call of sleepy birds and the splash of a waterfall. Later he lay warm and comfortable beside Grandfather under a *kapa* cover and watched the glow of the fire. *Ē,* this is good! he thought and fell asleep.

Birdcatching did not begin next day for other work needed to be done first. Līhau got fresh *koa* bark to mend the wall of the cooking shelter while the other helper gathered wood and stored it in a dry cave. Grandfather led Moku to the *lehua* trees. "We must know which have blossoms," he said. "We must remember where each blossom is, for our work is done before morning light brings the birds, the honey-suckers."

The two gathered gum from mountain plants. They heated *'ulu* gum in a large shell, added the other gum and mixed them with a stick. All was ready.

Everyday the four had prayed. Only with the *mana*, power, from the gods, could they get feathers from tiny birds. On the night before the work was to begin Moku prayed again and again. He thought he lay awake all night praying but suddenly Grandfather was waking him.

The boy shivered with cold and excitement as he pulled his raincoat about him and followed the old man into the fog. Only by keeping a hand on Grandfather could Moku find the trees.

"Climb," the old man whispered. Moku went quickly into a tree, found a flower by touch and gummed a twig just under it. A bird will light on this twig, he thought, and I shall catch it. As he worked he prayed:

> "O gods of the forest,
> Give me wisdom,
> Give me success.
> Send birds to my gum."

Dawn came and the fog lifted. All about were the calls of waking birds. Men and boy must leave the trees and hide or they would frighten the birds coming for honey. Moku hid behind a fern. He heard a flutter of wings and saw Grandfather climb. He watched as Grandfather took the bird in gentle hands, cleaned the gum from its feet and let it fly. He had not taken feathers, for the first bird caught must be an offering of thanks and prayer.

A sudden flutter of wings above Moku's head! In his tree! Panting with excitement the boy climbed. There was the little struggling bird. Gently he lifted it with his hands over the wings. He felt the frightened heartbeats, wiped the tiny feet on an end of his *malo,* lifted the bird and let it fly. "*Manu!* Bird!" he cried in excitement.

Moku was so excited and happy that he did not know he had spoken aloud but Grandfather knew. He came from his hiding place and took the boy in his arms while tears of joy ran down his cheeks. Then the birdcatching went on.

Again and again Moku climbed. Again and again he held a fluttering bird, pulled out a few feathers, cleaned the feet and let the bird fly. As he worked he prayed, then climbed from his tree to hide behind his fern and wait.

The boy was so excited that he did not notice the bright sunshine falling between leaves. He was surprised when Grandfather said, "The feeding time has passed.

We must break off the gummed twigs. Be sure you get every one."

Moku climbed quickly. It would be wrong to leave a single sticky twig. Perhaps a bird would light on such a twig when no one was near to take feathers and set it free. The bird would flutter, flutter and finally die. The gods would be angry that the life of a bird they loved had been wasted. Again the boy was praying:

> "O gods of the forest,
> Do not let me forget one twig.
> Give me success in all my work."

At last every gummed twig had been broken from his trees. Moku was sure. Then he went to the shelter where the others waited around the food mat. Grandfather held a small *'awa* cup and prayed:

> "O Mokuhāli'i,
> The boy has spoken.
> He is no longer silent.
> O great god of the forest,
> We give thanks.
> O Mokuhāli'i,
> You have given your name to this boy.
> He is yours.
> Give him more words.
> Grant him speech
> That he may pour out his thoughts.
> O Mokuhāli'i,
> Here is *'awa.*
> Here are *kalo* leaves.
> Drink and eat.
> We give thanks for the word spoken.
> Give the boy more words."

After the prayer Grandfather drank from the cup and passed it to Moku. "Drink," he said.

Wondering, Moku took the cup. "Drink," he repeated as he put the cup to his lips.

"Eat," Grandfather invited as he passed a bowl of *kalo* tops to Moku.

"Eat," the boy repeated as he tasted the *lūʻau*.

The men listened in wonder and tears came again to Grandfather's eyes. "Mokuhāliʻi has heard our prayer," he said reverently.

Life in the Forest

Every morning the men and the boy were at work before dawn. There were many blossoming trees and each man had his own part of the forest. One day he gummed certain trees. Next day he went to others. After a few days he came again to those gummed at first.

The afternoons were busy too. Feathers must be sorted and tied into bundles with a cord of *niu* fiber. Each man kept his feathers in a gourd—a gourd with a close-fitting cover, for the feathers must not get damp.

Everyday the men gathered wood. A rainy time might come when dry wood would be needed. They dug wild *kalo* roots and planted more, for they must never rob the forest.

They cut *olonā* stems and peeled off the bark. This was needed by netmakers. They gathered fern shoots for food.

Two or three times some of the men tramped the long trail back to the village. They carried down feathers and other things they had gathered and worked for a day or two in the home gardens. When they climbed the trail again each carrying pole was loaded with bundles of food—salt fish, *poi* and cooked *ʻuala*.

The long tramp tired Grandfather. Often he and Moku stayed behind in the forest. When the work was finished Moku sat beside a little waterfall and practiced talking. It was easy to form words with his lips, but it was hard to make the sound come out right. The boy liked to practice alone then surprise the others with new words.

Birdcatching in Other Districts

For two months the work went on. Every night it rained lightly and every morning the fog appeared. Then the heavy rains began. The four were glad for their well-thatched house and for the dry wood in their cave. It was good to sit beside the fire and talk quietly as they worked.

The men cracked *kukui* nuts. These nuts were needed for candles. Fishermen used the oil to quiet waves. Moku collected the shells. Later he would burn these to make charcoal for tattooing.

Suddenly he spoke. The boy had a question which he had practiced for days. "Birdcatchers," he said. The men looked up, surprised. "All—work—like us?" It was a sentence—more words than he had ever said at one time.

For a moment no one spoke. Then Grandfather answered quietly, "There are many ways. In one district men use gummed poles."

"That is more work," one man said. "Our way is better."

"Ours is the way of this district," the old man told them. "It is the way my father taught me. But gummed poles are easy to take away when the feeding time is over. A man will not leave his pole in a tree. There is no danger that a bird may be caught by gum to flutter and die when no one is near."

"Līhau," Grandfather added, "tell Moku about the snaring which you saw."

"That is interesting," Līhau said, "but takes much skill. Our way is better."

Moku moved closer to Līhau. "Tell," he said eagerly.

Līhau smiled at the boy. "My friend, Kaupua, showed me a cord of *olonā*. 'It is a snare,' he said. I did not understand so Kaupua took me to the forest. I hid among the ferns. Peeping out, I saw my friend tie a ripe *maiʻa* to a branch with a *maiʻa* blossom just above. The *maiʻa* was so ripe it was bursting from its skin. Below it Kaupua placed the small noose formed by his cord, then hid near me.

"I heard a *mamo* call from the fern where my friend hid. The call was clear and true. I almost thought a bird had whistled, but I knew it was Kaupua. Then I heard an answer from the forest. That was a real *mamo*. My friend whistled again. This time his call was soft as if he said, 'Come. Here is food. Do not be afraid.'

"The *mamo* came. It cocked its head and looked about, then flew to the food it loved. As the bird stepped into the noose Kaupua pulled the cord and the bird was caught."

"That way is not good," Grandfather said. "The bird is badly frightened."

"My friend was very quick," Līhau answered. "In a moment he had taken feathers and freed the bird. He did not have to clean gum from its feet."

"Some catch birds with a decoy," the third man said.

Moku's lips formed the new word but he made no sound.

"Have you seen that done?" Grandfather asked.

"No but an old man told me how he tied the first bird caught just above blossoms then gummed twigs nearby. Perhaps an *ʻōʻō* sees this decoy bird, flies down to drive it from the blossoms and is caught. The old man said he had caught several birds with one decoy."

"I have heard of a man who tamed a young bird," Grandfather added. "He made a cage for it and gave it food. The bird learned to love the man as our chickens do. That bird he used as a decoy."

"I like our way best," Lihau said.

And Moku repeated, "I like!" The words came suddenly and loud. The boy had not meant to say them. The men smiled.

"The life of a birdcatcher is good," said Grandfather, "and there is always need for feathers."

"Yes, I like to see a chief dressed for Makahiki or for war." It was Lihau speaking. "His cape shines in the sunlight and I think, 'There is nothing so beautiful. The feathers I gather will help to make such a cape.'"

"Or a feather god to lead our army in battle," the third man added. "It is good to be a feathergatherer."

The Great Surprise

The molting season lasted nearly three months. At last it was over. *Lehua* blossoms were gone. The birdcatchers could return to their homes beside the ocean.

Mats were rolled and *kapa* stored in big gourds. Nets were loaded with forest gifts and men and boy tramped down the trail.

Moku loved the forest. Now he found that he loved the ocean too. It was good to swim and surf, to race with his friends or lie on the sand in sunshine. It was fun to surprise the boys with words he could say. Yet Moku was eager to go on. He was eager to see Mother and Father and take his gifts to them.

The way home was long in the canoe and the paddle grew heavy. Then the home village came in sight and Moku forgot that he was tired.

He heard shouting. Children had seen the canoe and had run for Father and Mother. The whole village was at the landing place and they welcomed him noisily. Mother and Father wailed with joy.

After the wailing of welcome Moku ran to the canoe for the many *lei maile* he had prepared—some of his forest gifts. As he put a *lei* over his mother's shoulders everyone was watching. "Mother!" Had they really heard him speak? Then he put a *lei* about his father's neck. "Father! *Maile!*"

Suddenly there was excited talk and laughter. Moku felt his mother's arms about him. He felt her tears of joy.

Later there was a feast. Relatives came from upland farms. A black pig and *'awa* drink were offered to the gods. All the family gave thanks because Moku had begun to talk.

After the feast the boy asked the question in his mind, a question about his brother. "Kūpā—where?"

"He is learning to be a canoemaker," Father answered.

Grandfather's face was full of joy. "We are a forest family," he said. "We serve the forest gods."

Canoemaking

Palani *Fishing*

Kūpā stood on the sand, watching the canoe carrying Grandfather and Moku away toward the horizon. Moku had gone with Grandfather! He had gone to another village to be trained as a feather-gatherer. Moku is too young to go, Kūpā was thinking, why didn't Grandfather take me?

"*E*, Kūpā, I need help!" The boy turned quickly at the call. Haka, his cousin, was lifting a large basket into his canoe. It was a trap basket for catching *palani* fish. Several times Haka had let Kūpā paddle while he took *'uala* bait to feed those fish. Now he was going to catch them and was asking Kūpā, by a sign, to get paddles and bailers. All envy of his younger brother was forgotten as the boy hurried to obey. He helped carry the canoe into the water, then took his place in the bow.

Kūpā could paddle well for a boy and he understood this sort of fishing. For some time Haka had been taking partly cooked *'uala* to a certain place beyond the reef. *Palani* had become used to his big feeding baskets. A few days ago when Kūpā had gone with Haka they had seen many fish swimming about. Scared away for a few moments, the fish had returned for the fresh supply of the sweet potatoes which Haka had tied in his baskets. Now the time had come to catch these fish.

Haka steered and soon Kūpā saw the float that marked the place where the feeding baskets had been left. There were many fish swimming about. For three days Haka had brought no food and the fish were hungry.

They swam away as man and boy pulled up the baskets but they would return. Kūpā held the canoe steady while Haka lowered his trap baskets one by one to the ocean floor. The trap baskets looked much like the feeding baskets, large and deep, plaited of *ʻieʻie* rootlets. But the mouth was funnel-shaped. Fish could enter easily, but most of them would not find the small hole through which to swim away. Baskets were weighted with stones to hold them in place on the ocean floor. Partly cooked potatoes were strung on cord and tied inside. A cord attached to one of the baskets was fastened to a float of *hau* wood to mark their resting place.

Both Haka and Kūpā had been chewing *kukui* nut. Now they spat out the oil. It spread and calmed a little place among the waves so that the two could look down. *Palani* were already swimming curiously about the baskets, eager for food. Haka was pleased, took up his paddle and the two returned to shore.

After they had beached the canoe Haka pointed to a clump of *niu*. "When the sun has risen to shine above those trees," he said, "we shall go wandering again. It will be warm then in the upland." Kūpā understood. A man never said, "I am going fishing."

Father was planting *ʻulu* trees and Kūpā went to help, but his mind was on the fish and his eyes were often on the sun as it climbed the eastern sky. "Father," he said at last, "Haka is going wandering and wants me to go with him."

Father straightened up from the hole he had been digging. He looked at the sun and raised his brows for "yes." He understood.

Kūpā hurried to the canoe, but he was there too soon. The sun's rays still crept among the leaves and nuts of the *niu*. Haka had said, "When it shines above them." The boy must wait. He ran his hand along the side of Haka's canoe. How smooth it was! How thin its walls! The boy knew that the black part was hewn from a *koa* log, with side boards of yellow *ʻulu* wood fitted and firmly lashed in place. But he had never thought before of the canoe's beauty. It is pointed like a fish to slide easily through the sea. It takes great skill to make its walls so thin and smooth! For some time the boy stood, stroking smooth sides and pointed bow. Admiration woke in him for those who had made this thing. That is what I am going to be, he thought, a maker of canoes.

Then Haka came. The two paddled out once more. Haka lifted one of his trap baskets. What a splash and slapping of fish! And how Haka's face shone with delight at his good catch! He poured the fish into the canoe, baited his basket with a fresh string of *ʻuala* and carefully let it down once more. When each trap had been emptied of fish they returned to shore. There Haka made an offering of thanks to Kūʻula.

The two made several trips that day. Haka had many *palani*. He took a basket full to the chief's home—enough for the chief's household—and he shared with relatives and neighbors. Kūpā carried his share proudly. He had worked and earned those fish! Father cooked them over a bed of coals, for *palani* have a strong smell and are best cooked in the open. Kūpā was hungry and pride in his work added to his enjoyment of the food.

While the men laughed and talked, Kūpā was thinking. Suddenly he spoke, "How is a man trained to be a canoemaker?"

Some of the men in the eating house laughed at the sudden question but the boy's father answered seriously, "To learn that work takes years. Every boy learns farming, but only a few have the desire or patience to become expert canoemakers."

"Kāwai and Linohau are both canoe experts," the boy persisted. "Why are there two in one village?"

"Linohau and his men make canoes for the chiefs," the father explained. "Linohau is a famous canoemaker and his men are experts. But Kāwai makes canoes for commoners. He and his men are in the forest now cutting a *koa* tree to make a canoe for a relative of ours who is a fisherman. When it is done all our relatives will go up and haul the hollowed log to the sea."

"Shall I go?" Kūpā asked anxiously.

"Yes. All of us will go."

Hauling

A few days later Father said, "Tomorrow is the day. Help me make ready for the feast." Every boy loves a feast and now Kūpā was old enough to share in the preparation. He helped to prepare food for the *imu* and, when it was cooked, to wrap it in *kī*-leaf bundles to carry to the forest. As he worked he thought about canoe hauling. He remembered that he had helped before to haul logs when he was smaller. But then I was too young to understand, he thought. I did not know about the making of canoes. I had not chosen that as my life work.

In the red dawn of the next morning a crowd took the trail. Mother had given Kūpā a new *malo*, red printed with brown, and a *lei* of flowers for his head. All the relatives wore new clothes of *kapa*. All wore *lei*. It was a happy but quiet company that started up the trail. There was no shouting or loud laughter. No flowers were picked, no bushes broken. All were reverent in the presence of the forest gods.

They reached the *koa* forest. There, among great trees, lay the partly finished canoe—a hollowed log, pointed at each end but rough and thick-walled. It was not yet the smooth light craft that could slide through waves. Yet Kūpā looked at it with admiration. To cut a tree, to shape and hollow it! How did a boy learn such work?

"Come, Kūpā," someone called. "We must gather green *kī* leaves. They are needed for the feast." The boys gathered enough leaves to form two long food mats. Food for men and older boys was spread on one, food for women and girls was laid upon the other. All sat in their places about the mats. Talking stopped. There was no sound except the whispering of the wind high above them in the *koa* trees. Then Kāwai prayed:

> "O Kūpulupulu,
> O all you forest gods,
> You have shown us the tree.
> You have given sharpness to our adzes
> And strength to our arms
> That we should shape this canoe
> And hollow it.
> Now we haul it to the ocean.
> Clear our path.
> Make safe a way for this canoe,
> Yours and ours,
> That it may sail the sea—
> The deep sea, the calm sea,
> The billowing sea, the rough sea—
> For fish."

Then they feasted.

Satisfied with good food, the people made ready to haul the canoe to the beach. Knobs had been left at the prow and stern to hold ropes of *hau*. Before these ropes were made fast the *kahuna* prayed once more:

> "O Kūpulupulu,
> O all you forest gods,
> Care for this canoe.
> Guard it from bow to stern
> Until it reaches the canoe house."

Everyone took hold of the ropes; men in front, then women and, last, the children. Some of the canoemakers went ahead to clear the way of rocks and bushes. Kāwai and another expert held the ropes at the stern to steady the canoe and hold it back where the way was steep. Kūpā understood that behind these two, but unseen, came one of the forest gods.

A leader started the canoe-hauling chant and everyone joined. The chant was full of rhythm and helped men, women and children to pull together. Kūpā's heart swelled with joy that he had a part in the work and the chanting.

A shout ahead stopped the chant. "What is it?" people asked.

"The cliff! The trail leads over rocks, but this path is too steep and winding for the canoe. It must be lowered over the cliff."

Carefully it was pulled farther along the trail, then lowered broadside to the cliff by the ropes secured at either end. Slowly and carefully the men worked. Many held the ropes while others steadied the canoe as it went down the cliff face. Strong men waited below with arms upraised. Now the canoe rested on their hands! Now on their shoulders! They were carrying it safely to the trail below. Kūpā scrambled down with others, thanking the gods that the canoe was safe. On went the happy throng, chanting, toward the sea.

The Moʻo of Nuʻuanu

That night, in the eating house, the men talked eagerly of the day's hauling. "Kāwai is a wise man," an uncle remarked. "The lowering of the canoe over the cliff was well planned."

"And the gods were helping," another added, "while no enemy worked against us. Brother!" The young man turned to Kūpā's father. "Isn't there some story of an angry *mo'o* fighting against the canoemakers?"

"'The *Mo'o* of Nu'uanu'? Yes."

"Oh, tell it, Father," begged Kūpā eagerly. "I love to hear about *mo'o,* those huge lizards that live unseen in the forest. Tell 'The *Mo'o* of Nu'uanu'!"

"Yes, tell it!" urged the others.

The meal finished, they made themselves comfortable to listen. Father began, "The chief of Kou, on O'ahu, sent canoemakers into the forest above the Nu'uanu Stream. A tree was chosen, an offering made with prayers to the forest gods before men began to cut the tree. In a cave nearby lived a great *mo'o*. He was angered that men should come into the forest. He thought their chanted prayers and noisy chopping spoiled the quiet of the upland. 'I shall drive those men away!' he growled and sent a cold wind sweeping down upon them. But the work went on. Then the *mo'o* sent black clouds. Thunder growled and cold rain beat upon the men but did not stop them. The great tree crashed to the ground. Now they will go! the *mo'o* thought. But no! More prayers, more sound of adzes!

"Then many people came. Men, women and children feasted there in the forest where the *mo'o* had long lived in peace. Invisible to human eyes, he watched. He saw them fit ropes about the log they had been cutting. So that is it, he thought. They have shaped a canoe from that forest tree. They think that they can take it to the ocean. They shall not! The *mo'o* took the form of a mighty man but remained invisible. When he saw the ropes tighten to haul the canoe he seized the stern and braced his feet to hold it. He laughed within himself for the canoe did not move!

"Then he heard orders given. A chant rose and, as men, women and children pulled together, the canoe moved. The crowd was pulling both canoe and *moʻo!* The work was very hard. Rocks and bushes blocked the way and many times the *moʻo* braced himself and stopped the hauling.

"But the chanting crowd pulled with mighty power. The forest gods were helping and the canoe moved once more. At last they got it to the stream. 'The water will help us,' the *moʻo* heard people say and soon he found himself sliding over slippery rocks. The canoe was moving faster.

"The *moʻo* let go his hold to try another trick. He was very angry and meant to stop those men! He closed springs that fed the stream. It dried up and flowing water no longer helped the people. Now the *moʻo* seized the stern once more. The crowd had reached a very rocky place and there among the rocks the *moʻo* firmly wedged the canoe. The tired crowd struggled once more but could not loosen it.

"Darkness had come. People were tired and discouraged. 'Leave it,' the chief directed. So there it lies today, turned to stone. The waters of Nuʻuanu Stream continue to beat upon it but have never been able to carry it to the sea."

Pupils of Linohau

Years passed and Kūpā was almost a man. His boyhood wish to become a maker of canoes had increased. Today, with all the villagers, he had helped in hauling a large canoe for the chief. As men, women and children turned away from the long canoe house Kūpā walked slowly, thinking. "It is always the same," he said, unconscious that he spoke his thought aloud. "I may not watch the shaping in the forest. I may not watch the finishing here, beside the sea. All this work is sacred. It is *kapu*. How then can a boy learn?"

"That is what I have wondered many times." Kūpā looked up, surprised. Moho had come beside him and heard his words. Moho was a tall boy a little older than Kūpā. Kūpā did not know him well because Moho did not often join in the sports of other boys but worked alone or wandered in the upland.

"I did not know I spoke my thought aloud," said Kūpā with a laugh. "Do you, too, long to be a maker of canoes?"

"Yes," Moho answered, "and there is just one thing to do. Let us go to Linohau and ask him to take us as his pupils."

"Linohau!" Kūpā exclaimed. "He is a very great man. My father says he is one of the best canoemakers in all our islands."

"That is why I want him for a teacher," Moho replied. "Let us ask him, Kūpā. If he will not take us then we can ask Kāwai, who makes canoes for commoners."

Several days passed before the boys found a chance to speak to Linohau and in those days they were joined by ʻĀluka. "You two are going to be canoemakers?" he said. "I also. I shall go with you and ask Linohau to teach us all." The boys agreed.

Later the two talked together about ʻĀluka. "I like him," Kūpā said. "I have surfed with him and played games. He is good at sports."

"He likes to win," said Moho and would say nothing more.

These words set Kūpā thinking. Yes, he admitted to himself. ʻĀluka gets angry when he loses. "But canoemaking is not a sport," he said aloud. "ʻĀluka is strong and quick. I think he will be a good canoemaker."

"Did you ever see him work?" asked Moho.

The next day the three boys found a chance to talk with Linohau. "We three long to be canoemakers," ʻĀluka said. "Will you take us as your pupils?"

The tall gray-bearded man looked the three boys up and down. They stood quietly before him but Kūpā's heart was beating heavily. He will never take us! the boy thought. He is too great a man.

At last Linohau spoke, "You two I have been watching," he said to Kūpā and Moho. "You both belong to families who worship the forest gods. You each have shown great interest in the making of canoes. But you, 'Āluka? I did not know that you wished to learn this work."

"Indeed I do!" 'Āluka answered eagerly. "I think it is the most important work in all the world—to shape a strong, swift canoe that shall sail the whispering sea! Oh take me, Linohau!"

"Very well," the *kahuna* answered. "I will try you three. I shall speak to your fathers."

The boys were filled with joy. Moho seemed to forget his doubt of 'Āluka and the three were much together. They knew that Linohau had gone into the forest alone. "He is choosing a tree from which to shape a fishing canoe for our district chief," 'Āluka told his companions. The boys understood that the goddess, Lea, took the form of a little *'elepaio* bird and showed the *kahuna* which trees were sound and good. Also Linohau must choose a tree broad, straight and tall enough for the canoe wanted by his chief.

Some days passed. Then a man came to the boys. He was one they knew well—a canoe expert. "Linohau has chosen a tree," he said. "We go tomorrow to make an offering and start our work. You three are to begin your training. Be ready before dawn."

With great excitement the boys prepared for their days in the forest. Kūpā made *kī*-leaf bundles of salt fish, cooked *mai'a, poi,* and *'uala* cut in thin slices and dried in the sun. He made a bundle containing clothing, sleeping *kapa* and a mat. "I must make sandals," he remarked.

"Oh no!" his father answered. "You have been to the *koa* forest many times and should know that the trail leads over no rough lava. You did not need sandals for canoe hauling when you were a little boy. You need none now."

Before dawn they started with the men. "Let us carry the adzes," Moho offered. Kūpā did not notice that 'Āluka failed to take an extra load.

In the Upland

Whenever he had visited the forest Kūpā had been filled with wonder and awe. Now he stood looking at the *koa* trees stretching upward toward the sun. Here is the chosen tree, he thought. As it has grown straight in the great winds of the upland, it has gained strength to sail safely through the great waves of the sea.

"Come, Kūpā!" Moho's call broke into the boy's thoughts. "Help dig the *imu* at the foot of the chosen tree." A moment later both boys were hard at work. While they dug others gathered wood and stones. Soon the fire was kindled and stones heating, then all were busy preparing food. Kūpā worked steadily and took no notice of how little 'Āluka did. But Linohau was watching all his boys.

When the food was cooked an offering was laid on *kī* leaves at the foot of the chosen tree. The pig lay in the center. The good smell of roasted meat must be pleasing to the gods! About this principal offering there were laid a bowl of *'awa* drink, red goatfish, *kapa* garments, and *niu*. Then Linohau prayed. He offered the food to Kūpulupulu and the other forest gods and asked their help to make a canoe that could ride:

> "The towering waves of the ocean,
> The sleeping waves of the ocean,
> The drawing current of the ocean."

After the prayer they feasted. Then the *kapa* offered to the forest gods was buried at the base of the chosen tree along with bones and other leftovers, for food shared with the gods is sacred. Scraps of sacred food must never be left where men might step on them or animals feed on them.

Linohau divided the men into pairs. Kūpā watched earnestly as the *kahuna* himself and one of his men raised their adzes and began to chop around the trunk of the great *koa*. Often the boy had gone with men to cut *wauke* saplings or small trees to use in house building. But the cutting of a huge tree required a different kind of skill.

Kūpā noticed how the men stood and how they cut into the trunk with short firm chopping strokes of the sharp stone adzes. For a time the two worked steadily, then hot tools were laid aside to cool. Linohau and his assistant rested and another pair took up the work.

When Kūpā's turn came he seized the heavy adze eagerly and tried to use it just as the men had done but the stone did not bite into the wood. No chips flew. Still the boy chopped and chopped, trying to keep time with the expert who worked opposite. When his turn was over Kūpā was panting. Sweat ran down his body and his back and arms ached.

"You are learning," Linohau said as the boy sank down to rest and watch. Kūpā paid little attention to the work of Moho and 'Āluka for he was watching the experts to see how each used his adze.

He noticed their prayers.

"O Kūpulupulu,
Give strength to my arms," one prayed.

Another voice was raised:

"Make sharp our adzes.
O Kūpulupulu,
Give us power."

I did not pray enough, Kūpā thought. Even skilled workers need power from the gods. I, who have no skill, need more.

The workers changed places and Kūpā heard the voice of Linohau:

> "Guard this tree when it falls.
> O forest gods.
> Do not let our canoe be broken."

Was the tree ready to fall? So soon? The boy was filled with wonder at the skill of the experts and the power of the gods.

Linohau waved his hand. Silently the men moved to one side and the boy moved with them. No one stayed in the open space where the tree was to fall. The chopping continued. Linohau and a companion were working together, keeping perfect time. Suddenly they drew back. Kūpā saw a trembling seize the tree. Its leaves shook as if with fear. There was the cry of breaking wood and, with a crash, the great tree fell.

Strange feelings swept through Kūpā—grief that this great chief of the *koa* forest must fall and triumph at the power of gods and men. Kūpā glanced at Moho and saw tears in his eyes. He feels as I do! Kūpā thought. It was good to have Moho for a friend!

At a sign from Linohau all fell to work cutting off branches.

> "O Kūpulupulu," Kūpā prayed as he worked,
> "Teach me.
> Give me skill."

He felt his adze bite into the wood.

When the branches had been cut from the trunk the men gathered silently to watch Linohau. He had put on a white *malo*. Now he leaped onto the trunk and stood, facing the top, adze in hand. His voice rang strongly as he prayed:

> "Stand up in your strength!
> Here is the canoe, a solid log.
> Arise! Stand up!
> Shape the canoe!"

He took a few steps along the log and prayed once more:

> "Grant us a canoe
> That shall be swift as a fish
> To sail in stormy seas,
> When the waves toss on all sides."

Linohau reached the place where the log was to be cut. One of the men handed him a *lei* of *'ie'ie* which he twined about the trunk. Men and boys were silent as he marked the spot where the top of the tree was to be cut off. Then a murmur of approval came from the workers. Kūpā was moved by the excitement of the crashing forest giant, the prayers for aid, the help from the gods and from the skillful men. In the fastness of the forest the men in turn worked, then stopped for food and rest. The first day's work was done.

In the days that followed the men shaved away the bark, pointed the bow and stern and hollowed out some of the center of the log. Because there were many experts the work went fast. With joy Kūpā felt that he was gaining skill. He was learning how to use the different tools. Constantly he prayed, for he wanted to work as the men about him did.

Often the men worked in shifts. Half of them rested while the others used their tools, for the work was hard. Kūpā spent his rest time watching the skilled workers. Each time that his turn came, he felt his skill increase. But oh, would he ever handle tools as Linohau did?

When the log was shaped with knobs made for the hauling ropes, the men rested and watched as Linohau planned the inside of the canoe. As it would be hollowed, brackets would be left to hold the seats. Linohau now drew with a sharp stone the outline of these brackets. Then the hollowing began. Kūpā found this work required the use of swivel adzes and new skills.

At last the canoe was roughly finished and the whole village came to haul it to the sea. This was always a holiday time but this canoe hauling was far more important to Kūpā than any he had helped with before. As Linohau prayed the boy was praying with him. The forest chief had given up his tree life. No harm must come to him as a canoe. The work of gods and men must not be wasted!

"See what a good canoe this is!" Kūpā heard 'Āluka telling some of his companions from the village. "I am one of the workers now. Very soon I shall be an expert."

Very soon? thought Kūpā. I have not noticed 'Āluka's work. He must be much more skillful than I am.

By the Sea

After the canoe had reached its shelter by the sea Linohau called Kūpā and Moho to one side. "You two are workers," he said. "Stay with me. To be an expert requires years of labor, but you know how to watch and work, then watch again. Such boys I need. The day will come when I shall lay down my adze. Be ready, then, to carry on the work."

"When are we going to finish the canoe, Linohau?" asked 'Āluka as he rejoined the group. "The work in the forest was slow but I think I shall like the finishing. When do we begin?"

Linohau looked at 'Āluka for a long quiet moment and, as he watched, Kūpā felt afraid. "You are no longer my pupil," the *kahuna* said. "Your talk is great but your deeds are very small." His voice was cold and hard like a stone tool. When he had spoken he turned and walked away. Moho and Kūpā also turned and neither spoke as they went toward their homes.

The seasoning of the canoe took months. It was soaked in the mud of a *kalo* pond which turned the wood a rich dark color, then it was left to partly dry in the shelter of the chief's canoe house. After that came the finishing. Some of this work the boys could do. Some of it took such skill that Kūpā watched it in despair. Sometimes the canoe lay bottom-up on wooden supports while experts shaped its sides with sharp adzes. "They cut from it shavings thin as a curl of hair," Moho said.

Kūpā's brow signed "yes."

Then it was turned over and the men finished the inside. The rough thick-walled canoe had become smooth and thin-walled. At last the polishing with pumice stone began! That the boys could do. It was slow and tiresome but, oh, the smoothness of the wood after the patient work. "Now it is ready like a fish," said Kūpā, "and can slide through the waves."

While some men bored holes with pump drills others made the trim of yellow *'ulu* wood. Holes were bored in this to match the holes in the *koa*. Meanwhile Moho and Kūpā mixed the paint. First they burned *lau hala.* Then the charcoal they collected was mixed with juice from *mai'a* stalks and *kukui* oil. With this mixture they painted the hull of the canoe. Next the yellow trim was lashed to the body of the canoe with cords of *niu* fiber. The even pattern of the lashing once more filled Kūpā with despair. "I did not know there was so much to learn," he said to Moho.

But Moho's eyes were shining. "That is what I like," he answered. "All our lives we shall be learning!"

An *ama,* or outrigger float, was made from a curved branch of *wiliwili.* The up-curve at the bow end would help it to glide smoothly through the waves. The boys knew that no slender canoe, hollowed from a tree trunk, could keep upright without an outrigger. Curved crosspieces, or *'iako*, of *hau* wood were lashed to the *ama* and then attached to the port side of the canoe. The *ama* was far enough from the canoe to hold it steady and to give free movement to the paddles.

It was finished! The two boys stood drinking in the beauty of this graceful craft. "We helped to make it," said Kūpā. "Gods and experts made it," he added reverently, "but we had a part."

"Tomorrow!" said Moho eagerly. "Tomorrow it will be consecrated."

The Consecration

All the village came to the consecration. "The crowd flows to the beach as water flows from a leaky gourd," remarked Moho with a laugh.

"But this canoe will never leak," Kūpā answered confidently as the two took their places with the experts. Kūpā's grandfather, the feathergatherer, had come from his distant village and joined the crowd, gay in his many *lei* and bright *kapa*. With him was Moku, Kūpā's brother. Kūpā remembered the day, years ago, when his brother had paddled away to be trained as a birdcatcher. How he had envied him! And now Moku was seeing him, Kūpā, wearing a red *malo* and standing among experts! This was a proud day.

The chief came wearing a yellow *malo*. When he was ready the canoemakers carried the new canoe from the beach until it "drank the sea." The chief stepped in, then Linohau. The men followed, took up their paddles and the canoe leaped through the waves as the crowd watched from the beach.

At a sign from the chief they paddled slowly. He threw his line. A moment later he jerked his pole and a fish flew through the air—a red-gold beauty. A good-luck fish caught in a moment! Kūpā's heart leaped with joy, for the sign was very good.

They paddled to the beach once more and carried the canoe up on the sand. Once more the villagers came close. Little ones were gathered in parents' arms and their cries hushed. The crowd grew silent. Kūpā held his breath and listened. There must be no sound—no bark of dog nor chirp of bird—only the lap of waves which were to bear the canoe "over the drawing current of the ocean." Then Linohau prayed:

> "O gods of the sea,
> Let our canoe
> Ride swiftly over the waves
> Let this canoe
> Carry our people
> Safely in calm and in storm."

The prayer was long and Kūpā found himself listening not to the words but to the silence. No sound broke through the prayer. The blessing of the gods rested on the new canoe and the crowd murmured their joy.

An Expert

As Moho said, learning to be a canoemaker was a lifetime's learning. Many trees were cut, many canoes hollowed and finished. The boys' skill grew. Now and then something special happened to give deep meaning to the work.

One evening, just as darkness fell, Kūpā and Moho returned to a half-shaped log to get a tool for Linohau.

Suddenly both stopped. There before them on the log an old man sat—an old man with a long gray beard. The boys stood watching him then slipped away without the tool. "That was Kūpulupulu," Moho said.

"Yes," Kūpā answered. "The gods indeed watch over all our work."

Sometimes when Linohau went into the forest to choose a tree he took an expert with him. Once he took Moho—and Kūpā prayed that he, also, might someday be worthy to go with the master. The day came when Linohau called the young man to sleep with him in the men's eating house before the shrine. Linohau prayed long and earnestly that the gods would show him two trees, for the chief wanted a double-hulled canoe. In the morning the old man's face was shining and Kūpā knew that the gods had spoken to him as he slept.

The two climbed the familiar trail to the *koa* forest. At a sign from the master the young man sat down beside him on a rock. They waited. Kūpā knew they were waiting for Lea. The goddess Lea must come as an *'elepaio* bird to help them choose a tree. As the men waited they were praying.

Kūpā felt a light touch on his arm. Following the master's eyes he saw the bird. He saw it run along a tree and stop to peck. A rotten spot! The bird pecked for a time then flitted off. The two men followed. The *'elepaio* led them to another part of the forest. It lighted and ran up a trunk. That tree was sound but Kūpā saw that its trunk was twisted and would not make a good canoe. Once more they followed the bird. This time it lighted on a tall, straight tree and ran quickly along its length. Linohau twined an *'ie'ie* vine about the trunk then stood still marking its location in his mind.

Meanwhile Kūpā had followed the bird. The master joined him and all day they followed. Sometimes the

goddess' sign was good but the tree was not a fit mate for the one already chosen. One tree was too slender and one not tall enough. Then the little bird led them to a perfect tree—straight and tall like the first but close to a cliff. Kūpā could see at once that, were they to cut it down, the trunk would be broken in its fall. For two days they searched. The goddess led them far and showed them sound trees, but they could not find two alike. The third day came. They had circled back to the grove where stood the tree already marked. The *'elepaio* ran up this tree again as if saying, "Look at this once more," then flew a short distance and ran up another *koa*. Quickly she ran. The tree was sound. The bird flew on but the master stood admiring the good tree. Then Kūpā saw that this tree was a twin of the one already chosen. It was near the other and not far from a good trail. The goddess had been pleased because they had followed patiently. They would have a double-hulled canoe fit for the chief!

The day came when the double-hulled canoe was finished. Its strong mast was lashed in place between the two hulls. Its sail was made of strips of *lau hala* firmly sewed together. The women plaited a mat covering which could be fitted over each canoe hull in heavy weather. Paddlers could slip through the openings in this mat and sit paddling freely while the firmly plaited mat, lashed to ropes at each side of the canoe, kept out the waves.

The work was finished just in time, for a runner came with a message from the high chief. "A fleet has been seen!" the runner said. "It is that young hot-head chief on the next island. One island is not enough for him to rule. He seeks to conquer and may be coming here. Our chief orders all canoes to be made ready. Let us show the young *maha'oi* we have no fear of him. The high chief's *kilo* says the heavenly signs are good."

Excitement filled all hearts. Food was made ready in haste and canoes launched. Kūpā and his brother, standing together, saw the district chief come, glorious in feather cloak and helmet. They saw the *kāhili,* the feather standards, shining red and gold. They saw the feather god, carried aloft on a stout pole, his feathers erect and gleaming like those of an angry cock. The paddlers, fierce-looking in their gourd helmets, stepped into the new canoe. The sail was raised. The great canoe seemed to spread wings and point her beak toward the attacking fleet, like a strong bird eager to protect its nest. The young men watched with beating hearts.

Two days later the canoes returned filled with exultant warriors. "The gods were with us!" they told their friends. "When that young hot-head saw our fleet he turned and fled. Soon Makahiki will be here. For four months there can be no war."

"It may be," others added, "that the gods will give wisdom to that young chief. Let him care for his own people as our ruler cares for all of us upon this island."

"We are indeed blessed," said Linohau, "for our high chief thinks of his people, not of conquest."

Shouts filled the air—shouts of pride in chiefs and warriors and of joy that all returned unharmed. The crowd scattered, talking of their fleet's success and of Makahiki soon to come—the best time of the year.

Makahiki

Purification

Kaiki, Keao's nephew, was trying to go to sleep, but his active thoughts kept him awake. Makahiki! Tomorrow Makahiki begins, the little boy was thinking. "Grandfather!" he whispered.

Puakō lay on the sleeping mats close to the child. He grunted, only half awake.

"Grandfather!" Kaiki repeated. "Will you wake me? I don't want to miss the purification."

"I shall wake you," his grandfather whispered. "Now go to sleep."

"I can't! I keep thinking about Lono and our gifts. Then I think about wrestling and boxing. And the feast, Grandfather and…"

"Hush! You will wake everyone in the sleeping house. Close your eyes. If you sleep the time for purification will come soon."

Kaiki closed his eyes. Still his thoughts raced. What would purification be like? He couldn't remember. But the games….

"Kaiki! Wake up, boy." Grandfather was shaking him gently.

"What?" the child asked sleepily. "It's all dark. It isn't morning."

"No. This is the night before Makahiki. We go to the ocean to bathe for we must be clean when the god comes to our district."

"The purification!" Kaiki was wide awake now. Running out of the sleeping house he found his friend Noe and the other boys. They ran into the water and dove under a great wave. They swam and splashed.

When they turned toward shore they saw fires. Small fires were springing up all along the beach. As far as they could see the shore was outlined by stars of fire. The boys left the water and each ran to the fire of his own family.

Kaiki was shivering a little in the cool wind and the warmth felt good. Flames darted up and disappeared into darkness. They were magic, the boy thought.

Everyone bathed, for they must make their bodies clean and pure before the coming of Lono, the great spirit of the Makahiki. Big boys swam far out, racing. Old people swam a bit, then came back to the warmth of fires. Babies were bathed by grandmothers or older sisters, then they slept. Small children splashed in shallow pools.

"Come, Kaiki!" Noe was calling and the boys ran down the beach again.

"See, the waves are on fire!" Kaiki cried. He was watching the fire light reflected in a great roller.

Noe laughed. "I'm going to jump right into the fire!" he shouted. Both boys were diving, splashing and swimming once more.

"The morning star has risen!" someone exclaimed.

That was true. The waves no longer reflected fires on the beach for those had died down. Now a bright star was shining and its light was in the waves. The morning star! The ruler of the dawn! Soon the sun would rise and Makahiki would begin.

The Coming of Lono

"Four days is very long, Keao," Kaiki said.

"It is long for waiting," she answered, "but the waiting is over. Lono is in the district next to ours. Already gifts are being carried to the place where his people will stand."

"Kaiki, come!" It was Noe calling. "See the fine gifts from our district. My mother made that sleeping mat," he added proudly.

"Ana is giving *kapa*. I guess she's the best *kapa*-maker in this district," Kaiki boasted. Then he exclaimed, "Just look at the *maiʻa, ʻulu, kalo!* There is…"

"He is coming! Lono is almost here." Children hurried up with the news. The next moment the boys saw the procession. Some of the men walking wore robes of dull red *kapa*. But Kaiki saw only the pole carried at the head of the procession. At its top was the small carved figure of a human head.

That was Lono! His spirit was in that figure while he traveled around the island. Beneath the figure another pole was tied. This crossed the long pole and from it hung a beautiful white *kapa* which blew in the wind.

The crowd grew quiet, for they stood before a god. The long pole was set firmly in the ground with shorter poles on each side, wide apart.

Already people were laying gifts between the poles: a beautifully polished bowl, a canoe, *kapa,* mats, a large ball of sennit! Kaiki looked up at Lono. Was he pleased with all these fine gifts? He must be.

Then the boy noticed a man with a bunch of colored cords. What was he doing? Puakō laid *ʻuala* before Lono. The man tied a knot in a blue cord. Ana came with her *kapa*. Another knot in blue. Suddenly Kaiki remembered! One color of cord stood for one family. A knot meant a good gift. The boy watched as knot after knot was tied.

Then there were no more gifts. Kaiki looked about. Every family had given, people who lived beside the ocean and relatives from the upland. There were many gifts. Surely Lono would be pleased.

The man with colored cords must have made some sign for now a *kahuna* came forward, one of the men wearing

dull red robes. He was white-haired but tall, straight and splendid. As he chanted a prayer to Lono his voice was deep and beautiful:

> "Your body, O Lono, is in the heavens,
> A watchful cloud,
> An overlooking cloud in the heavens."

Kaiki remembered that Lono was god of farming. His clouds brought rain for crops. Now the chant changed as the *kahuna* spoke to the people:

> "Stand up! Prepare for play."

And the crowd chanted happily:

> "Prepare for play!"
> "Hail!"

The *kahuna* was speaking again to Lono and the people repeated:

> "Hail to Lono!"

The gift giving was over. Lono had been pleased. The pole was taken from the ground, the white *kapa* wound around it, and the procession moved away.

"Why don't they hold it up?" Noe whispered. "I like to see that *kapa* blowing."

"They will," Kaiki answered. "Puakō told me all about it. When the procession gets to the next district the pole will be held up again. Lono is traveling all around the island. He will receive gifts in every district."

"But he didn't take ours, Kaiki. Look! Those men are taking our gifts the other way."

"They are taking them to the ruler of our island. Puakō says our chief rules for Lono, so he has the gifts. He will divide them among the other chiefs. Lono is a spirit. He takes the spirit of the gifts, but the chiefs eat the food and wear the *kapa*. It is hard to understand."

"I think I do understand," Noe said slowly. "It's like a feast. The *kahuna* offers food and drink to the gods, then we eat the food."

Games

"Aren't you going to the games?" a big boy called as he ran past.

Kaiki and Noe raced after him. Already people had gathered around a flat, open field. At one side stood a large carved figure. Noe stopped and stared. "I never saw that before. What is it?"

"That is Lono, god of games." The boys had not seen Malu, Kaiki's uncle, close beside them. He led them through the crowd which made a circle around the field. Now the boys could see well.

Noe was still thinking about the carved figure. "Are there two Lonos?" he asked.

"No," Malu answered. "Lono is a spirit. The *kahuna* prays and Lono sends his spirit into these wooden figures. One travels around the island receiving gifts. The other stays to watch the games."

"I guess he likes games," Kaiki said. "Who are those men, Malu?" he asked as two came into the circle. Each carried a spear hung with many *lei*.

"They are the referees who are in charge of the games. The contests are beginning now."

A stout man stepped into the circle. "I know him!" Noe whispered. "He's a boxer."

Kaiki was laughing. "Look at the high steps he takes! He looks like a rooster getting ready to fight."

Men in the circle were shouting, "Sick one! Take to your mats! A beginner could beat you."

"They are for another man," Noe explained. When a second man came forward others made fun of him. The boys did not know who was the better boxer and shouted with both sides.

The first man struck, but the other dodged the blow. Men and boys shouted. Kaiki and Noe shouted till they were hoarse. Finally the second man was hurt and carried from the circle. The games were rough but the boys loved them.

After a time they grew tired of the hot, dusty boxing circle and wandered off to see what others were doing. Small children were sailing *kī*-leaf canoes. Some spun tops of *kukui* nuts. One little fellow was trying to turn a somersault. Every time he tried he fell sideways on the sand and the other children laughed. The child did not mind but just laughed with them and got up and tried again.

"Oh, there is Keao!" said Kaiki suddenly. "She's learning a string game."

"I love string games!" said Noe. "Let's watch."

"I come for the house."

Keao was chanting as her fingers made the string figure.

"There is no house.
All broken to pieces!"

The figure was gone. Then a different one was made as Keao went on:

"I come for the rafters.
No rafters!
All broken!"

"I come for the thatch.
No thatch!
All scattered!"

"I wish I had my string," said Noe. "I'd like to learn that."

Suddenly he noticed a group of boys. "There are my cousins from the upland, Kaiki. Let's see what they want to do."

A tall cousin spoke. "You told us you had darts, Noe. Let us have a game."

Noe led them to his home and brought out the darts. They were the stalks of *kō* tassels. Each was about as long as a boy's arm. The cut end had been bound with string so it would not split. Then it had been dipped in water and stuck into the ground to be smoothly covered with clay.

"Let's go to the place where men slide *pahe'e*. No one is there now and it is a good, grassy course."

"Do you want the first turn?" Kaiki asked the tall boy when they arrived. "Visitors may always choose whether they'll be first or last."

"Let us go two and two. You who live by the sea are *'kai'* and we are *'uka.'* You start."

"Let me be first, Kaiki," Noe begged. "I'm not very good," he explained to his tall cousin. Noe balanced his dart, ran to the starting line and threw. The dart shot along the ground then turned and hit a stone and stopped.

The tall cousin picked it up and looked at it. "See, Noe," he said. "The darts are yours, yet you chose a crooked one. This stalk is bent a little. That is why it turned and hit a stone."

"You next!" he called to a small brother. The little fellow's dart went straight but not far. Noe had won the first point.

The game went on. Sometimes *kai* was ahead and sometimes *uka*. The darts went farther and farther as Kaiki and the tall boy each called on better players.

That tall boy knows the game, Kaiki was thinking when only the two of them were left. I must play my best. He chose a straight, smooth dart. He took his place behind the line, balanced the dart, then stepped back. He swung his arm, bent low, ran to the line and let fly. The dart flew like a bird, now touching the grass, now rising.

"*'Ā! 'Ā!*" shouted the *kai* boys.

Noe danced with excitement. "That's the best you ever did!" he told his friend as he caught him by the hands. "My cousin can't beat that!" The two danced together.

Suddenly Kaiki stopped. "What is he doing?" he asked watching the tall boy.

The *uka* boy had a string fastened to a slender green bamboo pole. He wound the string around the dart he had chosen. Stepping to the starting line he snapped the string so skillfully that the dart was hurled over the ground. It touched and rose as Kaiki's had, but it went farther. A shout came from the *uka* boys, "*'Ā!* Our side has won!"

Kaiki was angry. He cheated! he said to himself. He had no right to snap the dart with a whip. But Kaiki knew it was not cheating. That was the way older boys played. Suddenly Kaiki thought of Lono. Lono would want him to be fair. "That was good," he said. It was hard to say and Kaiki's voice was low. Then he added, "I've got to learn that trick."

"The feast!" The boys heard a distant shout, "Come to the feast!"

Away they went, winners and losers together.

'Ulu Maika

Moku, the birdcatcher, had come from the mountain forest. He was Malu's cousin and Malu was proud to invite him to the new sleeping house.

He enjoyed every bit of Makahiki—purification, the gift giving and now the games. "This is the way for *'ulu maika,*" Malu told him. "I hear shouting. Let us hurry to the *maika* course. We must have a good look at those who are to play. This is a good day for the game," he added. "Hot sun makes the grass slippery. The stones should go far."

Two players had already taken their places, each holding a disc-shaped *maika* stone. The two were strangers to Malu, but one look told him which would win. One of the two was tall with long arms while the other was short and fat.

Most of the crowd thought as Malu did that the tall man would win. They were making fun of the fat one.

"He's a low shelf!" someone shouted. Everybody laughed.

"That's right! called another. "He's a low shelf the rats can reach."

"I think so too," Malu told his cousin. "The tall man is sure to win."

"Fat man—strong!" Moku whispered. "Pray."

People always prayed before games as they did before work. Those who played needed help from the gods. "All right!" Malu answered. "The fat man has few backers. Let us pray for him."

Malu and his cousin found a place where they could see. They watched the tall man swing his arm, then let fly the stone, throwing underhand. The stone first shot through the air, then rolled along the grassy track. Men ran beside it, shouting and praying, "Go on! Roll farther! Farther! O Father Lono, let the stone roll far."

It did roll far, but stopped at last. The referee thrust a stake in the ground to show the crowd how far the stone had rolled. The friends of the tall man were very happy. "Our man has won already!" they were shouting.

"I think he has," said Malu.

But Moku answered, "Wait! And pray."

Now came the fat man's turn. "Don't roll, Low Shelf," someone shouted. "You are beaten before you start!"

The fat man only laughed. He swung his stone and let fly. It rolled swiftly. Wind flattened the grass and seemed to push the stone along. It passed the tall man's stone, turned a little, hit a tree and stopped.

"'Ā! 'Ā!'" shouted the fat man's backers. "The low shelf holds good things. We prayed for him and he has won."

"Not yet!" the crowd answered. "The game is not over."

Someone danced and chanted. His *hula* made fun of the fat man and the crowd laughed. The fat man was laughing too.

Malu looked at his cousin. Moku's eyes were bright with excitement. "Pray!" was all he said.

There was a short rest. Then the tall man took his place again and the crowd grew quiet. Men held their breath as the player ran to the starting line and hurled the stone along the course.

Everyone watched the stone roll. On and on it flew, past the fat man's stone. "We have won!" An excited shout went up. "You can't beat that," they called to the fat man as he took his place.

He only laughed. "We'll see what the low shelf can do," he said. "Pray for me, friends."

He swung his arm back and forth, then sent the stone spinning along the course. "Go! Go!" Moku whispered. Malu too was praying.

On rolled the stone. It passed that of the tall man, rolled up a tiny hill, then out of sight. The referee placed a stake to show where the stone had stopped.

The fat man's backers shouted, "Our man has won! We never saw such rolling. The low shelf is strong."

As for the backers of the tall man, they were saying sadly, "He is tall, but no stronger than a *mai'a* stalk."

Evening Games

Games did not stop with sunset. Sometimes people played by moonlight. When the night was dark, torches were lighted.

Tonight the moon would rise late, so torches stood beside the space where a girl was juggling. Her quick hands were keeping eight pebbles in the air. Keao watched beside Pua, her friend. She held her breath, for it seemed to her that if she breathed the juggler would drop a pebble.

A chant rose outside the circle of watchers. The girl who was juggling heard and a pebble fell. Everyone turned toward the chanter.

> "*Pūhenehene* is the game.
> Will you play?
> Will you play?
> *Pūhenehene* is the game.
> Will you play?"

"It is Kalei!" Pua exclaimed.
"Yes. Choosing players."
"I wish she would choose me." Pua's voice was eager.
Kalei came into the circle of light. She was tall and beautiful with black hair hanging loose below a head-*lei* of green leaves and red berries. Her eyes were shining with excitement and fun. She stood before Pua and chanted:

> "*Pūhenehene* is the game.
> Will you play?
> Will you play?"

Pua rose at once to go with Kalei and Keao followed. *Pūhenehene* was to be played in a house with sides uncovered, so that the cool wind could blow through. In the center of the floor-mat lay a long *kapa*. On one side Kalei and Pua joined three other women.

On the opposite side, five men were seated. Keao smiled to see that one of the five was Malu's friend, Kahana. Lately, Keao had noticed, Pua and Kahana liked to play in the same company.

The five women did a sitting *hula* and the men joined. When the chanting stopped the men moved close to each other. Three people stepped from the crowd and lifted the *kapa* which lay between men and women. They held it like a curtain so the women could not see the men hide a small black stone on the person of one of their players.

The *kapa* was dropped and the crowd watched eagerly. The men had bent over so that no one could tell from a man's face whether he had the stone.

A woman guessed. Her guess was wrong—a point for the men's side. Kalei guessed. Wrong again! Then it was Pua's turn. "Kahana!" she cried without thinking. Everyone laughed. When Kahana took the pebble from under his arm the laughter changed to shouts of praise. Two points for the men, one for the women!

Now the women, shielded by the *kapa*, hid a small black stone. Again the men were lucky, for their first guess was right. Three points for them! The game went on. In the end the women had eight points and the men ten. Another *hula*. Other players were chosen and a new game of *pūhenehene* began.

Keao and Pua wandered off and were soon joined by Malu and Kahana. The four stopped to watch two old men playing *kōnane*. "I like to see the little white and black pebbles on the *kōnane* stone," said Pua.

"So do I," Malu told her, "but I have never learned the game. I can't even tell who is winning."

"*Kimo!* Everyone come and play *kimo!*" The shout rang along the beach. People ran to their homes for *kimo* pebbles.

"Come, Mother," Keao called as she saw her mother comforting a crying child. "Pua is getting the pebbles. Here is a good place to play."

People were seating themselves in small groups on the firm sand. "Your turn, Ana," Pua said, holding out the black pebbles to Keao's mother.

"Oh, no!" Keao exclaimed. "Save Mother till last. Have you forgotten how well she plays? You first, Pua."

Pua scattered the pebbles. Then she tossed her *kimo,* a special pebble. While it was in the air she picked up one of those she had scattered, caught the *kimo,* tossed it again and picked up another pebble. As she tossed she chanted:

> "Child I am of this shore.
> I toss the pebble of this shore.
> I toss! I toss!"

"Oh, you missed! Kahana next."

"Do you want my *kimo,* Kahana?" Pua asked.

But that young man had already taken a small pebble from a fold of his *malo.* "This fits my hand," he answered and began tossing and chanting. Soon no pebbles were left. Then Pua scattered those she had won and Kahana went on with the game.

"There! I missed. Your turn, Keao!"

But Keao was unlucky. She got only four pebbles and Malu six.

At last it was Ana's turn. Keao loved to watch as her mother tossed and caught up pebbles to the rhythm of her chant. She is as steady as the waves washing on the beach, Keao thought.

When no pebbles were left on the sand Malu scattered his six, then Keao scattered hers. At last only Kahana had pebbles left. He scattered them with a quick throw.

> "Child I am of this shore.
> I toss the pebble of this shore.
> I toss! I toss!"

Chant and game went on.

"O gods, do bless Mother," Keao was praying. "Don't let her miss now."

Ana changed the chant. Toss, catch! Toss, catch! Then, at certain words, she caught up the one last pebble.

"You've won!" Keao cried happily. "I knew you would."

Other groups were finishing the game and Ana was called to join the winners. Some of those who had lost went on playing. But Keao and Malu answered a call from Kaiki, "It's hide-and-seek. I'm the 'spirit.' Come!"

Several young people joined the children's game, to Kaiki's great delight. "Here, Keao!" Malu whispered, drawing his wife down in the shadow of an overturned canoe. When Kaiki, the "spirit," came near the two tried to crawl under the canoe. However the space was filled by three small boys. All five burst out laughing and were the first ones caught.

The game went on until the moon was hidden by a cloud bank. "Too dark to play!" someone exclaimed.

"Yes. Real spirits are out now!"

As Keao and Malu started toward their sleeping house Keao almost fell. "What is it?" she asked. "What did I trip over?"

"A small neighbor," laughed Malu. "He hid here in the shadow of the *niu* and went to sleep. Let us take him home."

Hula

Even more than the games, Keao had always loved the dances. This year she looked forward to them more than ever—for her friend, 'Ilima, would take part. 'Ilima was one of the new group of *hula* dancers who had finished training a short time ago.

Their graduation dance had been before the chiefs, but during Makahiki they would dance for the people of their district. After that they would go to other districts and other *hula* groups would come here.

Keao was up at daybreak gathering flowers and making a *lei* for her friend. All forenoon she watched the shadows. "Noon!" she told herself at last. "My shadow is right under me."

"Where are you going, Keao?" Malu asked a little later.

"To the *hula*. I think it is time."

"I don't," her husband answered with a laugh. "Wait till the shadow of that coconut palm is longer than the tree itself."

But Keao could not wait. So what if she was first at the exhibition ground? She wanted to be early enough to find a good place. The large mat spread for dancers and musicians was still in sunshine. Malu had been right. The *hula* would not begin until that mat was shaded.

Where should she sit? Near the large mat for dancers and musicians several small ones had been spread. For the chiefess and her attendants, Keao thought. The dancers will face them.

Keao found a space behind and to the side of but near where the chiefess would sit. As soon as she was seated she pulled out the string she had tucked into the top of her *pāʻū*. Chanting softly she made one of the figures she had just learned.

Other women and girls joined her. They talked together, showed each other their new string figures or played with little children who crept among them. Isn't it time? thought Keao. The shadows of the palms are very long.

Others thought as she did. "If they wait until darkness we cannot see the dancers!" said one.

Then a hush! The wife of the district chief was coming, followed by her women and *kāhili* bearers. Men and boys moved to make a path for them. When the women were seated the chief with his sons and attendants entered the circle. During the Makahiki chiefs and commoners mingled as they did not at other times. The audience was ready.

"The *hula!*" men were calling. "It will soon be night."

Once more the shouts were hushed, for the musicians were taking their places toward the back of the large mat. There were six of these, all older men and women. All had large sharkskin drums before them and small drums of *niu* shell tied above their right knees.

The drumming began. The sharkskin drums were struck with the fingertips, the small drums with thongs of braided fibers. In this way the drums kept time to the chants.

As the first chant ended two more musicians entered and knelt behind the others. Each struck a polished stick held in the left hand with a shorter one. The clear note of the sticks was like a call. In answer the dancers came forward to sit on the mat in front of the drummers.

There was 'Ilima! Keao had eyes for no one else. At a soft drum tap the young women rose to their knees and the dance began. Chant and movement were quiet and graceful. Then excitement rose and the movement became quick and spirited.

How easily 'Ilima moved! Keao understood that her friend was not thinking of herself or even of her audience. Filled with the power of Laka, goddess of the *hula*, she gave meaning to every movement.

Keao hardly breathed. Everyone watched with full enjoyment. As the music died a murmur swept over the crowd. Then shouts arose;

"Good! Good!"

"*Ē*, these are fine *hula* dancers!"

"More! Let us see more dances!"

Next four men and four women faced each other to dance with split bamboos. Each *hula* that followed was different. Some chants were sacred, praising the gods, some praised a chief or chiefess. One was a spear dance in which young warriors charged and fell back.

The most exciting *hula* told of a storm at sea. Chant, music and gesture grew more violent and realistic. When

Keao felt she could not stand the terror of the storm, it was over. The music died away and the dancers lay still, covered by their *kapa* garments.

When 'Ilima was not dancing Keao was able to notice the others. Some wore bracelets of boars' tusks. Some had anklets of dogs' teeth or shells knotted into a fine net. Every dancer wore a beautiful *pā'ū* of *kapa* and a *lei* of vines or flowers.

Many instruments were used: great gourd drums, bamboo nose flutes, clinking pebbles and gourd rattles.

It was nearly sunset as five girls moved through the last dance to the music of the *'ūkēkē*. These little stringed bows held against the lips gave a soft, weird accompaniment to a love chant. Then the music died away and with it the clink of shells in the anklets. The dances ended amid shouts of praise for "the best *hula* dancers we ever had!"

Pahe‘e *and* Hōlua

"Come, Moku! This is the day for *pahe‘e*." Malu was calling his cousin, the birdcatcher.

"*Pahe‘e!*" Moku came running. "I know where! May I play?"

"Anyone may play. I have no skill at *pahe‘e* but Puakō is a good player and has darts. Let us go."

"Here we are!" Malu exclaimed as they reached the playing field. "This is where Kaiki and his friends slide *kō* tassels. Perhaps you played here when you were a little boy."

A sudden look of sadness came to the birdcatcher's face, like a cloud hiding the sun. "Could not talk then," he said. Malu understood. Because he could not talk like other boys Moku had not wanted to play with them.

The game had already begun. Men were sliding *pahe‘e* darts of polished wood for distance just as the boys slid darts of *kō*. For a time Moku stood watching. Soon Puakō offered him a dart which the young birdcatcher balanced eagerly. "You next, Moku!" someone called.

Moku ran to the starting line and threw. His dart shot along the grassy course. Sometimes it slid. Again it seemed to fly. The referee shouted, "*Lilo ka eo!* He has won."

Another contest. Moku won that also. Men shouted and Puakō made a chant in praise of the best *pahe‘e* player. Makahiki is a wonderful time! the birdcatcher thought.

"Now for skill!" the man in charge called out. He laid two darts side by side, some distance from the starting line. They made a kind of gate, little wider than a man's hand. The game of skill was to send a dart through this gate without touching either side. "You first, Moku?" the man asked.

But Moku made a sign for "no," a quick wrinkling of the nose. "I have no skill," he whispered. For a long time he watched the others. Many missed, but some could send their darts easily through the gate.

A sudden cry was heard, "*Hōlua!* Come and watch the chiefs."

"Let us go," said Malu.

Again Moku made the sign for "no." "You go," he said, "I stay."

Malu stood wondering what to do. Another shout and he ran with the other men. Moku was alone.

The "gate" still lay on the grassy course. The young man took his place behind the starting line, swung his arm and let fly his dart. It struck the right side of the gate, knocking off the course marker. Moku put it back and tried again. This time he hit the left side.

I am throwing too hard, he told himself. Again and again he threw, growing more gentle and careful.

There! The dart slid through the gate! From a distance came the shouts of those who watched *hōlua* but Moku did not hear. To slide through the gate once was not enough for him. Again and again he shot his dart until every shot was good. Now I can play *pahe'e!* he told himself and ran toward the *hōlua* slide.

The district chief and a visiting chief had been sliding. Now two young chiefs had a turn. As Moku joined the crowd the younger boy was sledding down the steep grass-covered course. His older brother followed.

A sudden gasp from the watchers! The small chief's sled must have struck a stone. It tipped and threw him. The sled went on, but the boy lay where he had fallen in the path of his older brother's sled.

Moku felt cold with fear. But the skillful older boy guided his sled past his brother and flew on down the hill. The small chief got to his feet unhurt. A great shout rose. There was thankfulness that the little one had not been hurt. There was praise for the skill of the older boy.

Attendants carried the long, light sleds back up to the starting point. This time the older boy went first. Moku drew a long breath as he watched the swift rush of the sled. It is like flying! the birdcatcher thought. It must be wonderful to be a chief.

As the young men walked back toward the ocean a sudden thought came to Moku. "Feather capes?" he asked his cousin.

"You want to see them? Of course you do, birdcatcher. They are not worn for games. But soon Lono will return from his travels around the island. The return of Lono is a sacred time and the chiefs will wear feather cloaks and capes.

"Now let us go to the field near the dwelling of our ruling chief. There will be games and worship. I have seen Lono's return only once and I am eager to go again."

The Return of Lono

Many people came to the village of the ruling chief to see the return of Lono. Some slept in caves while others built shelters of palm fronds. "We are lucky," Moku said. "My older brother has room for us in his sleeping house. He says we are just in time, for Lono will soon be here."

Next morning the young men joined the crowd. Moku had never seen so many people. All wore new *kapa* and numerous *lei* of vines or flowers. Suddenly he saw the feather capes of the chiefs. How beautiful the feathers looked in the morning sunlight!

And there was a chief in a long feather cloak and helmet. "Our great chief," Moku's brother said, "ruler of this island."

The crowd watched as the chief removed his cloak and helmet, stepped into a canoe and was paddled toward the open sea. "Where?" Moku asked.

"He goes to fish. While Lono traveled around the island all fishing was *kapu*. Our chief must catch one fish.

Then the *kapu* will be lifted." Moku knew that the chief ruled in the name of the gods so he must be the one to lift the *kapu*.

A line of warriors carrying polished spears went by. Then a shout! And Moku saw Lono's procession. There were the many *kāhuna* dressed in their dull red *kapa*. There was the pole with the little carved figure and the white *kapa* blowing in the morning wind. The warriors gathered about Lono to guard him.

"Look, Moku! Our chief is back. He has caught a fish."

The chief leaped from his canoe. He put on the cloak and helmet he had taken off to go fishing. How splendid he looked! I thank the gods that I am a feathergatherer, Moku thought as he admired the cloak made with thousands of tiny yellow feathers tied to a fine net. Crescents of red feathers and triangles of black feathers added to the color and design of the chief's cloak.

Suddenly a spear was thrown right at the chief. The chief caught and held it. A warrior ran forward and touched him with another spear. "Why?" Moku could not understand.

"Did the spears hurt him?" Malu's brother asked.

"No."

"That proves that he is able to rule for the gods. Come now," he added. "Here is a good place to see the sham battle."

"Battle?" Again the birdcatcher did not understand.

"Our warriors are on this side," Malu's brother went on. "Over there are the enemy."

A little while ago these were all friendly warriors. Now they were going to fight! It seemed very strange to Moku.

The two bands of warriors came toward each other. Some shouted angrily. Some boasted of their strength. Suddenly a spear was thrown. Then everything was a great confusion of flying spears, running and shouting! This was war! To the quiet young man from the forest the noise and anger were terrible.

He watched a tall enemy warrior rush forward and throw his spear. The warrior did not run back, but caught two spears thrown at him. He threw one and a man fell. He threw another.

"Our chief! Our brave chief!" Shouts rose on every side. There he was in the middle of the battle—the ruling chief in bright cloak and helmet. He threw his spear, then caught one thrown at him. Men fell around him. Down went a tall warrior!

Suddenly—as suddenly as he had come—the chief left the battle. "That is what he does in real war," Malu's brother was saying. "When his men are driven back he is suddenly among them, helping and giving courage. Then he is off to help other warriors.

"Look!" he added. "The enemy are trying to get their dead."

Moku was too excited to listen to what was being said. He heard only the one word, "dead." That tall young warrior had fallen. Many had fallen. Were they dead?

"'Ā! 'Ā! Our side has won!" shouts rang all about him. "Now they are dragging away those they have killed."

They were dead. Moku felt hot with anger as he saw the tall young warrior being dragged off by his feet.

"It's over." Malu spoke calmly. "But wasn't it exciting? Watch them now!" The "dead" men jumped to their feet and ran to the ocean to wash off the sand. There was the tall young warrior laughing and splashing among his friends. He hadn't been killed! No one had.

The warriors were beginning a contest of fencing with spears. Moku saw the young men choose partners and challenge one another. Each tried to win points by touching his opponent with his blunt spear as he warded off the thrusts directed at him.

The young birdcatcher felt as if he were waking from a bad dream. A sham battle! he said to himself. Not real! The spears they threw were not pointed. The warriors were not angry. It was a game.

Next day everyone went to the *heiau* of Lono. The crowd outside the *heiau* wall listened in silence as the chief prayed. He made an offering of food to thank Lono for his care of the people during his journey around the island.

Then the *kāhuna* put away the pole with its little carved figure. They put away the beautiful white *kapa*. This was done with care and reverence. The spirit of Lono was no longer in the little image. Lono's spirit was journeying over the ocean toward the island in the deep blue of heaven which was his home.

With loving care food had been made ready for this journey. The *kāhuna* had filled a basket with *niu* and other food. This rested on the outrigger of a small empty canoe. The canoe was launched and its sail set. As the crowd watched it start its lonely journey toward the horizon one thought was in every mind, Lono will come to us again next year.

"Now the net-shaking," said Malu's brother as people left the beach. He led the way to a large net filled with *kalo, maiʻa, niu, ʻuala* and *ʻulu*. A man stood at each corner of the net. A *kahuna* of Lono stood there too, waiting for silence. Moku remembered a story he had heard of a hungry time on the island of Hawaiʻi. The ruling chief had let down a net from heaven and had shaken food from it to feed his people.

Silence at last! No bark of dog, chirp of bird or crow of cock! In the silence the *kahuna* prayed:

> "Net of heaven!
> Green are the leaves of god's harvest fields.
> The net fills the heavens.
> Shake it."

At these words the four men lifted and shook the net. *Kalo, mai'a, niu*—everything was falling out. The year to come would be a good year! Crops would grow and people would be fed. Thankfully the crowd chanted:

> "Shake down the god's food!
> Scatter it, O heaven!
> A season of plenty this.
> Earth, yield thy plenty!
> This is a season of food.
> Life to the land!
> Life from Kāne!
> Life to the people!
> Hail, Kāne of the water of life! Hail!
> Life to the lord of the Makahiki!"

Prayers for the Year to Come

Kaiki and Noe watched men plaiting palm leaves. Over and under, over and under—the work went fast. "Whose houses are these?" Kaiki asked. "Palm and *kī* thatch look nice, but *pili* grass lasts longer."

"These houses don't have to last," his friend told him.

"They are to be used right now for offerings and prayer."

"Why?" Kaiki wanted to know. "Every family has its own place for prayer and offerings—in the men's eating house or in a special house. Each of the great gods has a *heiau*. I don't see what these are for."

Noe himself did not understand. "Malu!" he called as that young man came near. "Why do we need these houses?"

"At the close of Makahiki we all pray that the gods will bless our district in the year just beginning. Tomorrow we shall come to this house with a palm-thatched roof to pray for fish."

The next day the boys joined the silent crowd as the *kahuna* made an offering. They listened to his prayer:

> "Here is an offering, O Kāne!
> Drive hither the fish from Kahiki,
> The *'ōpelu,* fish that travels with the sun,
> The *aku* pulled in by the line.
> O Kāne, send us fish!
> Life to the land."

That evening was one of bright moonlight. People sat here and there on the beach chanting, playing games, talking. Small boys raced about. Young people walked together. Kaiki and Noe joined groups in chants and games.

At last Kaiki sat down beside Puakō. "I wish Makahiki would last forever!" he exclaimed. "Feasting, games, *hula!* That's what I like!"

"What should you feast on if no one worked?" Malu asked.

The boy was still, thinking. Suddenly he said, "The prayer today was about *aku* and *'ōpelu.* Isn't there a story about those fish? It seems as if I heard one when I was little."

Puakō smiled, then answered, "You are thinking of Pā'ao. When he came from far Kahiki his angry brother sent a storm. The wind roared and angry waves seemed ready to swamp the double-hulled canoe. Then Pā'ao's guardians came, the *aku* and *'ōpelu.* The *'ōpelu* skimmed over the waves, quieting them, and the *aku* pushed the canoe on its way to Hawai'i."

"Oh, how I long to go fishing!" Malu exclaimed. "Makahiki has lasted long enough for me. I am eager for *aku* fishing."

"So am I!" said 'Aukai.

Kaiki moved close to the head fisherman and looked up into his face. Often 'Aukai was as silent as the fish but the boy knew he could tell good stories. He waited quietly. Everyone turned toward 'Aukai.

Slowly the head fisherman began to speak. He seemed to talk to Kaiki but he knew the others listened also. "I was not born in this district," he told them, "but came here when I was small to live with relatives. My foster father was head fisherman. When I had learned to paddle he took me with him. I paddled and bailed. I learned to run out on the outrigger to balance the canoe. I learned how water could be splashed out of a swamped canoe by pushing it quickly back and forth. And I watched the fishing.

"I remember the first time I went *aku* fishing with the men. Oh, how we paddled! My back ached and the paddle burned my hands! The great, shining fish were all about us. As fast as the fishermen could throw their hooks, so fast they pulled in *aku*. 'That is what I shall be,' I told myself, 'a fisherman.'

"I practiced alone in the upland. I caught a block of wood on a bone hook that I had made. I pulled it up, catching the block under my arm as the fishermen caught the *aku*. I loosened the hook and pretended to drop my fish into a canoe. I did this again and again until I could land the wooden fish with skill. If only I might catch a real one!

"One day we had been *aku* fishing and our canoe was full. Our arms and backs were aching so my father set the sail. 'Take my place at the stern and steer,' he told me. We changed places and he bailed.

"Suddenly all about us *aku* rose. They were chasing little fish which are their food. My father lowered the sail and signaled to me to fish. My chance had come!

"I threw the pearl-shell hook. At once an *aku* took it. Using all my strength I pulled up the big fish just as I had pulled up my block of wood. I caught it under my arm, slipped out the hook and dropped the fish into the canoe. I was ready to throw my line again.

"'No more!' I heard my father's voice and turned toward him. I had caught one. I wanted to catch more!

I motioned toward them. My eyes were begging him to let me go on fishing.

"'No more today,' he told me firmly. 'The first fish of a new fisherman must be offered to the gods. He must catch only one. Learn the rules of fishing, my son. Obey them and the gods will bless you and make you a head fisherman.'

"It was hard to sit quiet when the fish were all about, but I obeyed. That night my father wrapped my fish in *kī* leaves and cooked it with hot stones. He offered it to the gods." In a low, reverent voice 'Aukai repeated the prayer that had made him a fisherman:

> "O fishing gods from the east to the west,
> From the north to the south,
> From high heaven to the horizon,
> Here is an *aku* complete from head to tail,
> An *aku* offered by the new fisherman.
> Take this *aku* fish
> And accept the new fisherman.

"Then we feasted. When we were done I bundled the bones and carried them out to drop into deep ocean, for they were sacred. The gods had made me a fisherman."

❦ ❦ ❦

"Another new *malo!*" Kaiki exclaimed. "Oh, Ana, that's another thing I like about Makahiki. I have a new *malo* for every special day."

"And a *lei*," Keao called, holding one up.

The little boy danced about enjoying the *malo* and the *lei*. They make me look fine! he was thinking.

Then he noticed how Keao stood looking off over the blue ocean. He went to stand beside her. He thought of Lono who had gone to his island in the deep blue of heaven. "Lono will come back?" he asked.

"Yes. Next year at Makahiki he will come again."

"This is what I don't understand, Keao. If Lono is far away on his own island how can he hear our prayers for fish and crops?"

"Lono is a spirit. He will hear."

Later, when people stood before the *kī*-thatched house, the boy remembered his aunt's words. In his heart he prayed with the *kahuna:*

> "O Lono of the broad leaf,
> Let the low-hanging cloud pour out its rain
> To make the crops flourish,
> Rain to make the *kapa* plant flourish
> Wring out the dark rain clouds
> O Lono in the heavens.
> O Lono, shake out a net-full of food,
>   a net-full of rain.
> Gather them together for us.
> Gather food, O Lono!
> Gather fish, O Lono!
> *Wauke* bark for *kapa* and *'olena* dyeing *kapa*
> *'Āmama.* It is free."

The Training of a *Kilo*

Some years before, there had been much talk in the district about Kūpahu's longing for a son. Kūpahu was the *kilo,* the one who watched for the heavenly signs through which the gods speak to men. He made offerings and prayed for the welfare of chiefs and people. The gods heard his prayers and sent blessings on the district. Now Kūpahu prayed that his next child might be a boy, for he had only daughters.

The villagers rejoiced, even while they chuckled, at the news, "Kūpahu has twin sons." While still small, the babies were taken, according to custom, to the home of their father's parents. They were chubby, healthy children who soon were crawling on the beach, digging in wet sand and laughing when a wave rippled about them.

'Aki and Haili grew. They swam with other little children in a pool near their grandparents' home or floated *kī*-leaf canoes. And they ran about the village, making friends with the other children, helping their grandparents by catching crabs, gathering seaweed and bringing driftwood.

Then came the solemn ceremony of their consecration. They were still little boys but their wrong thoughts and acts had been shut away in the sacred gourd and they were free to eat with men. "Now they must come home with me," Kūpahu insisted. "I have only daughters in my house. My sons must learn my wisdom."

Soon the two came to know the people of their home village. They played with other little children: Kahana, Keao and 'Ilima. The twins were strong and quick. As they grew older they became leaders at surfing and other sports. They made kites and called upon the mountain winds to lift them, then ran shouting and paying out the string, each urging his kite to outdo the other's.

The twins had much time for play. They also, as did all boys, had work to do—only their work was different. From the first day of their return to Kūpahu's home, he became their teacher. Night by night and year by year the twins learned to see and understand the heavenly signs.

While they were still little boys their father told them how all things began. "Wākea broke open a great gourd," he said. "Half he threw upward and that became the sky. The other half became the many-colored sea with all its islands. The seeds of that gourd became sun, moon and stars. The juice became the rain."

He told them how the sun, chief star above all stars, had hurried too fast across the sky till Māui caught him and broke his strongest legs. "Now the sun goes slowly in the sky," Kūpahu said. "Each night he goes to his resting place beyond the ocean. Watch the spot where he disappears. Each night till midsummer that place is a little farther to the north. After midsummer each night he goes beyond the sea a little farther to the south and a little earlier, until the days grow short. Then the nights are long and ruled by the moon and stars. The sun's changes mark the year. The moon, the great whiteness, divides our year into twelve lights. Learn the changes of the sun and moon so that you can teach men when to prepare their land and when to plant."

The boys learned the names of many stars. These were wise and powerful beings. They were the ones who guided the ancestors who came to Hawai'i long ago and they still watched over people.

Then there were wandering stars. Each had its name: Following-the-Chief, Red Star, Chiefess Star, Dripping-Water. These moved through the heavens, following paths of their own. As they passed through the constellations of fixed stars the *kilo* read the fortune of his chiefs. If a wandering star took a certain course, the gods were telling men of ill-fortune coming to the chiefly family. Another course and all was well.

There was much to understand and to remember! At times 'Aki and Haili were discouraged. At times they were filled with admiration for the great wisdom of their father and with strong desire to learn all he could teach.

Before they were four they learned of the Backbone-of-the-Lizard, that shining pathway made of countless stars. They learned the names and shapes of the constellations, especially Makali'i, the little cluster of seven stars whose rising announced the Makahiki and the beginning of a new year. They learned to read the star signs: their twinkling, the rainbow colors that sometimes sparkled from them and their misty look before a storm.

In the southern sky they sometimes saw Bright-Scattering-Mist, which protected earth from dangerous winds. Often flying stars flashed for a moment across the sky and then were gone. These too gave the wise *kilo* messages concerning winds or the fruitfulness of months to come.

Once a star with a glittering tail appeared. Night after night it moved across the sky and each night it grew brighter. The *kilo* knew that, long ago, such a star had dragged its tail across the heavens. It had been followed by fire spurting from a volcano, a great rush of red-hot lava, clouds, thunder and terrible storms.

Day after day, night after night, the *kilo* made offerings and prayed. The boys joined him. Fear gave great earnestness to their prayers. And the gods heard, for the tailed star grew dimmer and at last disappeared. No evil followed.

Sometimes a halo was seen around the sun or moon. Often these halos were signs of evil: an eruption, a terrible tidal wave which swept away houses by the sea or sickness and death in the chiefly family. Whenever signs were evil the *kilo* made offerings and prayed. Often his prayers were heard and the evil turned away.

There were also many cloud signs. The twins learned to watch for figures in the clouds. A cloud pillar told of the coming of a chiefly visitor. Every cloud figure of an animal, bird, canoe or person had its special meaning. The two young men learned to watch the color of the clouds, their movement, their place in the sky and the time of day when each formation appeared.

By the time Kahana had become a skilled woodcarver, by the time Keao was married and ʻIlima had learned the *hula,* ʻAki and Haili had gained much wisdom in heavenly signs.

Makahiki had just ended. The men gathered at one *heiau* to pray for fish and at another to ask that growing things be blessed. The following morning before dawn ʻAki and Haili joined their father in offerings and prayer. Then they followed him to his observation point.

This special observation point was a place where rocks jutted into the sea. Neither trees nor mountains shut out the full sweep of the sky. The young men listened as their father talked to Lono, asking for signs. Now they could understand these signs. They had learned to read the message of the gods.

The morning star dimmed in the light of the coming sun. The sea grew many colored. Clouds gleamed pink and gold as they billowed upward. For a long time the three stood, watching earnestly.

At last Kūpahu turned and walked away. "What were the signs?" he questioned.

"They were good," Haili replied, "good signs for chiefs and people. Men shall return to work in their fields. They shall prepare the land and plant. The gods will send a good harvest."

"And they shall fish," ʻAki added. "The time is right for *aku* fishing."

"You have read the signs correctly," their father told them. "I go now to tell our chief the message of the gods."

Aku Fishing

Aku fishing! No one said the words but the chief's fishermen all knew. Makahiki had been a time of games and feasting. They had enjoyed it but could any game be quite so glorious as the struggle with sea and fish?

'Aukai had brought out the gourds which held pearl-shell hooks. When his young men saw him busy with these they went for bait. Though the pearl-shell hooks took no bait, small fish, called *nehu,* were used to start the fishing.

Canoes were launched and paddled slowly a short distance from the shore. The paddlers were watching Puna who ran along the land. Puna stopped and threw something into the water. He waited, then ran on. Puna was chewing salt fish. Again he stood still and threw the chewed fish. He saw little *nehu* gathering about this bait. At his signal the canoes stopped and several men slipped into the water with a net. The men could not see the *nehu* but following Puna's signs they carried the net around them.

One edge of this net was weighted with stones. On the other were floats of light wood. Once spread in the water, the net made a fine-meshed fence around the little fish. When the *nehu* were penned into a small space the young men dipped them up with scoop nets and poured them into the bait box. This bait box was like a small canoe with holes bored in it so water could pass in and out.

When the canoes had paddled back to the landing place each young fisherman had his task. The bait box was taken to a tide pool among the rocks. There the *nehu* would live safely through the night. Nets were spread on grass to dry and canoes were made ready for tomorrow's fishing.

Meanwhile Malu went to help 'Aukai. Malu loved to work with the master in his house where the fishing gear was kept. Here all was clean and orderly—hooks, lines, nets and paddles.

From the time they were little boys these men had learned that all things used in fishing must have special care. They must be clean and must be treated with respect. One never stepped over lines or nets. One never threw or dropped a hook. All work must be done quietly. So the fish would not hear. A man who was careless or noisy would catch few fish.

'Aukai handed a gourd to Malu and the young man examined each hook. These pearl-shell lures were both hooks and bait. The *aku* would be chasing little fish for food. If a pearl-shell hook was tied just right it would seem to swim along the surface of the sea and a hungry *aku* would grab it. The fishermen used hooks of different colors. 'Aukai could tell from sky and sea which hook would best fool the *aku* on any day.

Malu remembered the day he had learned how a hook must be tied. He was already a fisherman and working at the stern of a single-hulled canoe. 'Aukai, at the prow, was using a white hook. So Malu also tied a white hook to his line. Great *aku* were all about snapping up the little fish. Malu could hardly wait for one to snap his hook. None did! The young man could hear 'Aukai pulling in fish and dropping them into the canoe. But not one *aku* came to Malu's hook.

The young man changed to gray. No luck! White was the color. 'Aukai's white hook was catching many fish. Malu changed back to the white one he had tied himself. No *aku!* Then the school of fish dived deep and swam away.

After the canoes had returned the young man saw his master take that white hook from the gourd and look at it. 'Aukai glanced at Malu, then put back the hook, saying nothing.

When he was alone Malu took out his white hook and held it as the master had. Suddenly he could see what was wrong! Hog bristles must be tied to each pearl-shell hook in such a way that the hook could swim along on its flat edge. The bristles of this hook were badly tied. Malu took them off and tied them on more carefully. Next time he used the white hook he caught fish.

So today Malu looked carefully at every hook. Some he retied. Then he took out the sacred hook 'Aukai had given him and tied that also. It was rainbow-colored. As he worked he prayed:

> "O gods who taught us to fish,
> Help me to tie
> So that this hook shall please the *aku*.
> Send fish to all our hooks
> That chiefs and people may be fed."

That night all the young fishermen gathered before 'Aukai's shrine. The head fisherman offered *'awa* drink and cooked *kalo* tops to the gods of fishing. He prayed:

> "O gods,
> O Kū'ula, O Hina, O 'Ai'ai,
> Help us to use the wisdom
> You have taught us.
> Send fish to our hooks
> That chiefs and people may be fed."

After they had eaten, the young men made ready for the great day. Each must have a new *malo* and a *lei*. Malu would wear the first *malo* Keao had made after she became his wife. His *lei* was *maile* which she had gathered in the upland.

The young men lay down in 'Aukai's sleeping house though the master himself slept near the shrine. Will tomorrow ever come? Malu was thinking. Shall I wake in time?

It seemed only a moment until each young man felt the master's touch. Each heard the softly spoken words, "The morning star has risen."

Now they dressed in their new *malo* and *lei!* Then all gathered around the shrine for offerings and prayer. Surely the gods will help us was the thought of every heart. Excitement drove away hunger yet they must eat for everyone must be strong to paddle or fish.

Again each had his task. The bait box was fastened between the two hulls of a double-hulled canoe. The precious hooks, water gourds, paddles and poles were brought.

Without a word the young men uncovered the canoes and launched them in the star-lit waves. Because 'Aukai steered the double-hulled canoe, it led. Others followed, both double- and single-hulled. Malu was steering a large outrigger canoe.

They headed for a part of the ocean where *aku* were often found at this time of year. The canoes moved swiftly, swept along by eager paddlers. There was the morning star, the ruler of the dawn. Malu searched the heavens picking out groups of stars he knew. I must learn more about them, he thought. If I should be head fisherman I must be able to direct canoes at night as the master does.

A sudden signal from 'Aukai! Malu had been so interested in the stars he had not seen a squall coming. Driven by a strong wind, it swept toward them. The young men met it with excitement, even joy. Malu swung the canoe to meet the storm, head on, while each paddler worked with all his might. The steersman of each canoe struggled to keep it headed into wind and waves. He could only do this if the canoe was paddled strongly.

The full power of the storm struck the small fleet. Waves like mountains rushed at them but the canoes climbed bravely then slid down the slope on the other side. A snap! Puna's paddle had broken and the canoe swung around. Water came in. "We can hold it!" Malu shouted. "Bail!" With all their strength the men turned the canoe to meet the waves again. They were praying. They felt the power of men helped by the gods. They loved this struggle with wind and mighty waves.

As quickly as it had come the storm was gone. Gentle rain followed, quieting the sea. 'Aukai's canoe turned back to help small ones that had swamped.

The big double-hulled canoe which 'Aukai steered was almost dry inside. At the master's signal the men in each part of the canoe had stretched a mat over their part. These mats had openings so that they could be pushed down over the paddlers and firmly tied to the side of the canoe. The mats had kept out the waves.

'Aukai soon found the small canoes needed no help. The paddlers of each had slipped into the sea and pushed the canoes back and forth so strongly that most of the water had splashed out. Then they had scrambled in and bailed. All were ready to go on their way. The storm had added excitement to the day's adventures. It had been fun!

Just as the sea was touched by the first long rays of the rising sun there came another signal. "The terns."

Long-winged birds circled close to the sea on the port side. From high above the ocean their keen eyes had caught the gleam of little fish leaping wildly to escape the *aku*. Those little fish were good food and the terns circled above the school, darting down to seize them.

This was the time! Malu headed the canoe toward the circling birds. The paddler in the bow dipped with all his speed and the others paddled with him. The canoe fairly flew.

Suddenly 'Aukai's double-hulled canoe turned. Malu understood. The *aku* were swimming toward them.

The canoes must paddle with the fish if any were to be caught. The young man used all his strength on the steering paddle and the others helped.

Suddenly they were among the school! All was noise and confusion as every man leaped to his own task. Two men in each canoe seized poles. As he had steered, Malu had watched the dashing waves. They are many colored, he told himself. I can use my sacred hook. As he fastened it to his line he prayed, "O gods, I thank you. Send *aku* to this sacred hook."

One man threw bait fish to lure the *aku*. The other paddlers worked with all their strength, for the school was swimming fast. All about was the roar and splash of big fish and the screams of darting birds.

The *aku* were leaping close to the ocean waves and the canoes, chasing the bait fish. Malu threw his hook. It struck the water with a slap which an *aku* heard. A great fish leaped for the sacred hook and, with a mighty heave, the young man lifted it. The fish flew in a half circle through the air. Malu caught it under one arm and held it for a moment while he pulled out the hook. The first fish must be kept in a safe and honorable place as an offering to the gods. The men passed it quickly from hand to hand and laid it in the prow.

Already Malu had thrown the hook for a second time. An *aku* took it, flew through the air in a half circle and was dropped in the canoe. Another and another! It was a wild scene of darting birds, swift-paddling canoes and leaping fish.

Suddenly all was still. The fish had sounded. The birds were gone. Only foam and blood on quiet waves told of the struggle. The canoe was full of fish.

The wind had risen. At a signal from 'Aukai sails were put up. The men still paddled but took time to drink, as water gourds went from hand to hand.

As the double-hulled canoe passed Malu's to take the lead the men could hear the prayer of the head fisherman:

"O gods,
We give thanks for a good catch.
You have sent *aku* to our hooks,
These canoes—yours and ours—
Are half full.
Send more we pray."

A long time passed. The fleet of canoes sailed steadily while men searched the sky for birds. Many were praying.

Then, off to starboard, terns were seen. In a moment they were darting down and at once the canoes changed their course. Sails were lowered for the wind could no longer help. Every paddler worked with all his strength. They must reach the *aku* and keep among them.

Once more the roar and splash! Once more Malu was pulling in great fish. All was excitement, joy and hard work.

Silence! Birds and fish were gone. Now the canoes were filled. Heavy with their load they rode low in the water. Home was far away and the wind was strong.

Paddling was slower now but steady. Malu saw the weariness of an older man. "Change places," he commanded and took the other's paddle. It felt heavy. But the catch had been good! What mattered tired arms and aching backs! Helped by the gods they had food for chiefs and people.

They paddled toward a cloud that seemed to rest upon the sea. Slowly they drew nearer and saw mountains half hidden by that cloud. Nearer still they saw the lowland with *niu* and houses. They saw waves breaking on the reef. Sunset light was on clouds and mountains as the canoes were carried to the beach.

The first fish caught in each canoe was offered to the gods of fishing. As the men gathered about a small shrine on the beach every heart joined the master's prayer of thankfulness.

Then the *konohiki*, the overseer, came. At his command, attendants carried away the chief's share of *aku*. The rest were divided among the fishermen. Malu took fish to Puakō and to other relatives. All the men did the same. Soon the whole village was feasting and busy cooking, drying or salting *aku*.

Nāwai the Netmaker

"Wait for me, Noe! I'm coming with you." Kaiki hurried up the trail that led past the *kalo* patch and toward the upland. Noe did not stop and Kaiki was panting when he joined him. "What is the matter?" he asked as soon as he could speak. "You look as fierce as a warrior going to battle, Noe, marching along and shaking your stick."

The trail rounded a thick clump of *kō* before it crossed the stream. Here some pigs were rooting. "Go on," shouted Noe, striking one pig and then another with his stick. "You can't stop here! Get across the stream, I say."

"What is the matter, Noe?" asked Kaiki again. "Why are you so angry with the pigs? Whose are they? Where are you driving them?"

"Clear up into the mountains!" Noe said and his voice was sharp with anger. "I don't know whose pigs they are and I don't care! They come around our house all the time. Two days ago they walked all over Mother's *kapa* which was spread to dry. Yesterday they rooted into our *maiʻa* pit and ate half the *maiʻa*.

"And this morning!" angry tears came to Noe's eyes, "I took down the food net to get some of the fish Father cooked yesterday and some *kī* root, sweet as *kō*. I left the food just a moment, for I heard shouts and barking down at the beach. When I came back there were these pigs and such a mess! They had spilled fish and *kī* and *ʻulu*. They had broken calabashes, smeared *poi* over everything and torn the food net. My father was angry and said it was my fault. I am going to drive these pigs up into the mountains."

"Get along, you brown-striped pig!" he shouted aloud, striking savagely at one that had stopped to root near a small tree.

"Don't you dare do that!" Suddenly a tall girl stood in the path before the boys, her eyes blazing. She caught Noe's stick and wrenched it out of his hand. "Don't you ever strike an animal as long as you live," she continued. "How would you like to be beaten so, right on your bare back?" For a moment, both boys thought the girl was going to strike Noe with his stick.

"Don't, Maile!" Kaiki stepped quickly in front of his friend. "The pigs spoiled all Noe's food, broke the calabashes and even tore the net. We don't know whose pigs they are and we are going to drive them to the mountains."

"They are Nāwai's pigs," Maile replied, "and we are going to take them home. Here's your stick." She threw her arms around the brown pig's neck and stroked it lovingly. "This one is Nāwai's pet," she said. "He's used to kindness," and she looked up reproachfully at Noe.

"I wish Nāwai would keep his pigs at home!" Noe's voice was sullen. "And feed them!"

"We'll ask him to," said Maile. "Go up and get the others. We've got to take them back."

Unwillingly the boys hunted out the other pigs and drove them all down the trail. Maile was a strange girl. She seldom played with others but spent her time with animals or in the upland. She was usually quiet and gentle, but when her anger blazed all the children respected and obeyed her.

Silently the three returned to the village, driving the pigs. They found Nāwai in his work yard, scraping *olonā*. "We brought back your pigs," Maile told him. "They are hungry and taking other people's food."

Nāwai leaned back against the tree to rest. "I forgot to feed them," he said. "Get some of the *niu* piled near my *imu*, break them and feed the pigs, you three," and Nāwai continued scraping.

Maile led the way and soon the three were watching the pigs devour *niu*. "Nāwai ought to feed his pigs himself," Noe repeated as Maile left them.

"Oh, he is working!" Kaiki laughed. "Nāwai is the laziest man in this village. When he does work we must not interrupt him."

"Let's watch him then," Noe suggested. The two returned to Nāwai's work yard and squatted quietly on the grass beside him.

Olonā stems had been cut in moist mountain gulches where they grew abundantly. The bark had been slit, peeled and soaked much as *wauke* bark was slit, peeled and soaked for *kapa*-making. As the two boys watched, Nāwai tied moist bark to one end of a long smooth narrow board and scraped it with a turtle shell. This separated the long fibers from each other and the coarse outer bark. It was fascinating to watch the swift movement of the scraper. Today Nāwai's hands aren't like those of a wooden image! thought Kaiki, remembering a remark of the overseer.

Noe had much the same thought. "I have seen other men scrape but no one worked so well as Nāwai," he said in a low voice. "I wonder if it is hard to learn?"

Nāwai looked up. "Want to try?" he questioned.

"Oh yes!"

Nāwai rose and stretched, then showed Noe how to sit at the end of the long board. Noe must hold the blade of the scraper against the bark. "Now scrape toward you," Nāwai directed.

Noe tried. Several times the scraper moved along the creamy fibers. "I'm not doing anything," Noe said in disappointment.

"Keep on," Nāwai advised, "you'll learn."

And now Noe did. Soon he was removing the dark outer bark. "Good for you!" Nāwai praised.

"Only I can't reach the other end," said Noe, bending over.

"I'll finish it," said Nāwai. "Then Kaiki can have a turn."

But Kaiki had no success. "Does every man have to do this?" he asked as he let Noe scrape once more.

"No. This takes skill and only a few men learn."

"But many people twist cord," said Kaiki. "Keao, my aunt, is learning to make cord for fish lines. She wants to do that because Malu is a fisherman. She let me try. It looks easy when Keao does it but when I try the cord is bunchy."

"That too needs skill," said Nāwai. He took several long fibers, laid them on his leg above the knee and rolled them with the flat of his hand, making fine, smooth cord.

"You are skillful at everything!" exclaimed Kaiki admiringly. "But these fibers aren't as white as those Keao was twisting."

"The fibers I have scraped may be bleached in the sunshine, then twisted into cord. But we do not bleach fibers intended for a fish net," he added. "Often a net is dipped in sea water in which *kukui* bark has been soaked."

"To darken it?" asked Kaiki quickly. "So the fish will not see it gleam? Do you do all these kinds of work yourself, Nāwai? I don't see how you get time to make your nets!"

"People give me cord of different sizes. Come into my work house."

While Noe scraped busily Nāwai took Kaiki into his work house. There the boy saw a great bunch of hanging fibers. Like a waterfall, he told himself. He saw many balls of twisted fiber. "All this for nets?" the boy asked. "Oh, Nāwai, how many nets will you make?"

Nāwai laughed. "I don't know," he replied. "People give me cord and I think about the net I shall make. Maybe I start but netmaking is slow. I stop to rest or swim or I must go with others to the upland. When I return I start another net."

Kaiki examined the balls of cord. "This is coarse and strong," he said. "You don't use this for a fish net."

"Yes." Nāwai spread a half-finished net before the boy. "Sometimes fishermen use a net to capture a shark or turtle. Such a net must be very strong. And here is one for catching tiny bait fish."

"Why the cord is almost as fine as spider web!" Kaiki exclaimed, "and the mesh is very small. How do you make it even?"

"Watch," and Nāwai took tools from a small covered gourd. He seated himself just inside the doorway where the light was good. Kaiki listened reverently to his prayer, then watched as Nāwai's shuttle flew, knotting fine cord into small meshes.

"Noe, come!" Kaiki called. The two watched the flying shuttle as Nāwai formed the mesh, measuring each opening with a tiny wooden gauge held in his left hand.

"That's enough for today," he said at last. "The light grows dim," and he rose to put away tools and net.

"See that dark cloud!" exclaimed Kaiki going out. "I'll help you carry in your things. It's going to rain."

"The rain will please the pigs," Noe said. "They like a muddy place."

"We all like coolness," Nāwai answered. He had carried his scraping board and now went to look after the pigs. "This is my pet," he added, scratching the brown pig's back.

"That is the one that tore my father's net," remarked Noe. He had not forgotten his father's scolding.

"Tore the food net?" asked Nāwai quickly. "Run and get it, boy. I'll mend the net. Hurry! The rain is almost here!"

Sitting inside the doorway, while the rain fell outside, Nāwai mended the torn net. The boys squatted near, watching. "That is sennit you are using and not *olonā*," Kaiki remarked.

"Yes, this food net is made of *niu* fiber," Nāwai answered. "For fish lines and nets we use *olonā* because saltwater does not rot it and it does not kink."

"I know!" said Noe. "My father told me about a net used three generations and it is still good."

"Fishermen take good care of their nets," Nāwai told them.

"I should say they do!" said Kaiki. "Malu spends almost as much time drying and mending nets as he does fishing! Yesterday I wanted him to show me how to catch tiny eels but he had to go to the chief's fishing house to mend a net."

For a long time the boys watched the netmaker's rapid work. "There!" he said at last. "Your food net is as good as new, Noe."

Noe thanked him. "Father will be pleased," he said, then added thoughtfully, "Why do we use sennit if *olonā* is better, Nāwai?"

"*Olonā* is better in saltwater," Nāwai replied, "but sennit, too, is good."

"And bigger rope is made from *hau* bark," added Kaiki.

"Yes," Nāwai answered, "the gods have given us many good fibers. Delicate cords of braided hair hold the neck ornaments of chiefs. With *hau* ropes we haul canoes from the upland. In house building *'uki'uki* and *'ie'ie* are used. From *olonā* we make fish nets and the net work for feather capes and helmets.

"Capes and helmets!" Noe exclaimed. "Can you make nets for those, Nāwai?"

"I have never made a cape or a helmet," Nāwai replied, "but I can show you what my master taught me." He searched in a large calabash and brought out a sample of the finest net work the boys had seen. "A cape is made in this way," he explained. "The tiny feathers are knotted in, a few at a time, by an expert. A helmet is made of *'ie'ie* rootlets and closely covered with such a net.

"Oh, that's too much work!" said Kaiki. "But beautiful," Noe added slowly. "Oh, Nāwai, I want to be a netmaker! Will you take me as your pupil?"

Nāwai looked thoughtfully at Noe. "Do you want to feed my pigs each day?" he asked. "Do you want to go with me to cut *olonā* stems and peel and scrape? Do you want to run errands and help in little ways?"

"Yes, I do," said Noe solemnly.

"Very well, help me for a time. If you work well I'll take you as a pupil—if your father likes the plan. I've tried to teach my son but he is even lazier than I," and Nāwai laughed.

"*Ē,* netmaker!" Lako was calling from the yard. "The rain has stopped. Make ready to go tomorrow to the upland. The twigs of *hau* and *kukui* we put on the *'uala* patch have rotted. They have given their strength to the field. Tomorrow the overseer commands that we go up and plant sweet-potato cuttings."

"It is always so!" muttered Nāwai. "Here I have bark to scrape and nets half-finished and now I must stop to plant potatoes."

Kaiki chuckled. "Nāwai is lazy!" he told himself. "But he's clever. Noe can learn much from him. As for me, I'd rather be a farmer!" and he turned a handspring as he hurried off to help Puakō get ready for the upland.

On Land and Sea

Signs

Keao sat beside her grandfather in the shade as he worked with the fibers of *olonā*. The girl watched the old man's hands as they steadily twisted the fiber into a smooth cord. He never seems tired! she thought as she leaned back against the trunk of a *kamani* tree. She closed her eyes and listened to the sounds about her.

Close by, Ana was beating *māmaki* bark. Her *kapa* log gave forth a strong booming note. Farther off, Keao could hear the rhythm of other beaters. Sometimes the beaters carried a message, telling of the coming of strangers to the village or of the return of the fishing fleet. But today there was no message, only the ring of many logs, some deep toned, some higher.

Other sounds joined, as chanting voices join the rhythm of drum or rattle. The leaves of the *kamani* rustled in a light wind, waves lapped on the sand and now and then children's voices rose in shout or laughter. Pigs rooted nearby, grunting contentedly as they ate, only to be driven away by the sharp bark of a dog.

The sound roused Keao. "Oh, I'm so hungry!" she exclaimed. "I seem to be hungry all the time. Today it is *'opihi* I long for."

Ana laid down her beater and rose quickly. "I'll get some for you," she said. "The child, soon to be born, longs for *'opihi* and that is well. As the *'opihi* shell clings to the rocks so will your child cling to his relatives and friends. He will never desert them so long as he shall live."

Keao smiled her thanks as Ana hurried away. She thought much about the one soon to come and was glad of this sign her first child would be loving and faithful. Malu too will be glad, she thought, then said aloud, "I long for Malu! Other men have time for sports and talk and song, but, since Makahiki ended, the fishermen are busy from dawn to dark."

"But your husband thinks of you," Grandfather told her. "Here!" Feeling about him, he found a smooth stone which Ana used to hold down her drying *kapa.* "This is Malu" he said, placing the stone near his granddaughter. "He is with you in spirit. Because you think often of him at this time he will be very dear to your child." Keao looked at the stone, then touched it gently. She seemed to feel Malu near her and was content.

A few moments later Grandfather said, "Give me your hand." Wondering, she stretched it toward him. "Palm up!" was the old man's comment. "Your child will be a daughter."

"I'd like a daughter," Keao answered. "Ana says a daughter is good because she stays in her parents' home while a son goes to his wife's family. But how do you tell, Grandfather? What is the sign?"

"I said, 'Give me your hand,'" the old man repeated, "and you stretched it out to me palm up. If the palm had been down that would mean a son. Both hands would mean twins."

"I too am glad it is to be a daughter." The old man continued softly as if talking to himself. "Another little treasure! I live to hold another great grandchild in my arms. The gods are good indeed! She shall be loving as Ana says and a good worker, for Keao and Malu love their work. *'Ā!* Life is good!"

For a time the two sat quietly, thinking happy thoughts. Then Ana returned with the *'opihi.* "And Puakō is bringing *lū'au* to eat with the shellfish," she said. "The child needs green food also."

Stilts and Flying Fish

That same morning Kaiki and Noe had been making stilts. "There! I have cut mine even." Kaiki said at last. "Now watch me walk!" He scrambled onto a rock, balanced himself carefully on his tall stilts, took a step and—tumbled on his nose in the soft sand! "Help me to get started, Noe," he begged. "If I get started I can walk."

Noe steadied Kaiki's stilts and watched his friend take wobbling steps. "Ē, I'm a giant!" Kaiki shouted—and fell again.

"Start here," an older boy advised. "The firm path is easier." Soon both boys were balanced on their stilts and stalking about among a crowd of envious companions.

"Giants! Giants!" they chanted, "Watch the mighty giants. Ho, let me try them!"

"I want to be a giant, Kaiki. I'll give you the red shell you asked for if you'll let me use your stilts."

"I'd like to make some of my own. Show me how, Noe."

"You have to find two straight saplings," Noe began.

"With a side branch growing out of each," added Kaiki.

"Yes, I see," the other boy agreed. "Then you cut them with an adze so they are the same length. And leave enough of the side branch to make a place for your foot."

"It's hard work," Noe finished.

"Where is everyone going?" Kaiki shouted suddenly. "Look Noe! Everyone is hurrying toward the landing place."

In a moment every boy was following the crowd.

Canoes had been launched and people were scrambling in—men, women and children. There was Ana, Kaiki's grandmother, in a double-hulled canoe. Without a word the boy waded out and climbed in beside her. When he had settled himself he looked around.

Not far away he saw Malu in a large single-hulled canoe. Malu was paddling with two other men. 'Aukai was also in that canoe—'Aukai the chief's head fisherman! There was a net in their canoe.

So this was a fishing trip. Perhaps to get a tiger shark! Kaiki hugged himself with excitement. No, that could not be. Much as the boy longed to hunt a tiger shark he knew that canoes loaded with women and children would not go after that fierce fish. *Aku?* He had heard stories of *aku* fishing. Were *aku* caught with a fine-meshed net? No, they were big fish and were caught with hook and line.

The canoes paddled over the reef and into the rollers of the great ocean. The sky was blue and the sea bluer still. Kaiki was deeply happy.

The men paddled fast. When the boy looked back at his island he could not see the beach. After a time the lowland disappeared and Kaiki saw only mountains. We are far at sea, he thought, farther than I have ever been. Again he hugged himself with joy.

The canoes were moving more slowly and changing course. 'Aukai was signaling. The canoes are forming a circle, Kaiki thought. But why? I don't see any fish.

As his canoe came into the circle, Kaiki did see something. A ripple moved through the water inside the circle. Malu and his companions lowered the net. "It is a bag net with a wide mouth," Kaiki said. "What is it for?"

Suddenly 'Aukai waved both arms. At this signal many people slipped into the water and swam toward the net. As they swam they shouted and beat the water with their arms.

Flashes of silver rose from the waves and darted away from the swimmers. All at once the boy understood. "*Mālolo,* flying fish!" he shouted.

One flashed close and he grabbed for it. He had it, struggling in his hands! His grandmother pulled him back into the canoe and the paddlers laughed. "You're not a flying fish," said Ana. "Keep your weight in the canoe."

Men gathered up the big net and Kaiki saw it was full of fish. The men poured their good catch into the canoes. Strands of *kauna'oa mālolo,* the yellow upland dodder, were spread over the fish to hold them.

A great shout rose and Kaiki joined with all his might. It was a good catch and he had helped. He had caught a fish.

'Aukai's canoe put up its sail. Some others did too. But the sail of the double-hulled canoe in which Ana and Kaiki rode was not raised.

"It is not worthwhile," said Puna. "The wind is light. Those who sail before the wind will not be carried to the landing place but must turn and paddle. Let us paddle all the way."

Water gourds were passed. "Do not drink much," Ana said. "Many must share."

"Let the boy have all he wants," said Puna. "We brought many gourds." So Kaiki drank, while the men paddled to the rhythm of a chant. The boy soon learned the words and, leaning against Ana, chanted happily:

> "Thanks to Kū'ula,
> Thanks to Hina, his wife,
> To 'Ai'ai their son.
> These are the gods
> Who taught us to fish.
> Our canoes are filled,
> Filled with *mālolo,*
> Thanks to you gods,
> Thanks, thanks to you
> Who taught us to fish."

The men in nearby canoes had joined the chant, "Thanks, thanks to you."

Kaiki must have slept. When he opened his eyes the scene had changed. Darkness was settling over the sea as a bird settles over her nest to shelter her little ones. Clouds were the purple and gold of sunset. Kaiki sat up, suddenly wide awake for there, not far away, an island floated on the sea.

"Ana," he whispered, "is it one of the sacred islands? Is it one of the floating islands of Kāne?"

"No, Grandson," she answered, her voice full of the wonder and beauty of the night. "That island is rooted firmly to the bottom of the sea. It is our home."

The Stonecutters

In the Master's Yard

Skrish! Skrish! Chip! Chip! Chip! A steady sound of grinding and chipping came from the stoneworker's yard. There three young men sat on the grass, each bent over his work. A sudden exclamation and the sound stopped.

"A flaw in this stone too!" exclaimed Pūpū crossly. "It seems every stone I try to shape has something wrong with it!"

"You should test a stone by heating it before you start to chip," said 'Eli, looking up from the lamp he was polishing with pumice stone.

"I did," Pūpū replied. "I heated every one of my stones till it was red-hot. This did not burst. But look!" The young man held up the partly shaped *poi* pounder, showing a hole in the lava rock. Then he made as if to throw it on a pile of broken rocks.

"Wait!" 'Eli rose and came to him to examine the stone, "I think there is no other flaw."

"What of it?" Pūpū asked. "My *poi* pounder is spoiled."

"A small pestle for crushing herbs can still be made from this good stone."

"Oh, 'Eli, don't you ever get tired?" asked Pūpū. "Chip, grind, polish! You work as steadily as the master himself."

"I love stonecutting," answered 'Eli simply. "I like to see a pounder or a lamp take shape as I chip and grind. But you two are tired and there is other work to be done. Remember, our master is sick. See if he has wakened, 'Oloa,' 'Eli directed speaking to the third young man. "Give him the herb drink left by Uka. And did you, Pūpū, take the finished *poi* pounders to our chief? Yesterday a message was sent asking for two." The young men started eagerly, glad of any change from their hard task.

'Eli examined the lamp he had been rubbing, a little stone bowl to hold *kukui* oil with its wick of *kapa*. He held it lovingly, turned it this way and that, examined it with care. "It is good" he said at last and carried it into the work house. There on a shelf were several finished objects of stone: two small dishes to hold dye for printing *kapa* and a smaller one with a tiny central hole—a candle holder. *Kukui*-nut meats, strung on a *niu* midrib, gave light at night. But they needed such a holder to keep the midrib upright. There were also several sinkers to be bound with cowrie shell and hook for catching *he'e*, a mirror of polished black stone and a stone head for a war club.

At one end of the shelf were several partly shaped *maika* stones. During Makahiki many of these game stones had been broken. Already men were asking for new ones. 'Eli picked up an unfinished *maika* stone then remembered the spoiled *poi* pounder and returned to the yard. Seating himself beside the rock he used for grinding he went to work, making the pounder smaller and changing its shape. Skrish! Skrish! 'Eli worked with strength and skill, shaping a small pestle.

Pūpū came leaping into the yard. "'Eli!" he shouted, "I have wonderful news! The chief is sending us to the adzemakers of Mauna Kea. He will give us *kapa* and vegetables as trade goods and we are to get adzes."

'Eli jumped to his feet. "Does the master know?" he asked.

"Let us go to him at once," Pūpū replied. "You tell him."

They found the master lying on his mats, warmly covered with *kapa,* for he was old and shivered when his young men were dripping with sweat. 'Oloa had given him the herb drink and now was setting the sleeping house in order.

'Eli and Pūpū stood a moment, hesitating to waken the old man. Perhaps he felt their presence for he opened his eyes and smiled a greeting. "Master," 'Eli said quietly, "the chief is sending us to Mauna Kea to trade for adzes for this district."

"It is well." The old man's voice was weak, but he spoke confidently. "I asked our chief to send you there. This is spring. At this season the snows on Mauna Kea melt and the adzemakers go to the workshop of the adzes. It may be one of you can go with them. Tell Nui you are my pupils. Nui is my relative. Long ago his father took men to the workshop far up the slope of Mauna Kea. It may be Nui will take one of my young men."

"But we cannot all leave you, Master," 'Eli said. "One of us must stay."

"Tell Lako you are going," the master answered. "He is my cousin. He and his wife will care for me. Take gifts to Lako's wife and she will give you a bed *kapa,* for you must have gifts to carry to Nui. Take the bed *kapa* to him, *kalo* and salt fish. Take *kapa* and food for yourselves, as well. Do not depend on the adzemakers to feed you, for food is sometimes hard for them to get.

"When the chief has given you trade goods, show the things to me. You must take food, *kapa* and mats enough to trade for all the adzes our district needs. To climb the mountain and chip adzes is hard and dangerous work. The food we take, the *kapa* and mats—all those as well require time and labor. We must pay generously in work for what we get."

The days following were busy ones. Pūpū and 'Oloa made ready the canoe, prepared food and brought the trade goods to their master for his inspection and then loaded them into the canoe. All the while 'Eli worked patiently in the stone yard to finish work already started.

When all was ready the young men helped the master to the eating house. "I shall make an offering," he said. As the four stood before the shrine his feeble voice was lifted in earnest prayer that the gods of stoneworkers should bless this trip, should give good adzes for the district and bring the young men home in safety. They ate. Then, before the sun had dimmed the morning star, the canoe was on its way.

The Journey

The sun rose in a clear sky and the sea smiled on the canoe as it moved swiftly over smooth ocean swells. None of the young men had ever before left for so long a journey. Still they knew they were never to be out of sight of land. With that knowledge and a steady wind no skilled navigator would be needed to guide them to the landing place nearest Mauna Kea.

They took turns paddling—two at a time, while the third rested. 'Eli, watching the steady strokes of his companions, asked enviously, "Do your backs and arms never ache?"

Pūpū laughed. "My back aches when I bend over the grindstone," he replied, "just as yours aches when you paddle. Sometimes I wonder if I was wise when I chose to be a stonecutter."

At last the young men reached the village where the adzemakers lived. "We have brought gifts from our master," 'Eli told Nui, master of the adzemakers. "He has grown old as a yellowed *hala* leaf and very feeble but he thinks of you and sends his *aloha*."

Nui listened eagerly and asked questions. Then he said, "This spring the cold has stayed long on Mauna Kea, the snow has melted slowly and we are late in going to the workshop of adzes. Tomorrow we shall start. When we reach that workshop many days must pass while we chip the hard black basalt. All those days you must wait, for we have no adzes left from last year's supply."

"We can wait," 'Eli answered quietly. "Perhaps there is a stoneworker in the village who would like our help. We are learners still, but strong to chip and grind. Every village, every worker has different ways. We could both help and learn."

Nui seemed pleased at the suggestion. He stood looking thoughtfully at each young man, as if a plan were forming in his mind.

The three waited quietly. Was Nui thinking he might take them up to the adze workshop? They had heard much of that strange place. From stories they knew the mountain was very cold, the climb difficult and strange gods lived upon the slope. I would rather stay here in warmth and safety, 'Eli thought.

I wonder what it's like—that workshop, 'Oloa said to himself. Perhaps I'd like to go there, yet I am half afraid.

But Pūpū felt no fear. He longed with all his heart to meet the cold and danger and to see the place where the hard stone for adzes was to be found. But I am not the one to go, he thought. 'Eli is the best worker.

Suddenly Nui spoke. He spoke to Pūpū. "Your back and legs are strong," he said. "One of our men has been injured and cannot make the trip at once. Suppose you come with us. Then, when enough tools are ready, you shall return bringing those needed for your district."

Pūpū's eyes were shining and his face eager but he said, "'Eli is a better worker than I. He ought to go."

"No!" 'Eli spoke quickly. "You are stronger, Pūpū. You go. I should like to stay here and work. You are the one Nui has chosen." So the matter was settled.

That night Pūpū joined the adzemakers for offering and prayer. He slept with them and started before day on the long trail. Pūpū loved to be out of doors. He was fearless, strong and a good companion.

At first some of the adzemakers did not like the presence of a stranger and watched him doubtfully. They saw Pūpū had brought both food and *kapa*. At least he would not depend on them for things he needed! When he offered to share the loads of older men, they were pleased.

Pūpū strode along with the strongest yet was willing to wait and help the weaker ones. He was quiet and reverent. When the men reached the lower forest he prayed, with the others, that the gods might not be angered by their passing. By this time each adzemaker was thinking it is well we brought this stranger. He will help us and will not displease our gods.

As for Pūpū, he had always longed to explore some new place and now that longing was being satisfied. He loved to tramp and climb. He loved new sights and smells. He even loved the thrill of fear as they passed through the forest where many gods lived.

In his own district he had never been above the lower forest. When the party came out, on the shoulder of the mountain, the young man's heart beat with excitement. The ocean was many colored in sunset light. How great it was! On and on it stretched till the dome of sky rested upon it. And Hawai'i was a large island with rugged slopes, green valleys and, out by the sea, gardens and palm-hidden villages.

Night came before the party reached their workshop. The men made a fire and were glad of its warmth and safety, for cold crept upon them through the *māmane* leaves. Pūpū, wrapped in warm *kapa,* rejoiced in the clear cool air. He slept soundly and wakened hungry and filled with longing to go on.

Before leaving the *māmane* trees, the men collected all the firewood that they could carry. "The nights are bitter at our workshop," Pūpū was told, "also we need fire to heat our stones."

Heavily loaded they climbed slowly, yet Pūpū soon found himself panting. The men stopped often to breathe and rest. All were puffing and one or two dropped down so weary it seemed as if they could go no farther. Why are we so tired? Pūpū wondered secretly. Why do we pant?

Nui sensed the unasked question. "The height makes us out of breath," he said. "A man can tramp all day on the rough trails of the lower slope and be less tired than from a short climb up here."

Perhaps it is the cold, thought Pūpū. Yet that could hardly be, he realized, for already the sun beat hotly. The rough tumbled rocks which stretched on either hand were burning hot. Though they had not far to go, this day's tramp was harder than that of the day before.

The Workshop of the Adzes

It was nearly sunset when they reached the workshop. Pūpū helped to store food and wood in a dry cave. Then he joined the others as they made an offering, prayed and ate. He shivered as he settled, close to his companions, in the sleeping cave. But weary muscles and the warmth of five thicknesses of bed *kapa* brought sound sleep. Morning found Pūpū rested and eager to look about him.

Here was the basalt, the hard black rock from which strong tools were made. The gods of adzemakers had put this rock in only a few places in all the islands. Here there was much. This rock will make tools for our children, for our grandchildren and for many great-grandchildren, Pūpū thought. The gods give us all the things we need.

He saw a pile where poor or spoiled stones had been heaped together. Pupu understood that a worker had found a flaw in an adze stone or that accident or careless work had spoiled a nearly finished tool.

It is like our work at home, he thought. Here too is labor and discouragement! But I shall love this work! Here are strange sights, cold, fear of angering the mountain gods! I love the cold and danger and long to work here all my life!

He was surprised to find much rock broken off, ready for use. He watched as Nui went among his men, planning which tool should be made from the stone each had chosen.

At last Nui stopped for a moment and Pūpū went to him with the question that was in his mind. He motioned to the many pieces of basalt which lay about. "Did you break these off before you left last fall?" he asked. "How do you break them?"

"The gods break them for us," answered Nui reverently. "They know we need this rock for adzes. Each winter they break off enough for the next season's tool making. No one sees the gods at work. Some say cold is the tool they use to break the rock. I do not know. We give thanks and use the gifts they have made ready."

The men chipped and partly shaped the tools. A rock was always heated to test it for air holes which would spoil its usefulness. Pūpū was ready to help in any way he could. He tended fires, helped prepare the food, and carried water from the pool.

Much of the time he watched the workers chipping the adzes. The others saw his interest. "Here," said one, putting a stone in the young man's hand, "I tried to make a scraping tool for smoothing the inside of a canoe, but this stone won't chip in the right direction. I think it can be used for a smaller tool."

"Do you want to try? Chip this way." The man struck the stone at a different angle and a small piece flew off. "Yes," he said, "you can chip in this direction. Perhaps you can make a small tool such as a man would need in carving a wooden image."

Pūpū took the piece of basalt and the chipping tool. He was eager to try, but doubtful. "I have no skill," he said. "I may spoil the stone."

"It is already useless for my purpose," the other answered, "so do not be afraid of spoiling it. We learn only by trying."

The skill that Pūpū had learned in working the softer stone helped him now. But the work went slowly. At first he was so careful that he chipped off only tiny pieces. Then he was too eager and used too much strength. "I have spoiled it!" he exclaimed, bringing the work to the man who had given him the stone.

"Yes," the other answered, "you chipped too deeply. Never mind. When you take this to the pile over there, you may find another piece that will do for a small carving tool."

So Pūpū started once more. He tried many pieces of basalt, learning that a man must study his stone. The gods plan each piece, he thought. A man must learn their plan. He must chip each stone in its own way. He must make from it such a tool as the gods would have him make. Only as a man worked with the gods could he succeed.

Pūpū's back and arms were aching—so he was glad to be sent with others of the younger men to the *māmane* trees for firewood. Though the trail was rough, the downward tramp was easy. He missed the green of growing things yet the rough black and gray or red and brown of lava rock, rising in jagged heaps or dropping away in rugged slopes, had a beauty of its own.

The very contrast of this hard and endless waste with the soft beauty he had known thrilled the young man. He saw strange flowers, large white ones with tube-like petals, growing here and there as if they too loved cold and barren lava. In my heart is great *aloha* for this place, thought Pūpū. I wish I might come here every year.

Back at the workshop after a two-day journey, Pūpū returned eagerly to chipping. Now and then cold rain put out the fire and kept the men in their cave. Huddled back where rain could not reach them they did little work, but talked of adzemaking and of their homes or told stories of long ago.

"Was this workshop covered by the flood?" Pūpū asked one day.

"We do not know," answered Nui.

"It must have been," an old man added. "Only the tops of the mountains were above the sea."

"Tell me about it," Pūpū urged.

"It was when Pele, the great fire goddess, fled from Far Kahiki," the old man said. "All to the northeast was waste, for there was neither ocean nor freshwater. So Pele's parents gave her the sea to bear her canoe and those of her brothers and sisters. On the crest of this ocean the canoes rushed along. As the sea covered the land the brothers chanted:

> 'Oh the sea, the great sea!
> Forth bursts the sea!
> Its borders reach to the hills.
> Twice it breaks forth!
> Thrice it breaks forth!
> The voice of the sea rings out,
> The sea rises up,
> The sea of Pele, the goddess.'"

The chant ended and the men were silent, picturing the flood. Then Nui added solemnly, "We never climb above our workshop, for on the mountaintop live many gods. If a man should go among them and anger them, he would be turned to stone."

Pūpū was still thinking of the flood. "It is strange," he said in a low voice, "to think that once only Mauna Kea, Mauna Loa and Haleakalā stood above the sea—three small islands in this great ocean."

"Some say that Māui tried to haul a great landmass from the deep," said Uli. "They say these islands of *Hawai'i-nei* are mountaintops of that great land. I do not know." Again the men were silent.

The Load of Adzes

Summer had come and there were many pleasant days. The cold of the night disappears when the sun comes, Pūpū thought, and was filled with wonder at the change. He finished a small tool. The men praised his work and he himself knew he had succeeded. Then he searched for another discarded piece of basalt. I wish I could make a strong adze for cutting down trees, he thought.

At that moment Nui came to him. "We have many finished adzes," the master said. "We have all that 'Eli asked for, for your district, and more beside. Two men will take them to the village and bring up food. Go with them, you have been gone from home a long time. Your chief and your master wait for your return. Be ready to take the trail at dawn tomorrow."

"I shall be ready," Pūpū answered. Then he stood looking about him at the workshop of adzes with its glowing fire and busy men and at the fields of lava stretching as far as eye could see.

Nui watched Pūpū as he gazed about. He saw in the young man his own love for this lonely spot on the great mountain. "You must come back," he said. "Stay with my relative, your master, while he lives, learn all that he can teach you, then return to us."

"That is what I want," said Pūpū solemnly, "to be a maker of adzes. I shall return."

'Eli and 'Oloa had had many days of work with the stonecutter of the village. Both had gained skill and wisdom. 'Oloa had enjoyed wrestling and racing with new companions. He had surfed with them and gone torch fishing. The days in the adzemaker's village had been pleasant days.

But 'Eli thought often of their master. What if the old man grew worse? Would he not be troubled because no work was done in his workshop? People would come for bowls, *poi* pounders or *maika* stones and none would be ready. 'Eli was impatient to return.

Then the three men came from the mountain trail. Pūpū took the heavy net from his back and spread its contents on the ground. Villagers gathered to admire the adzes and 'Eli felt each one lovingly as he went over, in his mind, the list of tools needed for his district. "They are all here," he said. "The gifts sent by our chief," he added, "were those enough?"

"Nui is satisfied," the adzemakers replied. "Your master knew how much to send. The making of *kapa* and mats and the raising of *kalo* and potatoes was hard work requiring time and skill. Yes, you have paid well for the adzes."

"And I am more than satisfied with the help you two have given me," added the village stonecutter. "Take my *aloha* to your master," and he gave each young man a tool he had made. That night the stonecutter made an offering and prayed that the three young men might reach their village safely with their load of adzes. Next morning before dawn he prayed again. Then the canoe was launched and on its way toward home.

The sun rose and clouds gleamed with light. The sea smiled and the canoe flew swiftly with both sail and paddles. As their course changed, the sail, no longer useful, was taken down. Still the canoe flew swiftly over smooth rolling waves. The young men's hearts were glad. 'Eli thought of his master and the work he loved—'Oloa of friends he was soon to see once more and of all he had to tell them. Pūpū was as eager as they to get home, but in him was a new longing to learn all his master had to teach and then return to the workshop of the adzes.

None of these young men had much knowledge of wind and weather. Busy with paddling and thinking and planning they gave no heed to changes in the sky. In the late afternoon Pūpū, relieved of paddling, took his place in the stern and looked about him. "The clouds ahead look very strange," he said.

'Eli glanced up anxiously. "I hope we don't meet a storm," he answered.

'Eli and 'Oloa paddled with all their strength while Pūpū watched the sky with growing anxiety. "A gale is coming!" he exclaimed suddenly. "Let me paddle, 'Eli, for I am strong. You spread the mat to keep out waves. 'Oloa, we must hold the canoe head-on to the wind. We must not let it swamp and lose the adzes."

The wind came bringing waves which rose like cliffs before the tiny craft. But the young men were strong and the canoe climbed each cliff and coasted down its farther side like a swift sled. Wave after wave rushed at them. The two dug in their paddles, praying silently, while 'Eli's voice rose above the storm:

> "O guardian spirits,
> Save us.
> Quiet the waves
> That we may reach our homes
> With adzes for our people."

The guardian spirits heard their prayers. The wind died, rain fell and slowly the cliff-like waves became smooth swells. "Now I can paddle," 'Eli said. "You two rest." Pūpū and 'Oloa lay back exhausted. In the excitement of wind and waves they had not felt fatigue. Now as they rested it seemed to each that he wanted never to move again. Both fell asleep.

Their sleep was short for their bodies were cramped in the small canoe. They woke stiff but rested. The mat cover was rolled up, the water gourd and the *poi* bowl passed. A little seawater had seeped through the stopper of the water gourd. Still the drink and food refreshed them. "Now 'Oloa and I will paddle," Pūpū said. "We must make straight for our own village." He looked anxiously about. "I don't see land."

"Clouds rest upon the sea and shut out the islands," 'Oloa said.

"I have had no sight of land," 'Eli told them. "Before the storm the wind struck my right cheek. So I have paddled, keeping my right side to the windward. I know no other guide."

"The wind may have changed," said Pūpū doubtfully. "I wish we knew more of weather signs."

The two paddled steadily but they were tired and not as strong as earlier. Fear gripped every heart. Perhaps they were paddling away from the home island! Fishermen went out of sight of land but they were wise in knowledge of winds and currents. And sometimes even fishermen did not return! The young men prayed:

> "O great god of the sea,
> Bring us safe to land
> With our load of adzes.
> O all you gods,
> Hear our prayer
> And grant us life."

All night they prayed and paddled but all night clouds hid the stars.

Lost

Just before sunrise the wind changed direction and blew more strongly. It swept away the clouds. Out of the sea came the gleam of the rising sun. "That way is east!" Pūpū exclaimed. "This is our steady wind that blows from the northeast!"

"All night we have been paddling away from home!" said 'Eli in a low voice.

As they turned the canoe no one spoke. How far had they come? Where was Hawai'i now? The ocean is very great! each thought. Only the gods can help us.

"Let us make an offering," said 'Eli after a little. They made an offering and prayed to the gods of the sea and to their guardian spirits. Then they ate. Sunlight danced on the waves, the sky was blue and the young men felt new courage.

"The gods will bring us home," Pūpū said confidently. "They know our village has need of adzes."

The sun grew hot. The young men paddled steadily, resting by turns, but hearts and paddles were not light. The ocean was great and empty! Every paddle stroke might be taking them farther from their village.

Afternoon came. As the canoe rose on a long swell 'Oloa gave an excited cry, "There is land!" The canoe rose again and the others also saw. They paddled eagerly.

"It looks small," said 'Eli.

"We are approaching a point of land," Pūpū answered. "The rest of the island is hidden by cloud. This must be some island of Hawai'i," he added. "For Kahiki is many days' journey across the deep blue sea."

"But there are small islands," 'Oloa reminded him. All had heard of small rocky islands sometimes visited by fishermen.

"We don't seem to get nearer to the land," said 'Eli after a time. "Sometimes men see one of the sacred islands of Kāne, but no canoe can reach those islands."

"Perhaps a current is carrying us away," Pūpū replied. "Or perhaps it is just that we are tired."

He and 'Eli tried to put more strength into their paddling and suddenly 'Oloa exclaimed, "We are much nearer than we were!"

After that the canoe flew over the waves as it had done before the storm. The island became more clear. Just a great pile of rocks it seemed, beaten by the waves. They heard the crash of surf and in every heart rose the same question, can we find a landing space?

"Let us circle the island to look for a beach," Pūpū suggested. "There must be some place we can land."

They paddled steadily, looking and listening. Steep cliffs and crashing waves!

"There!" exclaimed Pūpū suddenly. "I see a little inlet!"

The others saw it and their arms grew strong with hope. "We can land," said 'Eli. "Here we can rest and watch for a fishing canoe which can direct us."

The inlet was only a break in the rocks—small and narrow. At its head will be a beach, each thought eagerly. The canoe entered, pushed by great waves. There was no landing place—only rocks and cliffs.

"Look! There is one low rock!" 'Eli exclaimed. "Leap to it, 'Oloa, while we hold the canoe." 'Oloa leaped and landed safely.

"Can you keep the canoe off the rocks while I swing up the net of adzes?" panted Pūpū.

"I think so." 'Eli prayed as he struggled to hold the canoe steady. Pūpū, standing on a crosspiece, swung the net with its heavy load. 'Oloa caught it and fell with it to the rocks.

As he scrambled to his feet he saw that the canoe had struck and smashed. 'Eli was clinging to the low rock, but Pūpū he could not see.

'Oloa threw himself face down. His toes gripped a projection and his arms reached for 'Eli. A wave lifted 'Eli and, with 'Oloa's help, he scrambled up, then lay exhausted, hardly knowing what had happened.

'Oloa turned to look for Pūpū. Leaping from rock to rock he ran to the mouth of the inlet. His eyes swept the waves. Was that Pūpū? No, only tumbling gray water!

Suddenly, just below him, a head appeared. Pūpū had swum underwater. He grasped a rock but had no strength to climb. In a moment 'Oloa was reaching for him. He must be quick, for the next wave would strike his friend with killing force! 'Oloa's prayer was a cry and the gods heard. He never knew how it was done but somehow he pulled Pūpū up beside him on the rocks. There both lay panting.

"Where is 'Eli?" Pūpū gasped out after a moment's rest.

"He is safe," 'Oloa replied. "Back there by the adzes." Again they rested.

At last Pūpū tried to rise. "Let us give thanks," he said.

The tired young men crawled over the rocks till they found 'Eli. "I thought you were dead!" he cried. "Oh, Pūpū!" and 'Eli clasped his companion in his arms, wailing with joy. Then they all thanked the gods.

The Island

The island was small and hollow like a bowl. "Perhaps Pele came here once and dug a fire pit when she was fleeing from her angry sister," 'Eli said. And they prayed for the powerful goddess not to be angry that they had landed on her island.

The lee side of the bowl's rim was the home of countless seabirds which screamed and circled as they searched for food. As the young men approached, some birds rose into the air and flew away, while others sat quiet in the sunshine, their eyes fixed on the men, but unafraid. "They have never seen men before," said 'Oloa. "They wonder what we are. And look! Birds' eggs! Lying right here on the rock!"

"And downy baby birds!" 'Eli added wonderingly. He lifted a little bird from the shadow of a rock where it had found shelter and stroked its down with a gentle finger. "No nests!" he said. "The mother just leaves her egg on the warm rock to hatch."

Meanwhile Pūpū was searching the crater. "No water here," he shouted. "We must dig."

The three cut sticks from bushes that they found, but 'Oloa was doubtful. "It is useless to dig for water in this hard, dry earth," he insisted.

"Everywhere rain falls," Pūpū replied. "Water may gather beneath dry surface, resting in a bowl of harder rock. I have seen it so." He began to dig. His stick broke and while he cut a stronger one, 'Eli took his turn. Then 'Oloa dug half-heartedly. Making a hole in dry, hard earth was difficult.

"It is useless," 'Oloa repeated when he took a second turn. Then, "$\bar{E}$!" he shouted suddenly. "Here it is wet! Look! Water bubbles up as from a spring. Pūpū was right!"

It came slowly but it came. The young men cleared away the earth, waited till the water looked clear above the rock, then took turns drinking from their hands as cups. The water was cool and fresh! They drank until their thirst was satisfied.

Then, conscious of their hunger, they looked about for food. They heard a call from Pūpū. He had reached a broken place in the wall of the fire pit and was beckoning. They hurried to his side and looked down to the ocean. Here, in the lee of the island, was a narrow strip of level land and a sandy beach with reef beyond to break the force of waves. "Here we could have landed safely," Pūpū said.

"If only we had paddled farther we should have found this beach!" 'Eli added. "Our canoe would not have been lost."

But 'Oloa's voice was cheerful. "The gods have saved us," he said. "And the adzes. And look there!"

Quite near them on the slope they saw a man-made pile of stones. They hurried to it. "It is a shrine!" 'Eli exclaimed.

"Fishermen have been here," said 'Oloa confidently. "They will come again. While we wait the sea will feed us."

Day after day the three lived on the tiny, rocky islet, hoping for rescue. While one watched the sea for a canoe the others caught fish and gathered shellfish and seaweed.

One day when 'Oloa was collecting driftwood he gave a great shout, "Come and see what I have found!" He was holding up a piece of wood and pointing to something sticking in it. "Iron!" he told his companions.

"Iron?" asked 'Eli. "I have heard that iron sometimes comes in driftwood, but I have never seen it."

"I have!" Pūpū exclaimed. "I saw an iron fishhook. It had been in my friend's family for generations. It is stronger than bone or shell."

"Some say it can be heated and bent," said 'Oloa. "I do not know whether that is true, but it will make a good fishhook. I shall get it out of the driftwood and show it to 'Aukai when we get home," and he hurried to the adze net for a tool with which to pry the iron from the wood.

When we get home, 'Eli repeated to himself. That time may never come. He thought of his master, sick and frail. He must be troubled that we do not return. Already he may be dead.

And he felt anxiety for himself and his companions. The men who built the shrine may have been lost as we are. It may be years before anyone comes again. And what of evil spirits? They may be watching us. Some night they may steal upon us while we sleep. But 'Eli did not share his anxious thoughts with his companions.

The younger men talked eagerly of home, yet enjoyed this adventure on a lonely island. 'Oloa wanted to build an *umu,* a stone oven on the ground. "My cousins have one," he told Pūpū. "It is square and large enough to hold a good-sized pig, with fish and vegetables besides. Food is cooked in it by hot stones, just as in an *imu.* There are many stones here and I know just how to build it."

Pūpū laughed. "We have no pig nor vegetables," he answered. "Fish is good cooked over coals or in hot ashes. Why build an *umu?*"

Perhaps it was because 'Eli was most eager for rescue that he was the one who saw a sail. He shouted to his companions, pulled off his *malo* and waved it. The steady north-east wind blew out the *kapa* streamer. "They see it!" 'Eli shouted as the others joined him. "They see our signal!"

It was true. The sail was lowered and the canoe flew toward the island, paddled by strong arms. The young men directed it to the landing place, then rushed down the crater slope and waded out to meet their rescuers.

A little distance from the beach the canoe stopped and the paddlers shouted, "Who are you three? Give your family and district."

Quickly Pūpū shouted back, telling names, island and district. "We went to the workshop of adzes on Mauna Kea," he explained. "On our return we met a storm and lost our course."

The canoe crossed the reef and was quickly beached. It was a large single canoe with four fishermen. "We have heard of you," said the one who seemed to be head fisherman. He named the district from which the four had come. "Word of your loss had gone all about our island. There will be great rejoicing in your village at your return. Did you lose the adzes?"

'Eli told of their landing on the tiny island, of how the adzes had been saved but the canoe lost. Then the youngest of the four said, "We thought you might be evil spirits."

"Yes," another added. "We have heard that evil spirits live on some of these small islands. When you signaled, we thought you might be seeking to do us harm."

For the last time an offering was made at the little shrine. It was the head fisherman who prayed aloud, but in the hearts of the three stonecutters was such thankfulness as they had never felt before.

The journey home was shorter than the young men had thought possible. The head fisherman knew the sea and its winds and currents. Sunset light gleamed on their island. They paddled eagerly along the coast as the moon rose and lighted the palm trees sheltering their village.

The canoe flew over the reef on the crest of a wave. Shouts rose from underneath the palms as people ran to the landing place. "What canoe is that?" a strong voice shouted.

And the head fisherman replied, "It is the canoe that brings ʻEli, Pūpū and ʻOloa returning from Mauna Kea with adzes for your district."

For a moment there was silence as if those on shore could not believe the words. In that moment the canoe reached the sand, the men jumped out and carried her above the waves.

People had moved back, staring. Pūpū lifted the net of adzes from the canoe. "We must take these to our chief," said ʻEli.

Suddenly everyone realized that the good news was true. Voices were lifted in shouts and wails of joy:

"ʻEli, my son!"

"Run! Tell ʻOloa's grandfather of his return!"

"Where are Pūpū's relatives?"

"The chief must know!"

"And the master stonecutter!"

"Does our master live?" ʻEli asked eagerly.

"Yes, but he weeps for you, thinking you dead. He says he sent you to your death."

"Let us go first to him!" the young men cried.

The crowd followed to the old man's home, but stayed outside. The master had been wakened by the shouts. "Who comes?" he asked and his voice was very weak.

"Your men," ʻEli answered eagerly. "Pūpū, ʻOloa and ʻEli have returned with adzes." He took the thin form of the old man in his arms and held him close, while Pūpū and ʻOloa each took one of the master's hands and stroked it lovingly. ʻEli felt his master's tears, but knew that they were tears of joy.

Someone brought a *kukui*-nut torch. Others brought food and ʻ*awa*. The young men helped their master from his mats and led him to the shrine. There he made an offering and thanked the gods. "Now go," he said. "Take the adzes to our chief. After you have polished them he will appoint skilled men to lash on handles, then the tools will be ready for those who need them—canoemakers, woodcarvers, makers of images—for all whose old adzes are broken beyond repair. As commoners serve their district chief with gifts or labor, so it is his duty to supply things they cannot make.

"Go, greet your relatives and then return to me. My house and heart have been empty while you were gone. Now they are full of joy."

Hiwa

Kalo Wehiwa

Once more Kaiki was in the upland with the men. The *wehiwa,* the quick-growing *kalo,* had matured. "The overseer was wise," Nāwai admitted. "The upland patch means much hard work, but we need the food. Look at the *kalo* now!" he added proudly.

"You are right," replied Pakī, "this *kalo* is ready when there is little left in our lowland patch. We were wise to make an upland garden."

Lako and Puakō looked at each other smiling. They remembered how these men had grumbled over clearing land, over planting and mulching. Yes, the upland garden meant much work! But now it meant abundant *poi*. No searching in gulches for wild *kalo*.

As the sun slipped behind the trees of the forest close to the *kalo* patch, men and boys gathered together. They listed reverently as the overseer prayed:

> "O god, our *kalo* has matured.
> O Kū-the-producer,
> In the morning our *kalo* shall be pulled,
> Fastened into bundles, carried home.
> The wood shall be chopped,
> The *imu* lighted.
> The *kalo* cooked in the *imu*.
> The *imu* shall be opened,
> The *kalo* peeled.
> It shall be pounded
> And the *poi* placed in a calabash.
> Let men, women and children
> Eat of our *poi,*

The *poi* that belongs to the mighty planters.
O Kū-the-producer,
Bless us in little things and great."

As the others walked to the caves where they were to spend the night, the boys stood a moment looking at the garden. "It does look pretty fine," Noe remarked, "with the big *kalo* plants rising out of the earth!"

"Yes," Kaiki added, "and fine new shoots, white like the teeth of a big boar!"

Noe laughed. "The gods are mighty planters," he replied. "Men and boys help," and the two hurried away, Kaiki to join Puakō and Noe to sleep beside Nāwai, for he was his apprentice now.

As the morning sun sent long leaf-shadows across the patch, all made ready for the first pulling of their *kalo*. The boys had been given digging sticks. Each found a large plant and waited eagerly. All together men and boys lifted their sticks and plunged them into the earth. The earth was moist and soon the plants were loose and could be pulled.

At every home in the village fires blazed that afternoon. The *kalo* was washed and the *imu* filled. While the *kalo* steamed, men bathed and surfed.

Kaiki and his friends had a game of splashing water, then they lay resting like lizards in the sun. Suddenly Kaiki remembered the *imu* and looked about. The men were gone. Puakō might be opening the *imu*. I want to help! the boy thought, brushed sand from his body and raced to the sleeping house. As he came out, wearing a dry *malo,* he stopped suddenly. What was that sound? He heard it again. Where did it come from?

His great-grandfather, that gentle white-haired man, sat in the shade nearby. Kaiki went to him. "Do you hear something, Grandfather?" he asked. "Some little animal?"

The old man raised a smiling face. "It is a sound I have longed to hear," he answered. "It is your cousin's cry. I have a great-granddaughter."

"Oh!" said Kaiki. He had known a baby was expected. There had been talk of it. Puakō had said that Keao must have much green food and little salt or raw fish. But Kaiki had not thought much of the matter. And now the child had come! She was in the women's house with Ana and Keao.

The boy straightened himself to his full height. "One more mouth to feed!" he said cheerfully. "I must go and peel the *kalo*."

Prayers for the Precious One

Keao lay on a comfortable pile of mats. Sleepily she watched Ana working over the tiny one—her child, her little daughter. Ana wiped its eyes, then rubbed its tiny body with warm *kukui* oil. She wrapped the little one in soft *kapa* and laid it beside its mother. Happily cuddling her baby, Keao slept.

She wakened to the sound of pounding. Puakō and Kaiki were pounding *poi*. Throughout the village pounders sounded. Keao opened her eyes. After a long look at the sleeping child, she turned a questioning glance on Ana.

Her mother understood. "The first of the upland *kalo* has been pulled today," she said, "the *wehiwa;* soon the whole village will offer thanks and feast."

"*Wehiwa*," Keao repeated in a whisper. "*Kalo wehiwa. Hiwahiwa,* the precious one. Ana!" she said, raising her voice a little, "that shall be her name, Hiwahiwa."

"A good name!" her mother answered. "My grandfather was Hiwahiwa. It is good that the name should live once more. Father will be pleased."

Two days later the villagers, decked with *lei* and new *kapa,* feasted. The *kahuna* made an offering and prayer of thanks for the good *kalo* harvest and then the feast was enjoyed.

Not long after another feast was held by Keao's family and relatives—the path-clearing ceremony for little Hiwahiwa. This was a ceremony for the first-born, a time of prayer that the gods would remove all evil from the child's path and from the paths of brothers and sisters who should follow.

Still in the women's house with her precious baby, Keao heard the greetings as relatives arrived. After a time of talk and laughter—silence. And, in the silence rose the voice of the *kahuna.* Keao could not hear the words, but knew he prayed for blessing on her first-born.

> "Clear this child's path,
> O guardian spirits.
> Keep all evil from her!
> O all you gods,
> Guard this child from evil—
> This child
> And those who shall come after.
> Let goodness cling to them."

The prayer that formed in Keao's mind was a little like the long prayer of the *kahuna.*

Voices rose outside. The offering and prayer were over now and the feasting would begin. Someone brought food and Ana carried it to Keao. "This is your special portion," Ana said. "This food the *kahuna* set apart for you. Eat all of it."

And Keao ate, with a prayer for her child at every mouthful. There was a special portion of the pig which Puakō had raised before Hiwahiwa was born. Keao remembered the day her father had shown the pig to her.

"That one," he said, "is for the path-clearing ceremony for the first-born child of Malu and Keao."

Reverently the young mother ate her small portion of mullet, the "sea pig," and of *lū'au,* the "plant pig." All three "pigs" belonged to the path-clearing ceremony. She ate her bit of shrimp. Its name meant to "peel off." "So may all evil be peeled off from my children," Keao prayed. And so with crab and seaweed. "May bad behavior and ill luck be loosened from them." Slowly she ate a kind of shellfish never used as food except at the path-clearing ceremony. This means "hold fast," thought Keao. So may all goodness "hold fast" to Hiwahiwa and to the sisters and brothers who follow her.

Keao had eaten all her portion. Now she rested content, knowing that Malu shared the feast. She was glad that the relatives also were sharing the joy and prayer of this ceremony. Now the baby was being formally named Hiwahiwa, The-Precious-One.

A *Kahuna* of Healing

"Funny Child"

'Ēwe had spent the morning gathering herbs in the upland. As he came slowly down the trail he watched and listened to the sounds of the forest.

Suddenly he stood still, stopped by an odd clucking noise. It was like the soft call of a mother hen to chicks, yet different. Silently the young man made his way around rocks in the direction of the noise. Peeping over a large rock, he saw a sight that made him smile. A little girl of four or five years sat on the ground, holding a young hen in her arms. She talked to the hen with soft clucking sounds. 'Ēwe was fond of children and had none of his own. For some time he stood, watching the child as she gently stroked the feathers of the hen and talked to it. Small children are rough with birds and animals, he thought, because they do not understand. But this child is gentle.

That night 'Ēwe told his wife and his father about the little girl. "Let us watch her," said Uka, the father, "such gentleness is rare. It may be the gift of Lonopūhā, god of healing."

Uka had studied healing from childhood. He was a *kahuna* of great wisdom and power. 'Ēwe loved and admired his father and listened reverently to all the old man said. But it was Lola, another pupil of Uka, who next brought word of the little girl.

Lola was a fat, lazy boy. People said that he was stupid and sometimes teased him. Uka and 'Ēwe were patient with him, not only because he was a relative, but because of his gentleness. The boy learned slowly, but what he had mastered, he remembered.

One night, in the men's eating house, Lola put down his *poi* bowl and sat chuckling. "Funny child!" he said with another chuckle, then stuffed food into his big mouth and said no more until the food was swallowed. Then he repeated, "Funny child!" After a moment he went on, "Today a small girl came to me crying. She caught my leg and tried to tell me something I could not understand. When I bent down to her she caught my hand and pulled me. 'Come! Come!' she said. That much I understood and followed her. She led me to a half-grown pig lying beneath a bush. The child talked to it. I think she told the pig not to be afraid of me, for I would help it. She looked up at me and showed me that the pig's leg was broken. I don't care for pigs, for they are mischief-makers. But when that child looked up at me with tears in her eyes, I wanted to help. I did what you have taught me, Master. I pounded roots of the upland morning glory. I set the bone and bound on the pounded root. The child held the pig still and kept talking to it while I worked. Funny child." And Lola stuffed more food into his mouth.

'Ēwe looked at his father. "It must be the same little girl," he said.

Two nights later Lehua, 'Ēwe's wife announced, "I know who that girl is. I don't wonder Lola called her 'funny child.' Today as I was hunting for the brown hen's nest, I met Ke'ala with several little girls. They are relatives whose grandmother died and Ke'ala has taken them into her home. You have heard?"

'Ēwe and Uka made a sign for "yes," a quick lift of the eyebrows.

"You know what an idle fellow Ke'ala's husband is. The children don't have enough to eat, I'm sure! Well, I told Ke'ala what I was hunting for. 'Maile can help you,' she said and turned to the smallest girl who trailed along behind the rest. 'Lehua is looking for the nest of her brown hen,' she told the child. 'You know where it is?' The tiny girl raised her brows. 'Yes,' she knew, but she spoke not a word."

"I took her hand and she led me off among the bushes. She would bend back a bush and hunt among the leaves, then lead me on again. We did not find the nest. 'You don't know where it is?' I asked at last, 'The brown hen's nest?' "

"Again she made a sign for 'yes,' and said some words which I could not understand. 'Poor little girl!' I thought. She is so pale and thin. The hand I held was just a little claw. I put my arms around her to show my love. 'Does Maile know where the nest is?' I asked again. 'Tell Lehua slowly. I did not understand.' "

"She said the words several times until at last I understood. Yes, she knew the nest, but it was a secret—the brown hen's secret. As I looked into her big brown eyes and felt her thin body in my arms, I forgot the hen, in love for the child," Lehua told her husband.

'Ēwe understood. "Keʻala is your relative," he said. "Let us take this little one as our foster child. Here there is enough food."

"Yes," Uka agreed. "It may be Lonopūhā, god of healing, sending her to us."

A Pupil

So Maile came to a new home. She thought little of the change, but wandered about the village just as she had before, making friends of pigs and dogs and chickens. She was shy with the family, but came to feel safe in their love. One day she asked 'Ēwe for scraps to feed a hungry dog. He gave them gladly. After that she came to him often, asking for food. "We shall soon be starving!" 'Ēwe joked, but was pleased by Maile's care of animals.

The child talked little and played or wandered by herself. "Day by day she grows more fearless," Lehua said. "Today I saw her playing with a lizard which many dare not touch."

"Have you seen her climb?" asked ʻĒwe proudly. "She can't be more than four or five years old. Yet she can walk far up the trunk of a *niu*."

One morning, as Uka started for the upland to gather herbs, he heard a sound behind him and there was Maile. She followed quietly. As Uka dug roots and gathered leaves, he talked to the little girl. He prayed to the forest gods that they might share the plants with him and give healing power to each.

He told Maile about the gods who lived in the upland. "We never crush the plants they love," he said, "nor pick them carelessly. We ask the gods for each leaf or root we take, for every leaf and root is precious. The gods give to plants the power to heal disease."

He told the child the name of each plant he took and explained its use. Just as Uka had talked to ʻĒwe and Lola, he talked to Maile and she listened gravely with big brown eyes watching all he did. They did not go far that day, for Uka feared the child would grow too tired.

The next morning Maile came to him with both hands full of herbs. As she gave them to him, one by one, Uka wondered at her memory. Some of the names she knew. She remembered what diseases certain plants could heal. And she had brought the right portion of each plant, root, stem or leaves. She had remembered which parts he had taken. "The prayers," she said, "I told the gods I do not know them all. They said that you would teach me."

Maile came to love the forest. She went with Uka and ʻĒwe whenever they would take her. She followed Lehua and her friends when they went up for dye plants. And sometimes she went alone. She was learning the proper prayers and went, unafraid, where many would not venture.

One afternoon she came to Uka. "I met someone in the forest," she said, "a wise old man. He showed me this." Maile brought a hand from behind her back and held out some leaves.

Uka took them eagerly. "These leaves are very rare," he said. "Did the man give them to you?"

"No. He showed me where they grew. Close by the stream where the water tumbles among rocks. I'll take you to the place, for there are many plants with leaves like these."

"That man must be a *kahuna* from another district," said Uka, puzzled.

Maile's hand signed "no." Her great eyes looked into Uka's as she said, "He is a very wise man."

Then her grandfather understood. "Lonopūhā, god of healing, came himself to teach you, Maile," he said reverently. "It was he who sent you to us."

Sometimes Maile played in the upland, swinging all alone on a strong vine and chanting as she swung. Once she saw a little rat peeping from a tree fern, then darting off in search of food. She stole quietly to the fern and there, just above the ground, she found the nest, lined with soft *pulu*. The little girl stood long watching the squirming naked little rats, then went home happy in her secret.

Uka was mashing roots in a stone bowl one morning when Maile came to him. "Uliki has come. He has a mat for you." Uka went out. As Uliki laid the mat in the arms of the *kahuna* he said, "Nani, my girl, is sick."

"I will come to her," Uka promised. Maile watched which offering and prayer Uka would make for wisdom. Then she followed him. She went with him into the sleeping house where Nani lay. The girl's face was flushed and Maile saw how she had pushed off the *kapa,* as if she were too warm. The little girl watched gravely as Uka ran his hands over Nani's body. He stroked her hot forehead and asked questions, then hurried home. Maile ran after him.

She watched him make a fire and heat stones. He took salt from a large covered bowl and wrapped it firmly in many *kī* leaves. After the fire died and bits of smoking wood had been removed, Uka laid the salt bundles among the stones to heat. Then he prepared a drink of herbs. As he worked he prayed. He had little thought of Maile, but the child watched every movement and listened with deep interest.

As they returned to Nani, Uka let Maile carry the gourd which held the herb drink. He prayed that it might cure Nani, then gave it to her. After that he wrapped the girl in *kī* leaves and packed the hot salt bags about her. Maile heard him pray that sweat might come and carry the sickness from Nani.

The next day Uliki came again to Uka's home. His face was shining. "She is well," he said. "The fever and pain are gone. Nani wants to swim and play."

"Swimming and play are good," said Uka, "but tell the child to wait until tomorrow. Let her rest today. Tomorrow she can surf or lie sunning on the beach. Today give her much water to drink and green food. Let us make sure the sickness is all gone before your girl returns to work and play."

Maile listened to this talk, then ran into the sleeping house for the gourd that held her treasures. Carrying this, she ran to Nani's home.

Nani was feeling cross because her father had repeated Uka's words, "Rest today." She smiled at Maile, a welcome playmate. Maile waited on her and followed her directions and so the day passed quickly. Maile herself was filled with wonder that one so sick could become quickly well and full of energy.

That night, sitting at 'Ēwe's side, Maile said, "Uka is a very great *kahuna*. Nani was sick and Uka made her well."

"Yes," 'Ēwe answered, "with help from the gods."

"I know," Maile replied. "As he works, he prays." The child was silent, thinking. Then she asked, "Are you a great *kahuna*?"

"I can heal some sickness," 'Ēwe told her. "Father teaches me, but he still has skills and secrets I have not."

Again, the child was silent while 'Ēwe stroked her hair. At last she lifted her eyes to his and he saw that her face was troubled. "A girl?" was all she did say, but her foster father understood. "Oh, yes," he told her, "a woman can be a *kahuna* of healing. That is what you want to be?" Maile raised her brows in a quick sign for "yes," her face alight with happiness.

"We knew that you would be a *kahuna*," 'Ēwe said. "Lonopūhā, god of healing, sent you to us to be trained."

Maile Becomes a Kahuna

In the years that followed, Maile learned. Now Uka and 'Ēwe had two pupils. They understood that Lola would never be wise, but he was kind. He was useful in certain work, even though he was slow and lazy. It was a great joy to the men to teach the eager girl. At times her quickness filled them with surprise. "She knows a hundred plants and the use of each," 'Ēwe told Lehua. "At her age I knew not more than fifty."

"Noe's dog is sick," Maile said one day. "May I give him medicine?"

"Yes," 'Ēwe told her, "cure him if you can." Later he asked, "How about Noe's dog? Did he get well?"

"Oh, yes. That dog ate too much spoiled fish. Someone had thrown out the fish." She told 'Ēwe what herbs she had used to cure the dog.

"That was right," he said. "Sometimes Father tries new herbs on dogs and pigs. If animals are cured, it is safe to give those herbs to people."

Maile listened thoughtfully. Not long after, she came to Uka sobbing. "I killed the hen," she told him. "Lehua's small brown hen she loves. I gave her this to see what it would do." She showed a root. "It killed her." Again the child sobbed bitterly.

Uka took her in his arms. He told her about the root and how to use it. Maile was interested and forgot to cry. "I too have killed animals," he said. "I too have given medicine that was wrong or was too powerful. I was sorry to kill a chicken or a dog, but suppose I had made the mistake with a sick child. The life of a person is more precious than the life of an animal." The two were quiet, thinking. After a time Uka added, "You are a big girl now. You must learn what animals are like inside."

"I know about chickens," Maile answered. "I have watched 'Ēwe when he made them ready for the *imu*."

"Yes. And pigs?"

"I know a little."

After that the men called Maile when they dressed a pig for cooking. They showed her all the organs and explained their use. "Animals and people are much alike," said Uka, "and yet different."

"Have you ever seen a person's organs?" the girl asked.

"Yes. Sometimes my cure fails and someone dies. His family may let me examine the body, then I can see the organs. Sometimes I find the sickness was not what I thought. So I learn things that help me cure others."

Again Maile was thoughtful. "When can I see?" she asked.

"From this time you share all our work," the old man promised solemnly. "You must know how a person's organs are placed, so that you can locate disease or massage back to place a misplaced organ."

From that day Uka and 'Ēwe took Maile everywhere. 'Ēwe taught her how to help a mother dog give birth to pups. She learned the care of a woman before her baby came. The neighbors sometimes smiled as they watched the serious young girl or listened to her words. "Before Hiwahiwa was born, Maile asked about my food," Keao told Lehua. "'Does Puakō bring you green food everyday?' she wanted to know. '*Lūʻau* and *ʻuala* greens are better for you than too much *poi*.'"

From the time she was five, Uka had taught Maile to "see" with her fingers. Now, blindfolded, she could tell different kinds of stones by means of a light touch. "This is pumice," she might say. "This is the hard lava rock used for adzes. This is coral."

One day Uka took pebbles from a special calabash. There were twelve fours of these, red, white and black. Uka laid them on the floor mat of his work house, making the figure of a man. Then he told Maile where each organ was: heart, lungs, stomach and all the rest. "This is why you have learned to see with your fingers," he explained. "To feel a person and so learn the nature of his sickness is the work of the *kahuna hāhā*. Because I had two teachers, I learned the work of the *kahuna* who finds the cause of a disease and also the one who heals it. So you have much to learn."

Maile was a well-grown girl, almost a woman. As she went about with Uka she learned to set a broken bone. She learned to feel the organs in their place and to tell when one was not where it belonged or was diseased and swollen. Uka taught her to oil her hands and gently push an organ back into its place, chanting as she worked, to cheer her patient. Sometimes her massage cured sore muscles or reduced swelling. But sometimes all Uka's wisdom was not enough and a patient died. Death always saddened Maile but now she seldom cried.

One day a man had died—a young man of the upland. Maile had listened to the wailing of his wife and children. When evening came she was still very sad. "She did not eat," Lehua told the men. "I think Maile is too young to share all that you see and do."

"Maile will be a very great *kahuna*," Uka answered gravely. "I am an old man and have not long to live. I must teach her all I know. Soon she will be a woman."

Later he found the girl. She was holding Noe's dog and sobbing while the dog licked her hand to comfort her. Uka seated himself beside her and asked gently. "You weep for Wao?"

"Yes. Now his wife and children have no one to get food. There is no loving father in that home. Why did you fail?"

"I do not know," Uka said. "I too am sad. I did not find the real cause of his sickness, so my treatment did no good. Sometimes, Maile, there is no disease. Sometimes a person has broken a *kapu* or in some other way displeased the gods. Then angry gods send sickness to him or to a member of his family. Such sickness I cannot cure. A *kahuna nui* must be called. He knows diseases of the spirit and makes offerings and asks the gods to forgive the wrong and cure the sickness. With Wao there was no time, his sickness came so suddenly."

For a long time the two sat silent as daylight faded and stars appeared. Then Uka spoke again in a low tone. "The day has come when I must share with you and 'Ēwe all the secrets that I know." Maile lifted her head and looked at Uka, then took his hand and gently rubbed her face against it. The old man knew his grandchild understood.

In the days that Uka remained strong he taught 'Ēwe and Maile the few remaining prayers and secrets he had kept till now. "The gods have been very good to me," he said, "for I leave both a son and grandchild to carry on my work."

Fishponds and Torches

Malu sat on the wall of the chief's pond and watched fish come in with the tide. It was good that mullet and other food fish should come, even small ones. In the pond they could grow until they were large enough for the chiefs to eat.

But Malu's spear was ready for an eel or other enemy which would kill food fish. The chief's fishermen took turns watching the pond as tide and fish came in. The strong wall had been built long ago, but Malu had helped to repair it after a storm. Its stones were laid so that waves could wash through easily, but fish could not swim through to leave the pond.

A sudden swirl of water told the young man the tide had turned and was flowing out. He quickly lowered the gate of strong sticks. Food fish must not swim away. Malu's work was done. Tonight Puna would raise the gate. The young man stopped to get shrimps hiding under rocks. Each one who watched the pond might get shrimps and certain kinds of fish.

It was late. He must take the shrimps to Puakō, then hurry to see if 'Aukai had other work for him. On the way he met Puna. Puna looked at the cloudy sky and said, "The night will be dark, a good night for wandering."

Malu lifted his brows for "yes." Torch-light fishing! Glorious fun! As he hurried home Malu prayed silently: O gods, I thank you that I am a fisherman. A fisherman's work is full of adventure.

When he reached 'Aukai's house where fishing gear was kept, Malu found the men at work. *Kukui* nuts had been roasted then strung on *niu* midribs to make candles. Puna and others were wrapping *kī* leaves around these.

They were making long, thick torches. Malu's work was to tie the torches to bamboo poles so they could be carried.

'Aukai came. He made an offering and prayed. The men ate quietly. No loud talking should tell of their plans. Darkness settled over the village as a bird spreads wings over her young.

The fishermen walked quickly along the shore to a place where the reef was wide. Here they stopped to make fire, then with a bit of twisted *kapa* lighted their torches. Good! each one was thinking. The torches burn smokily, but their flame is yellow and bright. That means good luck tonight.

The men separated as they waded out. They moved slowly along the reef, all going in the same direction, but not too close together. Malu's torch was in his left hand, in his right a spear. There was no sound except the wash of waves and the splash of feet stepping carefully.

In a deep pool Malu saw a fish, quiet, dazzled by the light. He speared it easily and slipped it into the bag fastened to his *malo*. He waded around the pool and went on.

He saw another man dip a scoop net into the water. Small fish lay close to its mouth and Malu dropped a stone behind them. Frightened, they swam into the net. Good!

Nearby a loud splash! As others looked they saw one of the fishermen scrambling from a hole. His torch was out and his knee skinned on coral but the man did not cry out. Such accidents were common.

A quick flash just ahead! An eel! Malu's spear struck quickly, but the eel was quicker and was gone into the dark.

A low cry from one of the men was hushed at once. Perhaps his toe had gone too near a crab. Spearing, netting, sometimes missing a fish, the men waded on.

Malu's bag was heavy. He looked around—all the bags were well-filled and the torches burning low. "Let us go back," he said.

The men talked quietly as they waded out. "I almost got the biggest—" began the boaster. Splash! Into a hole he went! Boast and light were ended.

As the fishermen reached the village a rooster crowed. Others answered. Pigs woke and squealed. The village was suddenly filled with sound. The men made an offering at the beach shrine and took fish to the chief's attendants.

My wife must be asleep, Malu thought as he reached their home.

But Keao stirred. "Did the gods send fish to your spear?" she asked.

"Yes. All bags were well-filled." Before he slept the young man prayed:

> "O Kāne, O Kū, O Lono,
> O gods in the great night,
> Grant life to me and to my family
> In the world here, and peace."

Year's End

Hukilau

Kaiki and Noe had been helping to gather *niu*. Now each carried a heavy net-load to his home. "*E*, Kaiki!" Noe had stopped and was staring toward the top of a little hill. "What is Malu doing?"

Malu stood on the hilltop looking out to sea. "He must be watching for fish," Kaiki answered. "There is a canoe carrying a long net. Let us hurry home with the *niu* and come back to watch."

"Many people are coming," he said as the boys raced back. "A canoe is paddling into the bay and the men in it are watching Malu."

"He has a bamboo rod with a *kapa* streamer at one end. He is signaling with it!"

"I know!" Kaiki was excited, but he spoke quietly. "It is a *hukilau*. Malu can see a school of fish. He is sending the net-carrying canoe beyond them."

"There are two other canoes," Noe added. "I remember now. One takes the net to the right and one to the left. The weights carry one edge down so the net makes a fence around the school of fish. But why are *kī* leaves tied on the net? Do you know, Kaiki?"

"They move in the water and the moving shadows scare the fish. The whole school will swim before the net and we can catch them." Both boys were jumping with excitement but they kept their voices quiet.

The two canoes were coming close to shore. Now one turned to go around some fish at a signal from Malu. Men swam or waded beside the net to keep it from catching on coral. Both ends reached the beach and

Malu signaled as if in a hurry to have it pulled in. "We can't pull it in," a man said to the boys. "It is too heavy. Run for more help. Get my wife. Get everyone."

Kaiki and Noe ran. "Come!" they said to those they met. "The *hukilau!* Everyone is needed."

People came eagerly. Some took hold of one end of the net, some of the other. *"Huki! Huki!"* they shouted, "Pull! Pull!" Slowly the net was being drawn to shore. The men in the water splashed and shouted to drive the fish before the net.

"Ē, the signal! Stop!" someone called. Malu was holding up his bamboo rod. Somewhere the net had caught on coral. Men freed it. Then the pulling began again.

"Huki! Huki!" the boys shouted and pulled with all their might. The net was almost in and they could see the frightened fish swimming in shallow water.

The *konohiki,* the overseer, had come to divide them, but a baby boy ran into the water before him. The child seized a fish and waded out.

"He ought not to do that," Kaiki said. "He should wait for the *konohiki.*"

"He took the prettiest one!" Noe exclaimed and ran to take it from the baby.

"Let him alone," the *konohiki* said. "You two are big boys and take your turns with grown-ups. A baby may pick up any fish he wants."

Now the *konohiki* divided the fish. He gave two to Malu to carry to the shrine. Some were given to the chief's attendants, for chiefs must have a share. "He is throwing some back over the net," Kaiki said. "Why does he let them swim away?"

"Those are small," a man answered. "It is better to let the little ones grow big before we catch them."

"Why did the *konohiki* give so many to Haka?" Noe wondered. "He is lame and hardly pulled at all."

"I know why," Kaiki answered. "Haka has a big family. Many, many mouths need many fish."

"Here is one for you," the overseer said to Kaiki. "All your family helped and have many fish. Run home, Noe, for a gourd. Your family is large and only you were here to pull."

"The others are in the upland," Noe panted as he brought the gourd. Carrying it home full of fish he thought, it is lucky I was here.

Kaiki stayed to watch the men untie the nets which had made up the long one. They even save the *kī* leaves to use again, he thought as these were taken off and spread to dry. How carefully Malu looks over every net! *Ē,* a bad tear! That must be the one that caught on coral. Other men picked off bits of seaweed and spread the nets in a sunny place to dry.

"Bring your fish, Kaiki," Puakō said to his grandson. "Our family has many. I want to clean them right away and dry them."

Surfing

That afternoon the wind rose as the *kilo* had foretold. Great waves rushed into the bay and, until moonrise, commoners were free to enjoy them. Small children splashed at the water's edge. Young swimmers ventured out, threw themselves before an oncoming wave and were carried headlong up the beach. Some older people, too, were bodysurfing but nearly everyone else, from boys and girls to grandparents, used surfboards.

Swimming with their long narrow boards of *wiliwili* or *koa* wood, Kaiki and his friends reached the place where an oncoming wave broke before rushing to the beach. Kaiki stood holding his board. "Here comes a big one!"

Noe shouted and every boy threw himself flat on his board. One was just too late to catch the wave, one tried to stand and tumbled, but the rest came with a glorious rush all the way to the beach.

"Look out!" and the boys scattered before a canoe racing in from the outer edge of the reef. "I long to do that!" Noe remarked enviously, watching the young men paddle out once more.

"Yes," Kaiki replied absently, "but what I want now is to stand up on my board. Let's all try!"

Again they paddled out, each lying flat on his surfboard. A great wave came and, as he rushed toward shore, Kaiki tried to scramble to his feet. He slipped and found himself underneath the board as he struck the sand. "I couldn't stand at all!" said Noe. "But Pai did."

"They fell!" said Pai, laughing. "Let's go and watch the men who come in among the rocks. Those are the best surfers."

Climbing high the boys watched a group of young men paddling out, some on *koa* boards. When they reached a line of breakers each slipped off his board and dived under the splash and swirl of breaking wave, then paddled on. The group reached the first line of surf where great ocean rollers broke, then paused, waiting for the right wave. "There!" Noe shouted as a huge one neared the men. "Now they're off!"

Many of the young men had caught the wave. Small distant figures, they rose to their feet and came thundering toward shore. At the second line of breakers one fell off but the rest rushed on. How beautiful they looked! Like images carved from wood! Kaiki thought. I want to surf like that!

Through the third line of breakers the young men came. Now they were close, headed for the rocks. Noe was dancing with excitement and Kaiki felt shivers of

delightful fear go up and down his back. Skillfully the young men turned from the rocks and reached a narrow strip of beach, while two of them slipped underwater and swam to safety, still clinging to their boards.

Before the boys could draw an excited breath, another group came flashing in on the next wave. Oh, glorious sport!

For hours the villagers played—surfing, racing, splashing. Now and then a group gathered on the sand to rest while they told jokes and riddles, then back again to surf. At sunset they scattered to their homes, hungry for food.

Other Pastimes

As moonlight touched the breakers, the chiefs came and the commoners knew that they must spend the evening elsewhere. Kaiki and his friends followed 'Aki, Haili and others toward the upland. The young men carried a huge kite. Kume held the string, bound round a stick, as well as the long tail.

"The wind is just right!" said 'Aki. "You run, Kume, and we two will pitch the kite into the wind." Several times they tried. "Now!" one would shout, hoping a strong gust would lift the kite, but in vain.

"Perhaps it is too big," said Kume as the young men gathered round the kite. It was made of *kapa* over a framework of light bamboo.

"That's not the trouble," Haili answered. "I've seen larger ones lifted by the wind. Run that way, Kume, down that little hill, straight toward the wind. Now! Toss it up!"

At last! Watching boys shouted with joy as the kite rose, tugging at its string and gleaming in the moonlight. The young men, too, were shouting as they ran. Kume paid out the string and the kite rose up and up.

"It's like a bird," said Kaiki. "Struggling to free itself and fly over the mountains."

"As Māui's did!" By now the running men were far away but their kite still gleamed aloft. "I'm glad Māui invented kites," Noe added. "Let's fix ours and fly them, Kaiki!"

Keao, with Hiwa in her arms, had joined a group who were swinging. The swing was a single rope of *hau* bark, firmly fastened in a tall palm. Kahana was swinging. He sat upon a wooden crosspiece at the rope's end, holding firmly with knees and hands. His friends swung him by two other ropes, attached to the crosspiece. Moku and Malu held these two ropes, alternately pulling in opposite directions. A chant rose and, to its rhythm, the young men pulled, sending Kahana high and higher, then slowly they brought the swing to rest.

"That was the best swing I ever had!" Kahana exclaimed as he leaped off. "You be next, Moku. You'll think that you are flying!"

"No, Pua next!" Moku insisted.

"I'd like to swing, but not so high," Pua told them.

"What is the sickness without pain?" As the young people, tired of swinging, joined a seated group they heard Keao's grandfather ask this question.

"Riddles!" said Keao softly and added, "I know that one."

Others knew the riddle and a voice called eagerly, "Sickness without pain is baldness. That's the riddle the old nurse guessed. She knew the chief was sick at heart because his head was bald."

"Let me tell a riddle," said Malu as the young people found places in the group. "What has gray hairs when it is born?" No one knew so Malu proudly gave the answer: "The flower of the *kō*."

"My little man which cannot be cut?" This was Nāwai's riddle.

Again no one knew the answer but Laua'e asked, "Does your little man run and play upon the beach on moonlight nights?"

Still no one could guess. "You have the answer," Nāwai said at last. "What is the name of my man, Laua'e?"

"A shadow?" and everyone knew she had guessed right.

"Now you give one, Laua'e."

"My bird that walks on its beak."

"There is no such foolish bird," Puakō declared and everybody laughed.

At last Laua'e had to give the answer. "A top. That spins on its beak, doesn't it?"

"My *kapa* log that sounds without rest," said Lako.

"It is sounding now," Ana replied, for everyone knew that riddle and was silent for a moment to listen to the booming of the surf....

Suddenly a different sound! From the far edge of the village a real *kapa* beater struck insistently, sending the message, "Visitors are coming."

Quickly the villagers gathered to welcome guests. Young men came running from the upland or from the wrestling ring. Boys and girls left a ball game and a contest of skipping ropes of braided vine. All waited expectantly.

"Why, it's Kaipo!" 'Ilima exclaimed.

"With the *hula* dancers from the next district! Why did you come afoot?"

"We came by canoe," Kaipo explained, "but found your bay *kapu* because the chiefs are surfing. So we turned back and landed near the salt pans."

"A long walk!" Puakō exclaimed. "Run, boys, and bring water gourds and food."

"No food," said Kaipo, "until we've done our *hula!*"

The villagers spread a mat for their guests, then gathered round it, sitting or standing. Musicians took their places and began a rhythm which mingled with the distant boom of waves and the swish of nearby branches. The dancers seated themselves and told, by chant and gesture, how Laka had taught men the *hula*. She had sent wind to set the trees dancing and vines swaying, just as they did tonight.

Keao laid her sleeping baby in Malu's arms and leaned her head against her husband's shoulder. Oh, the beauty of the moonlit night, the music and the dancers! Oh, the happiness of family and friends! "The gods are very good to us," Keao murmured.

Glossary
of Hawaiian Words and Names

In Hawaiian "s" is not used to form the plural of a noun. Such Hawaiian words as *lei, heʻe, menehune* and *moʻo* may be either singular or plural.

The *ʻokina,* also known as the glottal stop or hamzah (ʻ), and the *kahakō,* also known as the macron (¯), are both necessary for correct pronunciation. The *ʻokina* indicates that at one time a consonant appeared in that place and has since been dropped. It indicates a break such as between oh's in "oh-oh." The *kahakō* indicates a stressed vowel pronounced somewhat longer than other vowels.

Pronunciation of unstressed vowels:

a as *a* in *a*bove *o* as second *o* in bronc*o*
e as *e* in b*e*t *u* as *u* in p*u*ll
i as *i* in s*i*t

Pronunciation of stressed vowels:

ā as *aa* in baz*aa*r *ō* as *oh* in *oh*
ē as *ey* in th*ey* *ū* as *oo* in m*oo*n
ī as *ee* in s*ee*

Diphthongs are ae, ai, ao, au, ei, eu, oi, ou.

Most consonants are pronounced much as they are in English, however, informed speakers vary in their pronunciation of *w*. After *i* and *e* the letter *w* may have a *v* sound. After *u* and *o* one may use the *w* sound. The initial *w* may be *v* or *w*.

Most of the capitalized Hawaiian words used in this book are the names of characters in the story. See the *Hawaiian Dictionary* (revised and enlarged edition) by Mary Kawena Pūkuʻi and Samuel H. Elbert (University of Hawaiʻi Press, ©1986) for more complete or alternate meanings of these words.

ʻĀ: oh!; ah!
ʻAiʻai: son of Kūʻula the god of fishing.
ʻAki: nip or nibble.
aku: bonito, a food fish.
aloha: love, greetings.
ʻĀluka: crowd.
ama: float on the outrigger canoe.
ʻāmama: amen.
Ana: cave.
ʻAukai: seafarer.
ʻauwai: ditch.
ʻawa: ceremonial narcotic drink.
E: "O," as a marker to designate the one spoken to.
Ē: denotes emphasis; exclamation.
ʻĒ: yes, in mild agreement and as an acknowledgment of another's speech.
ʻEā: "tra-la," sound used in chants and songs to maintain rhythm.
ʻelepaio: a flycatcher bird.
ʻEli: to dig.
Ēwe: place of birth.
hāhā: to feel with the hands.
Haili: the loving memory returns, precious, beloved.
Haka: perch; shelf.
hala: the pandanus tree.
halapepe: tree sacred to the *hula* goddess Laka.
hālau: house used for canoes or *hula* instruction.
Haleakalā: house-of-the-sun, extinct volcano on Maui.

GLOSSARY

hau: tree which furnishes bark for rope.
heʻe: octopus.
heiau: place of worship in old Hawaiʻi.
Hepa: stupid one.
Hiʻiaka: youngest sister of Pele.
Hina: a woman's name.
Hīnano: blossom of the male *hala* tree.
Hiwahiwa: precious; beloved; also "Hiwa."
hōlua: long, narrow wooden sled.
huki: to pull.
hukilau: fishing with a large net.
hula: Hawaiian dance.
ʻiako: boom which joins the outrigger to the canoe.
ʻieʻie: a vine with aerial roots which are used in basket making.
ʻIlima: yellow blossoms used for lei; flower symbolic of Oʻahu.
imu: underground oven in which food is cooked by hot stones.
Kaʻeha: the pain.
Kahana: the work.
Kahiki: land beyond Hawaiʻi.
kāhili: feather standard.
kahuna: an expert in some profession or skill.
kai: the sea.
Kaiki: the little one.
Kaipo: the sweetheart.
kala: to loosen.
Kalei: the lei.
kalo: starchy root-like corm which is cooked and pounded into *poi*.
kalo lehua: variety of *kalo* used for red *poi*.
kalo wehiwa: a quick-growing variety of *kalo*.
kamani: a large tree.

Kanaloa: one of the great gods; god of the ocean and its winds.
Kāne: one of the great gods; god of creation and of living things.
Kāneiki: little Kāne.
Kānepua'a: the pig form of the god Kāne.
Kanoe: the mist.
kapa: bark cloth.
kapu: sacred; forbidden.
kauila: a tree furnishing hardwood.
kauna'oa mālolo: yellow upland dodder.
Kaupua: flowering season.
Kāwai: the water.
kāwa'u: wood used for *kapa*-beating anvil.
Ke'ala: the fragrant.
Keao: the cloud.
Kehaulani: the dew of heaven.
Kekoa: the fearless.
kī: useful plant, leaves used in food preparation.
kīhei: cape.
kimo: a game similar to jackstones.
kilo: one who reads signs and omens.
kō: sugarcane.
koa: fearless; a large forest tree.
Kona: lee side of an island.
kōnane: a game somewhat like checkers.
konohiki: overseer.
Kou: a tree furnishing soft wood; old name for the harbor area of Honolulu.
Kū: one of the great gods; god of war.
kukui: a tree with many uses.
Kūpā: the swivel adze.
Kūpahu: stand-by-the-drum.
Kūpulupulu: Kū-of-the-undergrowth.
Kū'ula: the fish god.

La‘a: dedicated.
La‘ahana: dedicated to work.
Laka: goddess of the *hula*.
Lako: wealth; provisions.
lama: a hardwood tree; light.
lau hala: leaf of the *hala* tree.
Laua‘e: fragrant fern.
Lauhuki: to soak *kapa*.
Lea: goddess of canoe builders.
Lehua: blossom of the *‘ōhi‘a* tree.
lei: necklace of flowers.
Leimomi: necklace of pearls.
Līhau: cold with dew.
lilo ka eo: to win.
limu: seaweed.
Linohau: well-dressed.
Loa: tall one.
Lono: one of the great gods; god of peace, agriculture, games.
Lonopūhā: god of healing.
Lola: lazy.
lū‘au: kalo leaf.
maha‘oi: disrespectful or arrogant.
mai‘a: bananas.
maika: game similar to bowling.
Maikoha: god of *kapa*-makers.
Maile: fragrant vine used for *lei*.
Makahiki: year; long holiday of gift-giving, games, relaxation.
Mākālei: fish trap.
Makali‘i: the constellation Pleiades.
malo: loin cloth for men, usually of *kapa*.
mālolo: flying fish.
Malu: shade.
Māmane: a forest tree.

mamo: bird which furnished yellow feathers for royal garments.
mana: divine power.
manu: bird.
Māui: a great hero with sacred or magic powers.
Mauna Kea: white mountain, highest peak in Hawai'i.
Mauna Loa: long mountain, second highest mountain in Hawai'i.
Moho: a flightless bird, the rail.
Mo'ikeha: famous voyager.
Moku: island.
Mokuhāli'i: god of canoemakers.
mo'o: lizard.
Nani: beautiful.
Nāwai: the waters.
nehu: bait fish.
Niu: coconut.
no'a: game using a stone or small piece of wood.
Noe: mist.
noni: Small tree whose bark and root are used for red dye.
Nui: great.
Nu'uanu: cool heights, valley and stream on O'ahu.
O'ahu: the most populous of the Hawaiian Islands.
'ōhi'a 'ai: mountain apples.
'Oloa: fine white *kapa*.
olonā: strong cord for lines and nets.
'ō'ō: a digging stick; bird with both yellow and black feathers used in royal garments.
'ōpelu: a fish.
'opihi: edible shellfish.
pahe'e: smooth, slide.
Pai: to encourage.
Pakī: to splash.
palai: a fern.

palani: a surgeonfish.
pāʻū: women's skirt.
Pele: goddess of the volcanoes.
piko: the life cord of a person or a house.
pili: favorite grass for thatching houses.
poi: cooked and pounded *kalo* corms.
Pua: flower.
Puakō: sugarcane blossom.
pūhenehene: a game in which a pebble is hidden on the person of a player.
pulu: floss at the base of the tree-fern frond.
Puna: coral; spring of water.
Pūpū: shell.
ʻuala: sweet potatoes.
uhu: parrotfish.
Uka: toward the mountains.
ʻūkēkē: musical bow with three strings.
ʻukiʻuki: broad leaves from this plant are used for thatching.
ʻulu: breadfruit.
ʻulu maika: game similar to bowling.
ulua: large food fish.
umu: a type of fish trap constructed of rocks; an above-ground cooking oven constructed of rocks.
Wahi: place.
Wākea: the sky father.
Wao: mountain region.
wauke: the paper mulberry, bark used for kapa.
wiliwili: tree with light-weight wood.